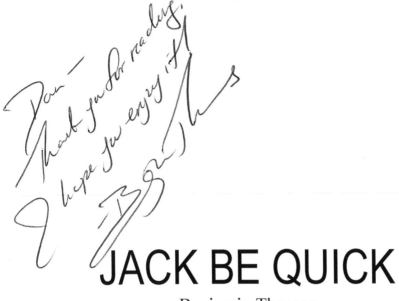

Dan—
Thank you for reading;
I hope you enjoy it!
—Benjamin Thomas

JACK BE QUICK

Benjamin Thomas

OWL HOLLOW PRESS

WORLD-ALTERING STORIES, REAL AND IMAGINED

Jack Be Quick

Library of Congress Number: 2017938607

ISBN Print: 978-1-945654-04-6
ISBN E-book: 978-1-945654-05-3

Cover by Les Solot

For Mary Ann, Annie, Elizabeth, Catherine, and
Mary Jane

ONE

Noah McKeen pulled the paramedic fly car, an abused Ford Explorer that needed an oil change and new brakes six thousand miles ago, into the parking lot of a twenty-four hour gas station. His phone rang as he stepped out and watched a car blow through a red light, hammering around a country corner with an accentuated exhaust that sounded like a vibrating metal shell. Despite the obnoxious noise, it was a gorgeous night. Crisp, fall, New England air. Revitalizing to the lungs with every breath.

"What's up?" he asked with the phone pressed to his ear. Before Amber could answer, his pager volleyed out a series of tones and beeps.

In the brief pause before the dispatcher's voice came across, Amber asked, "Bad timing?"

Noah waited, his hand on the still open door of the SUV as a woman, laced with static, gave Buckland Fire Department the first motor vehicle accident of the night.

"Nope. Not yet anyway," he said and headed inside.

There was an electric chime as the door closed behind him. He surveyed three isles filled with junk food, basic household items, and the row nearest him almost completely filled with obscure, useless gadgets. Pay-as-you-go phones meant for runaways or teens with poor parents. Gift cards and charge cables whose packaging had more Chinese symbols than English letters.

The clerk—a pimpled teenager with greasy hair—glanced at Noah and, without nodding or smiling, returned his attention to whatever video he was streaming on his phone. Noah chuckled to himself. Wondered where the usual guy was— friendly enough to bullshit about politics and laugh at news headlines, yet still not on a first name basis.

"So, is Jade able to come in early?" Amber asked.

Noah pursed his lips and poured a coffee. Buckland's fire captain signed on the air, stating that he was responding to the wreck. Noah turned his radio down and contemplated. He could lie, say he had asked her and that she had said no, or there was always the truth.

"Noah?"

"I didn't call her," he said quietly.

He heard the hiss of a sharp inhale. "Noah, we have plans tomorrow. I took the day off and everything. There was no reason for you to volunteer to cover a sick call tonight."

"Yeah, I know." While there was remorse in his voice, he knew it wouldn't be enough without a little added effort. "Just hold on one second."

Noah pressed the phone to his ear with his shoulder and placed his coffee on the counter. The kid pressed pause on his video and rang the coffee up while Noah scanned the row of colorful scratch tickets, motioning for number seven.

He pointed to the kid's screen. "Saw that episode last night. Fuckin' hilarious."

The cashier laughed. "Yeah, not bad so far."

Back outside he picked up the conversation with Amber. "Sorry about that."

He put the coffee and the lottery ticket on the hood of the SUV and fished a coin from his pocket. Through his radio came the call signs for Buckland's fire engine and heavy rescue. "It'll be good; I promise."

"No, I know," Amber said. "But it's a four hour drive to Camden, and if you need to sleep for a bit first… It just would have been better if you could have gotten out before seven."

A husky voice came over the radio. Buckland's assistant chief. Worked in fire and EMS, yet still smoked a pack and a half a day. "Car 172 on scene. One vehicle over the embankment, possible entrapment."

Noah stopped scratching his ticket. Gray flakes blew off the hood of the car. He mentally calculated his response time to Sawyer's Ridge from where he was in Caligan. Employed as a fly-car medic, Noah technically belonged to no specific ambulance company, yet when the EMTs needed advanced life support skills, he covered ALS calls in the entire tri-town area: Caligan, Buckland, and Sara's Point.

"Noah? Noah, are you there?"

"Yeah." He hopped in the Explorer and pulled out of the gas station parking lot. "Sorry. I heard you."

"Mhm. What'd I say then?"

"You said that I wouldn't be able to drive that far unless I take a nap. So that means you're just going to have to keep me awake."

He made a clicking noise. An exaggerated audible wink. Amber giggled. Said his name. He could see her shaking her head on the other end of the line. Lightly kicking her foot against the floor the way she did when bashfulness crept through her and her cheeks turned red.

"What? Not like it would be the first time."

"Excuse me, that was once and the only reason it even happened was because—"

"Because you like the thrill," Noah laughed.

"Because it was after Craig's party, and you got me drunk."

"Sweetie, I had very little to do with that."

As he turned onto the highway, his pager beeped and toned a second time. Dispatch came across, "CN Dispatch to Alpha One Medic. ALS requested on scene of Sawyer's Ridge, vicinity of Harken's Overlook, single vehicle rollover with entrapment."

He had called it. Had the feeling the second Buckland's Chief said possible entrapment. This meant the car was bashed. Spider-webbed windshield, crumpled roof. That, or it was down the embankment. Deep, deep down.

"Hey, I gotta go," he said.

Amber had become accustomed to sudden interruptions. Regardless, there was deflation in her voice. The playfulness gone. "Be safe."

"Of course. You should start drinking now."

"Really? Why's that?"

Before he could answer, Buckland's assistant chief was back on the air. "Dispatch from Car 172."

"Dispatch is on."

"Requesting med flight. LZ will be the overlook. Fire police will have the road shut down."

Amber was saying something. Possibly something flirtatious and lustful. Noah cut her off. Said a quick goodbye and threw his phone to the passenger seat while pushing the gas. The speedometer arced. The vehicle's emergency lights reflected off mile markers and exit signs. Each blue and red flash lasting as long as a subconscious calculation.

Med Flight equaled a three-minute prep, seven-minute flight from St. Vincent's Trauma Center in the city. A two-minute landing time meant they'd be on scene in twelve minutes. Still, four minutes away meant eight minutes on scene before the flight crew was there. A lot could happen in eight minutes.

Noah slowed the SUV as he took the off-ramp. He followed the curve and hit the gas as the road straightened, catching a quick glance in the side mirror as he blew past a yield sign. Buckland's heavy rescue radioed dispatch to inform them and any other units that they were on scene. Noah reached the top of Sawyer's Ridge and let off the gas as he followed the winding drive. All he needed was a deer to jump out or to come around a corner meeting someone head on, walking his or her dog. A swerve. A skid. An overcorrection and a crash into the river with blood on his hood.

His stomach tingled. A decade as a paramedic and certain calls were met with jaded eye rolls, but ones like this, serious wrecks and heart attacks, abdominal aortic aneurysms and active strokes, legitimate medicine still made his veins pulse. Like Christmas morning when you know what you're getting, and you can't wait to tear it open.

Then you should go to medical school. Amber's words were in his head. *I make enough as a nurse to get us through until you graduate, and you love it enough to stay with it. You have the pre-reqs done; take the MCATs while your sciences still count and go to medical school.*

The conversation would have continued . . . had he not hugged her and bit her shoulder. Her hands instantly up the back of his shirt, and his down the back of her pants.

He stowed thoughts of sex and school and career growth as he wound down the serpentine road, his windshield illuminating with an array of flashing lights. Cops and cones with silver reflective bands across the bottom. Firefighters rushed to different compartments, pulling tools and rope from the rig.

Noah threw the SUV in park, shouldered his med bag, and headed for Buckland's assistant chief, a meaty man standing with his heavy bunker jacket open and one foot on a rock where a guardrail should have been.

"Anderson," the chief bellowed. "Tie the fucking trunk off. Use a damn wedge, would you?"

Noah stopped at his side, leaning over to look down the embankment as two light poles flicked like bright artificial suns. He felt the chief's hand hit him in the chest. "Some broad drove by, saw the headlights and called it in. Unresponsive. Don't know how long."

Noah was over the edge and sliding before the chief could add anything else. A sedan. Tire marks were carved into the ground. The car was wedged between a tree and a large rock. This far from the road meant whoever was in the driver's seat had been hauling.

His boot slid on dry leaves and loose dirt. He tried to shift his weight, but he had too much momentum. Rotating at the last second allowed him to throw his shoulder against a tree to stop from tumbling the rest of the way. He hurried to the back of the car while motioning for a firefighter to move out of the way. Noah wedged his bag through a shattered rear window and climbed through after it.

A volunteer first responder was in the back seat holding the driver—a young woman—by the head and neck to prevent further injury. He sucked himself into the seat as Noah crawled like a spider over a carcass to get across him and into the front seat. He was talking. Noah caught the words *breathing, pulse*; enough to know the woman was alive. But he knew that without the first responder stating it. His eyes had already traveled down the woman's torso, saw the faint rise and fall in her chest.

"You get vitals?" Noah asked.

"Nothing." The first responder wiped his cheek against his shoulder. "They're grabbing a back board."

"Well, let's keep her alive first." He slid a sensor on the woman's limp finger to measure her heart rate and oxygen saturation. Both low. He put his hands on her collar bone just below the other man's grip, wrapped his fingers around and felt his way down each arm, her torso, and onto her legs. No broken bones . . . that he could feel.

He pulled a penlight from his pocket and checked each eye. Pupils were reactive. The first responder shifted, his hands slipping. The woman's face slumped forward, and Noah dropped his penlight and scrambled to keep her head straight while the man in back repositioned his hold on her neck.

"Keep your hands steady," Noah said.

He unzipped his bag and pulled out a cervical collar. Blue plastic and thin padding. Noah ripped the cellophane off and slid it around her neck, adjusting the Velcro and repositioning the MRT's hands over it as a reassurance.

"Good?"

The first responder nodded.

Noah fished through for an IV kit. Just as his hands hit the plastic, the car rocked. Metal screeched as it dragged across what he could only assume was the large rock holding them in place. His eyes locked with the first responder in the back seat. The world outside the car went still. Every firefighter and technician stood frozen as the scraping metal sound faded to nothing. The car moved slightly. A sway, like the Titanic beginning to lift from the water. Noah's stomach lurched, and though it was a ridiculous idea, he thought the mere motion of his insides moving could potentially send the car toppling down the rest of the way.

He heard the crunch of leaves, the snaps of branches, as the crew outside the car slowly began to move again. The assistant chief's voice echoed from the top of the embankment. Zeus with red and blue lightning. But any discernable words were lost amongst tree trunks and the bustle outside the car.

"No coins on the eyes tonight," Noah whispered. The first responder looked at him confused. "Never mind."

The voices outside the car grew louder as the half-a-dozen firefighters and EMTs worked to stabilize the vehicle and give Noah any supplies he didn't have in his own bag. Truth be told, the EMTs were of little help at that moment. The car jerked to the side. Noah quickly glanced out the window as two firefighters jammed wedges between the car and the tree it rubbed against. There was a snap against the hood of the car. He turned to see hydraulic lines trailing across the front end of the sedan.

With the backseat responder occupied holding c-spine, preventing potential fractures and paralysis, what Noah really needed was a second set of hands; those outside the car did him no good. But he had to make due. The woman groaned. He rolled her sleeve the rest of the way, tied a tourniquet, and drove the IV into her arm, taping the small tubing to the inside crook of her elbow.

A knock on the passenger window caused Noah to look up. A woman firefighter with a window punch in her hand. They were prepping to get the Jaws of Life in place. Sever the posts and cut the roof from the sedan.

"Passenger window going!" the woman shouted.

Glass shattered.

Med Flight *thwup-thwup-thwupped* as it approached. Behind him came a jarring metal bang as a firefighter jammed the Jaws of Life, a massive pair of hydraulic cutters, against the post separating the windshield and the now shattered passenger window. They had to get her out of the car. Out and stabilized and intubated. Her oxygen level was dropping and there was no safe way for them to wedge a backboard into the car. They could pop open the driver's side door, but with the angle of the car, they would be pulling her weight up onto a backboard and run the extreme risk of losing balance and dumping her. With the posts severed and the roof rolled back, they would be able to recline the driver's seat, slide a board behind her, pull her up and strap her in.

Hands were slapping his wrists. The woman shoved him, pushing at his arms to get him away. He attempted to hold her wrists together against her stomach as he connected a bag of saline fluid to the IV line. Next would be a nasal airway and high-flow oxygen.

Noah repositioned himself. Caught sight of the flight crew running over the embankment. Medical special ops. The woman slapped at him again. She needed to stop jerking and lay still, or there wouldn't be a chance to do anything else before the flight crew was at the car.

"They're going to cut," the guy in the back seat said. His eyes were wide. Was this his first accident? Noah tried to place him but drew a blank.

"Okay," he said.

He stuck his foot in the corner where the passenger door and the dashboard met. There came the whine of the hydraulic tool. A lobster claw the size of a grown man's chest. The metal in the post resisted, crumpled, and—

A deafening bang exploded in his ears. A soldier's flash grenade if he were in combat. Pressure and pain slammed into his right knee, driving it backward, bending, bending, until it snapped.

***

Noah woke groggy. There was a haze over his eyesight; everything looked *blurred*. Each part of his body slowly came to life, tingling at first, but as he flexed his fingers, patted the . . . bed? He tried to look to his side. A bed rail obscured his view. There was an end table with a phone and what looked like a list of numbers.

He was in a hospital. A lump formed in his throat as everything came at him: the television hanging above his bed, the gold cross next to the dry erase board that said who his doctor

and nurse were. *Gold cross*. He was in St. Vincent's Trauma
Center.

Before he could open his mouth to ask a question, a blur
from the corner of his vision rushed toward him. Slim in a
sweatshirt and jeans. Her smell hit his nose, and he recognized
the perfume he had bought her last year. Amber's face came
into focus. Tired eyes, half-hidden under auburn side-swept
bangs. She pushed her face into his shoulder and sobbed. A
dull pain pulsed in his right knee, and as he tried to move
there was resistance. His knee wouldn't bend. *What the?*
There it was, a cast from his thigh to his shin.

"What—" He tried to speak, but her lips were on his.
Pressed there with her palms on the sides of his face. When
she broke away, he stared at her, shocked. "Amber? What
happened?"

She told him between halting sobs. "The doctor said you
suffered blunt trauma to your leg. Your knee, femur, and the—
"

"Tibia." He said, his voice flat.

"Yeah, that one. You broke all of them, but your knee got
it worst of all. Whatever happened had pushed it backward
until it just—" her voice trailed off.

Everything flashed through his mind; he replayed everything he could remember about the call until it finally dawned
on him.

"The guy cut through the airbag," Noah said softly. "And
no one disconnected the battery."

Had the person been a probie? New to the department?
New to the fire service in general? Had it been the same one
who broke the passenger window? Not like any of it mattered.
Whoever had handled the tools, didn't cut low enough on the
post, causing the cutter to slice through a pressurized cylinder
filled with inert gas. With the battery still connected, the system had been ready, and when the cylinder was cut, it must
have blown the tool outward and into his knee. The person
who had been holding the tool—it must have pulled their
damn arms out of their sockets.

Amber blew her nose. Cleared her throat before she started talking again. "Doctor said it's going to take a year of physical therapy, maybe more. Said you're lucky. He thinks that you'll walk fine if you work toward it. I laughed and told him you'd be running in six months. Okay so I didn't really *laugh*."

Noah dropped his hand against the rail of the bed. *Okay, one year.*

TWO

The sound of Noah's pager pierced the pre-dawn morning. He dumped out his glass of water, ice clacking in the break-room sink, and turned the dial. Static gave way to a female voice. "CN dispatch to Sara's Point. Respond with Alpha-One Medic: 137 Oak Street, 43-year old female, abdominal pain, shortness of breath."

It was three-thirty in the morning. A 43-year-old female should have been asleep. Everyone should have been asleep, just like the firefighters in their bunks one room over. The station was so quiet at night. Almost creepy, with the only sounds being the occasional call sign on the radio and the humming vibration of the bay vents above the rigs.

He slapped at his radio. "Alpha-One responding."

Dispatch repeated, "Alpha-One responding. Zero-Three-Twenty-Four."

Stepping on his right foot caused him to limp; the exertion forced the muscles around his knee to contract in a tight, merciless band. He was living with it: a constant, dull ache that amplified when he became active. A year of physical therapy had been the supposed cure. What a fucking joke that had been. And the six months after he walked out of his last appointment had been spent in dull, aching misery. He clicked the Explorer's seat belt, the lap strap feeling a little snugger with each passing day. Two switches on the center console gave him lights and sirens.

Noah pulled out of Caligan Fire Department's main station, leaving the crews asleep in their bunkroom. Bunker boys and girls need not apply.

His eyes traveled to the glove box of the SUV. Inside was a white envelope that held his letter of resignation. The date at the top had been whited-out three times. Handing it to his supervisor would kill a part of him. But, now at thirty-one, when he could barely walk at the end of a twelve hour shift, it may very well be a part of him that needed to die.

He pulled an orange pill bottle from the center console. It rattled like a baby's toy. That was bad. The more it rattled, the less it held. With a swig of coffee he swallowed one down, knowing the ache in his knee would dissolve in less than half an hour.

Noah cut the wheel and pulled onto the highway. An exit hop from densely populated Caligan, Sara's Point was a small town whose acres covered more water than actual soil. It had been named after the wife of a wealthy man who'd built his house on the sole peninsula jutting into Aurora Lake. Romantic. Pathetic. Two sides of the same coin. Local schools used the mansion and its spring tours as field trips for American history classes. Several years ago, three sophomores had gotten arrested when they attempted to break in and spend the night. Now it was rumored to be haunted. The very idea of such a thing absurd.

Voices over the radio pulled him from his thoughts. He picked up the receiver, half of the conversation missed, and added, "Alpha-Medic on scene."

137 was a cape on the right side of the road. Two cars were parked half on its lawn, both with flashing blue lights in their rear windows. Small town volleys. Sara's Point Ambulance had been backed into the short, slightly inclined driveway. All the windows on the first floor of the house were dark, however the top corner window

glowed yellow. Noah gulped down a mouthful of coffee. Lowering his gas station cup, he caught sight of himself in the rearview. His hair had gotten long and his face was covered in stubble—direct violation of corporate policy. When was the last time he had shaved? He squeezed his cheeks. Even they had begun to look fat. With a groan he dropped the grip on his jaw and grabbed his med bag and a portable heart monitor.

He passed a male volunteer leaning against the trunk of a sedan, steadying himself as he took off his EMS jumpsuit. Slim face. Narrow jaw. Noah returned the man's nod and kept walking. That feeling of recognition without actually remembering. Two years ago he knew every name of almost every volunteer in the area, but that was two years ago. And two years can be a lifetime.

A blonde woman—Miranda—shut the back door of the ambulance. She taught rock-climbing during the day and owned her own gym closer to the city. To call her arms defined was an understatement.

"Already loaded?" Noah asked, a little surprised.

It would have made for a quick response from a paid town, let alone a volunteer department whose members were at home sleeping when the three-thirty calls came out. Miranda shook her head, palms up, and walked to the other side of the ambulance.

Odd. Overtired or pissed at something? He scoffed. Either way he didn't need the attitude.

Footsteps thudded above him. Boards creaking under weight. A quick pause let him look around both sides of the stairs: living room, kitchen, no signs of anything odd. The kitchen table had a margarita glass on it, but nothing seemed out of place. There was no smell of cigarettes or marijuana. No animal toys.

A right turn at the top of the stairs led him into a bed-room where the 43-year old female with abdominal pain and shortness of breath lay on the floor, unmoving, her stomach cut open and her throat slit. The skin of her ab-domen had been pulled back like someone had intended to remove the things inside. Noah lowered his bag to the floor and leaned against the doorframe, his usual quick-thinking mind a sudden black slate.

Rogers, a middle-aged, balding EMT crouched in the corner of the room, taking pictures on his phone.

"You found her like this?" Noah asked.

He tried to analyze. To take in every inch of the scene. A bed pushed against the far wall. A window on either side of the room. No weapons. No hiding places, except for the closed closet. Over his shoulder he could see down the hall, but in the darkness, that was as far as his eyes would allow.

He clenched and unclenched his fists. If she was dead, then who called 9-1-1? Shifting on his feet, he looked down the stairwell, barely able to see into the living room. Had he missed something?

"Rogers," Noah snapped. "Want to tell me what happened? Did you find her like this? Was the front door open?"

"Right," he stowed his phone. Rubbed his hand over a fully-formed beer gut. "Yeah, she was like this when we got here. I wasn't first on scene, so I don't know about the door, but soon as we got up here—*pfft*—called med control for DOA and asked for the cops. You didn't hear that?"

"No," Noah said. His cheeks burned. He should have been listening. Should have been paying attention to what he was walking into. "Couple other calls going on, was listening to them, too."

He knelt by the body. Shards of glass surrounded her pale, upturned palm. A pocket mirror, or what remained of a pocket mirror, lay a few inches away. Near her head was a plastic comb and a white handkerchief smeared with red lipstick. A bruise had formed on her jaw. A wound like spoiled fruit. Only beneath her skin there was bone, and Noah bet that was broken. Shattered like the little mirror.

The slice across her neck was almost knuckle-deep. Noah stood, his knee popping. He forced an exaggerated grimace just in case Rogers was watching him. The meds had started taking effect, pushing the pain in his knee away, but no one else knew that.

His head spun as he tried to figure out what he had missed walking in. There was nothing down the hall. Nothing near the bed. Nothing obviously wrong, but the air in the room made his skin crawl. What was it? What was he overlooking?

DOA calls were DOA calls. Heart attacks who had no family and whose neighbors had gotten nervous. Overdoses because one more bag of heroin would just hit that sweet spot. His hands had treated people who had been shot or stabbed and eventually dubbed 'murder victims' but never someone who had been so *skewered.* Noah shuddered.

Rogers cleared his throat. "She must have been dead a while, which makes me wonder who found her? And who called us, you know?"

While it was a fair assumption based on the state of the woman's body. Blood no longer running on the floorboards, no one present in the house. But it was wrong none-the-less. Noah forgave the mistake. Rogers hadn't been on many DOA calls as a volunteer.

Noah shook his head. "I *don't* know. I'm trying to figure that out. But you're wrong; she's been dead fifteen minutes tops."

A new set of flashing lights shone through the bedroom window. In the glow, he noticed several drops of blood dotting the floorboards, nearly hidden against the hardwood. He followed the trail above her shoulder and past her head.

"How do you figure?" Rogers asked.

"Because." Noah's voice was low. He remained focused on the trail of blood that stopped just shy of the closet door. "Her lips still have color. If she'd been dead a while, they wouldn't."

With his hand on the closet doorknob, Noah looked back and was met with a puzzled look on the EMT's face. A quick flick of his wrist and Noah yanked open the closet door, bracing himself for someone to lunge.

No one did.

Rogers gawked, staring along with Noah at the inside of the closet door. At the dark-red drawing of three deer, large antlers protruding from their heads. The crude image drawn in blood, smeared against the wood by someone's finger.

"That." Noah lifted his chin. "You might want to get a picture of."

***

Noah sat in a small room at a metal table that was cool against his forearms. The walls were the same interior-cinderblock walls in gym locker rooms and morgues, coated with puke-beige colored paint. Detective Alyssa Madsen sat across from him. Her brunette hair fell just above her shoulders, brushing the collar of her navy button-up blouse and black blazer as she stared at her laptop's screen. She didn't look up as she drank coffee from a Styrofoam cup. Noah took a sip from his own—one offered by the officer that had lead him to the room—and fought the urge to spit the bitter sludge on the table.

When Detective Madsen finally looked up from her computer, she skipped the small talk and reached over to place a tape recorder on the center of the table. "This is Detective Alyssa Madsen with Sara's Point Police Department. The time is zero-six-forty-five, and I am here with Noah McKeen, a paramedic employed by New England Medical Response to work overnights in Caligan, Connecticut. For the record, please state your name."

Noah leaned forward and spoke. "Noah McKeen."

Detective Madsen nodded. "And please state that you understand that you are not under arrest, that you are here willingly to provide a statement of what you observed this morning."

"I understand." The detective nodded, waving her hand in an effort to usher Noah. "That I am not under arrest and am here willingly."

And while it was true—technically—Noah could argue that he'd wanted to give a statement on scene. However, since he'd felt compelled to open the closet door, and thus located a macabre shrine of some sort, the beat officers felt it best if he met with the detective who would be handling the case. He offered an insincere smile and leaned back in his chair.

Detective Madsen typed something, giving Noah the chance to really take her in. He couldn't argue the fact that she was attractive. Thin lips, narrow face, and hazel eyes. There was a hardness to her, as would be expected for a detective, but at the same time something about her features ate at him. Was it her eyes? The way she kept them narrow despite their apparent beauty in color? Eyes were supposedly windows to the soul; if she constantly squinted hers, it gave people less of a chance to see inside. Or was it the way she tapped her finger? It wasn't in an impatient way, more of a trying to keep her mind from something way.

"So, Mr. McKeen, please walk me through, in your own words, what happened this morning."

He cleared his throat, sipped the disgusting coffee in front of him, and reiterated the basic details. "I was dispatched to a 43-year old female with abdominal pain and shortness of breath."

"Do you know what time the call went out?"

The time should be on your report was his first thought, but it wasn't what came out of his mouth. Try as he might though, Noah couldn't come up with a precise recollection of what dispatch had actually called. "Um, I know it was about three. Maybe a little after."

The detective typed something into her computer and waved him to continue.

"Right. When I arrived on scene, I went inside to find a volunteer from Sara's Point Ambulance in the upstairs bedroom. On the floor of the bedroom was a woman, presumably the woman the call was regarding, and she was dead."

Madsen folded her hands on top of one another. "Did you feel for a pulse? Or evaluate in any way?"

Had he? For a split second he couldn't remember. Had he touched the woman's body at all?

"No."

"Why not?"

He pursed his lips. Spoke slowly and nodded slightly with each word. "It was fairly evident that she was dead."

She spun her laptop and on the screen was a photograph of the body. "Showing Mr. McKeen photograph 36. Is this the woman you saw?"

Noah nodded and swallowed. Madsen urged him to state out loud if it was the victim. When he said yes, she thanked him.

"Can you describe her state when you arrived?"

Noah looked at her with his head slightly tilted. Was she serious? Of course he could describe the woman. But was it really necessary? Madsen had his run form. Obviously plenty of pictures. He stared at the table, fighting not to look the detective in the face.

"She was lying on her back, her legs open. Her throat was cut, I never got close enough to really see but it looked pretty deep. There was a bruise on her—actually a few bruises I think—on her face, near her jaw." He circled his own jaw with his finger and paused before continuing. Took another breath. "Her abdomen had been cut open—crudely. It looked like whoever did it had wanted to pull the skin back for some reason."

"Anything else?" she asked.

"Not really sure what else you want."

The detective straightened in her chair. "What else did you find in the room?"

At first the question puzzled him, but then Noah saw it in his head. Hidden between weaves of exhaustion and chemical compounds that had attached themselves to the receptors in his brain. The *fog*.

"There was a drawing—at least I guess you would call it a drawing—on the inside of the closet door."

The detective nodded. She leaned forward. "What was the drawing of, Mr. McKeen? What was it drawn with?"

Noah looked at the clock on the wall: seven on point. That anxious feeling began creeping up. The same one that hit him when he was stuck on a last minute call. It was seven. This part of his day was done, and he should be onto the next. Though recently his days were comprised of nothing more than sloth, not the worst sin but one of the seven nonetheless.

"Mr. McKeen? Am I keeping you?"

He shook his head. "No, I'm sorry. What was the question?"

"The closet, Mr. McKeen, how did you know to look inside of it?"

"I saw drops of blood on the floor. Didn't really think anything of it, except they were in kind of a line." But had they been? Or had they been just a spray from the slice in the woman's throat? Why was it so hard to remember? Actually, Noah knew why, but it beat having pain in his knee. "When I followed them, they led to the closet. I thought maybe the guy who did it was hiding in the there. I didn't think I would find . . . that."

Detective Madsen shifted in her seat. She rubbed her thumb and index finger together. A look of mental calculation on her face. "You saw drops of blood on the floor?"

"Yeah."

She typed something on her keyboard, turning the laptop back toward him; the screen displayed a picture of the floor and the dots of blood. The woman's neck and head were just visible in the corner of the photograph.

"You saw these drops of blood but were never close enough to see how deep the wound in her throat was?"

A sudden tightness in his throat paused his breathing. Surprise more than anything. "I—um?"

She spun the computer back to her side of the table. "I'm just wondering, Mr. McKeen. That's all."

Noah gripped his coffee, never lifting it from the table. He squeezed, careful not to crush the flimsy cup. He saw her look at his hand, and he quickly let the beverage go. She smiled.

"What was the mural of?" she asked.

"Deer," he said quickly.

Noah felt her eyes on him, studying his reactions, his words, searching for ticks and lies. He wanted out. This was voluntary, and he was being pressured by a hundred-and-forty pound woman in a blazer.

"What was the mural drawn with?"

"Blood." He exhaled. "It looked like it was drawn in blood."

She nodded. "Thank you, Mr. McKeen."

***

The second he sat in his Tacoma, Noah flipped open the center console and threw back a pill. He bent forward, head against the steering wheel, then started rubbing his knee, breathing heavily.

What the hell had he just sat through? They didn't label it an interrogation, but they sure as shit may as well have. Regardless, it was now past seven, which marked another day that he had missed his supervisor. Noah reached for his letter of resignation on the passenger seat, only to have his fingers touch nothing but cloth.

The seat was empty.

A wrench twisted his stomach. It was still sitting in the glove box of the SUV. He had left it there like a fucking idiot. His nerves were suddenly on edge at the thought of Jade—the paramedic who had met him at company headquarters two hours before her shift started—jumping in to cover him and pulling away with the letter still tucked neatly between the vehicle manual and a hazmat guide.

Noah threw his truck in drive and pulled out of the police station while twisting open the pill bottle and dry swallowing a second dose.

It slid down slowly, pushing against the sides of his esophagus. A quick cough and the feeling dissipated. There. That would do it. As he pulled into the parking lot of Mary's Cathedral—sparsely populated, as expected— he recognized Father Michaels' Honda in the far parking spot.

At such an early hour, the cathedral would be next to silent. In its silence, there would be beauty. Molecules of quiet air would move down the aisle, circulating in candle flames that dotted the altar, watched over by the statue of the Virgin Mother to the left, before rising to the feet and body of Jesus Christ.

If he went in, Noah would gaze at the Son of God, a man suspended in agony, feet and hands punctured with a broken crown digging into his scalp. He would stare and feel questions burning inside. Stirring in contempt and frustration.

But Noah didn't go inside. Instead, he sat in his truck and thought of the woman's body on the floor of her bedroom. Sliced open like a cadaver.

A car pulled into the handicapped spot just in front of the cathedral. Out of the driver's side came an elderly woman. She walked around to help her husband from the passenger side. His head trembled as he walked from the car to the ornate wood doors.

In his head, Noah played out the scene inside. Father Michaels sitting with the old man in a pew, offering comfort before walking to the back and finding Noah in the last pew, leaning forward with prayer pressed hands.

"You mustn't be discouraged at the trials of others, Noah."

An easy thing for the Father to say. But a domestic abuse. A fall down a flight of stairs resulting in a broken shin. A kid on his mom's hip who knocked a boiling pot of water off the stove and onto himself. The look in the flight nurse's eyes when she took the child from him and headed back to the helicopter. It was all engrained in there. Carved with a knife.

In a flat tone, Noah would ask, "At what point are they no longer trials and just misfortune? Needless suffering?"

"That point, my son, does not exist. Remember: Trust in the Lord with all your heart and do not lean on your own understanding."

Noah would nod. Mumble Proverbs, even though he didn't have to prove a damn thing to the Father, let alone that he knew the book backward and forward.

"That is right." Father Michaels would put a gentle hand on Noah's shoulder. "The road is long, Noah. Without His guidance, our burdens will overbear us. Misguide us. We mustn't let that happen, for if we do, then our way on this path is as good as lost."

He would get up and leave. Heed the Father's words and drive home, probably passing Amber on her way to work. He'd get up and go through it all again, only to have Father Michaels utter the same words the next time. Maybe that was why Noah had stopped going: the lessons were always the same.

His phone vibrated in the center console, the sudden plastic rattling startling him back to the present. He picked it up to find his brother's name on the display.

"Hey, Robert," Noah said.

"You still going to make it?"

"Make—shit—I'm sorry. I completely forgot. I had a late call and well, actually, you wouldn't believe the morning I've had."

"Try me," Robert said. "Please. I could use a good story to shake up the day."

"It's only eight."

"Right, and it's already boring as all hell. I have a class at ten. Can you make it to Crossing's by then? I'll wait to order."

Noah looked at the clock on his dashboard. The medication had begun to make his movements feel amplified. His eyelids fluttered. With a hand on the wheel he steadied himself. "Yeah. Yeah, I can be up there soon. Sorry again, just out of it."

"Yeah," Robert said. "Well third shift does that to you. I'll order you a coffee."

THREE

Noah pulled open the door to Crossing's Diner, causing bells to clang against the metal frame. It was a small place on the edge of Northern University's campus that smelled of eggs, bacon, and syrup. He caught sight of Robert in the farthest booth and walked down to slide in across the table.

At five-eight, Noah was a few inches shorter than his older brother, who was just shy of six feet. His hair was still solely brown, but his short beard was beginning to gray. He grunted as Noah sat down. Rather than look up, he used the back end of a red pen to push his glasses up the bridge of his nose, before leaving bloody slashes across a term paper.

"Jesus, Rob," Noah said. "Go a little easy on them."

He pointed the pen at Noah's chest, finally meeting his eyes. "Read enough of these bloody things, and you'll realize the scope of their idiocy."

"You're the one who keeps doing it. Isn't the defini-tion of insanity repeating the same thing over and over, expecting different results?"

"So you can remember Einstein's most overused quote." He capped the pen and grumbled. "While that doesn't make you a scholar, I suppose you're right. If there was something else I could settle on, believe me, I would. Unfortunately, the humanities don't offer the broadest scope of job security. Something I should have realized when I went into this."

"You're doing what you like. Or at least what you used to like."

"Yes, well, the upper-class is not as awful as the freshmen. That lot is terribly misinformed about everything. I've given up trying to hold their attention. If they'd rather tweet their education away, then so be it. Perhaps they can get fifteen dollars an hour at McDonald's."

Noah shook his head. "Is McDonald's really paying fifteen dollars an hour?"

A young waitress appeared. College student that greeted mornings without a hangover. "Coffee?"

"Yes," Noah said. "Thanks."

She turned to Robert. "Refill? Would either of you like a menu?"

This time it was Robert who spoke first. "Yes, both of us, please."

She slid a pair of single-page menus onto the table and told them she would be back in a few minutes.

"So," Robert said. "Was it at least a good call that held you or another routine round of bullshit?"

And from there, Noah's mind was led down mental tributaries until it came to memories of the morning's mutilation. How many years had it been since there was a homicide in the small lake town? Had there ever been one at all? Things like that were normally reserved for the city. He stirred his already blended coffee and put the mug to his mouth.

"Noah?"

"Yeah—sorry. Rough morning."

Robert lifted his head from the menu. "So you've said."

The waitress re-appeared as if she could smell the tension and came to quell it with the promise of food in exchange for good behavior.

"Alright," she said. "What can I get you guys?"

Two omelets, two orange juices, and two sides of hash.

"Such individualism," Robert said as they finished ordering. He slid his ungraded papers into his briefcase and stirred a packet of sugar into his coffee. "Well, what was it?"

Noah looked at him, confused. His body tingled in that odd state where exhaustion felt like intoxication. He yawned, and as he stretched, he felt another familiar feeling: the fuzziness brought on by opioids. His knee no longer ached. His skin, his muscles, everything existed in a comfortably numb state of subtle pleasure.

"Noah?"

"Hmm? What was what?"

He snapped to, refocused on his brother and the conversation. All the while, the pleasantness inside his body rose from his feet to his knees, from his waist to his chest, and through his neck like a volcano of peace. The euphoria wrapped itself around his brain, where the medication masked away any and all pain.

"The call. Jesus, Noah, are you alright?"

Noah pulled his phone out and slid through several messages until he found the pictures Rogers had sent him, then passed the phone to Rob. "Like I said, it was a long morning."

His brother flicked through the photos. Noah slumped back in the booth and fought to keep his eyes open. He let his gaze bounce from head to head around the diner, trying to focus on anything to keep them from closing. A young man was standing next to the counter. Their eyes met and something felt off. It could have been the gauges in the guy's ears or the tattoo crawling up the side of his thin neck, but normally those things didn't take a second of Noah's attention.

"Where was this?" Robert asked.

"Hmm?" *The phone. Focus.* "Sara's Point. Near the lake."

"Were you the first one there?"

Noah shook his head, looked back up and once again saw the kid looking at him. "Couple volunteers."

"Who called 9-1-1?"

Robert's rapid-fire questions along with the sudden overwhelming feeling of being watched caused Noah to shift in the booth. "I have no idea. The detective that questioned me never said. She was too busy leaning toward, you know, me." He forced a laugh. "But it must have been her—the dead woman."

An arm brushed against his. He looked up to see the kid from the counter now standing next to him. Noah immediately slid farther into the booth. Not in a polite, *here, let me give you some room*, way either. Robert shot Noah a look before turning his attention to the young man.

"Case, what can I do for you?"

Noah noticed flakes of dandruff on the shoulders of the kid's black hoody and felt his lip instinctively curl upward. Matted hair, clinging together with the shine of grease. Had he never heard of a shower? Shampoo wasn't that expensive.

Robert's palm hit the table, and Noah jerked backward, his reactions delayed by the medication. The kid had been talking. What had he said? What had Noah missed this time?

"I'm sorry, Case. No extra credit. If you do well on the exam and turn your final paper in on time, I am absolutely certain you will do fine."

The kid nodded. Dejected like a miscreant on Christmas. He walked back to the counter, shoulders slumped, and picked up a bagged container of take-away.

"Noah," Robert hissed.

"Who was that?"

"Huh? What are you—?"

"The kid. Who was he?"

"He's from my medieval history class. Why?"

Noah dragged a hand through his hair, heard the bells near the door rattle. "Because he was fucking staring at me."

Robert's face contorted. "What? Case? He's harmless. Jesus. A little weird, but trust me, he's normal compared to some of these kids. Now, anyway, back to this. You think the woman in these pictures was the one who called the police?"

Noah shook away the thoughts of being stalked. Being watched by some punk shit who probably had both nipples pierced with a fucking chain holding them together.

"Yeah—I don't know. I mean, it had to have been. There was no one in the house, and it makes no sense that the guy who did it would have called it in. But, at the same time, how could she have called? There was no way someone left her like that and she was alive long enough to call 9-1-1. Plus, there was no phone anywhere in the room."

Robert pinched the screen and zoomed in on one of the pictures.

"Alright." The waitress was back and holding two steaming plates. The smell hit Noah like a fist. Robert quickly pressed the sleep button on the side of Noah's phone. "Let me know if you boys need anything else, okay?"

As she turned, her fingertips grazed Noah's arm. The drugs amplified the feeling of her touch. Each millimeter of soft contact like orgasms on his skin. Robert sat poised, ready to eat, utensils over his plate.

"So you saw a murder and were questioned by a detective? Interrogated, actually?"

Noah shook his head. "I didn't see a thing. I found the body. Well, the ambulance crew found the body a few minutes before I got there."

Robert raised his eyebrows, a sly smile on his face. "So you were meant to find her. You or one of the ambulance crew."

"Huh?" Noah stuffed a forkful of omelet into his mouth. Chopped peppers and warm, melted cheese inside of fluffy eggs. He barely needed to chew.

"Someone called 9-1-1 to get you there, and when you got there, she was dead."

Noah paused before taking another bite. Opened his mouth to say something but stopped.

"What?" Robert pressed.

"What if the call was a call for help? Like she was being beaten or something but couldn't say *help I'm being beaten*, and we didn't get there in time."

His older brother shook his head. "Don't do that. Your response time would have been the same, regardless of the complaint. Besides, the guy beating her would have known she had called 9-1-1."

"True, but if it's a medical complaint, an ambulance is dispatched, whereas a domestic automatically triggers a cop. May have given her a chance at least."

"Really," Robert said and took a bite of his omelet. "Don't do that to yourself."

Noah stretched. Felt the euphoria in his muscles. A billion tiny hands massaging his entire body. It was unlike marijuana, and it was nothing like alcohol. He felt complete control over his body and the words that left it. It was just . . . a calm. He was effectively numb. Complacent and happy. Just like the song. He queued Pink Floyd's *Comfortably Numb* in his head. Made a mental note to put it on during the drive home.

"What'd the detective say?" Robert asked.

Noah squinted and rubbed his eyes. "Nothing really. She just had me describe what I found. She seemed surprised I found the closet."

Robert put his fork down. "*You* found the closet?"

"Yeah? There were drops of blood leading to it. I thought maybe whoever did it was still there, and I wanted the upper hand. Why is that surprising? You may be a genius in history and literature or whatever, but I can read a scene better than anyone."

Robert said, "And yet you opened the closet door rather than wait for the police?"

Noah sat back and folded his arms across his chest. "Why is it a big deal? At least I found it. Everyone else overlooked it. And what if she'd had a kid hiding in there or something?"

Rob held his hands up. "Point. I'm sorry. It's not that you did anything wrong; I'm just jealous, if we're being honest. You get to run around and have all this fun while I'm stuck lecturing to a hall full of zombies. It's bloody boring."

"Again," Noah said. "You are the one who continues to do it. Besides, you have a wife, two kids, and you teach dark history."

His older brother held up a sole finger. "I teach *a* dark history class. Only one a semester. It's all that bastard Melvin would allow. Despite the fact, mind you, that it is the most popular history class at the university. Haven't had less than a full roster in three semesters. Wave killers and tragedies in peoples' faces, and they are instantly addicted. Talk about the dawn of civilization or the feats of the Mesopotamian Empire and well…" His voice trailed off, and he shoved a forkful of eggs into his mouth.

"Sorry," Noah said.

Robert waved the apology away. "I have a great job. I shouldn't complain."

They ate the rest of their respective breakfasts in silence. As the moments ticked by, so did the numbness humming underneath Noah's skin. He finished the last of his meal as a dull ache returned to his knee. He stretched under the table, but the muscles refused to loosen.

"Leg still bothering you?" Robert asked as he slid his credit card inside the black bill holder.

"Sore. Just bothers me after back-to-back runs."

"Eh. Sore beats painful enough to take meds or need physical therapy anymore. Little progress is still progress."

"Yeah," Noah averted his eyes. "Thanks for break-fast, by the way."

"Don't mention it."

Outside in the cool morning air Robert added, "You should send me those pictures. Maybe I can figure out what the deer mean."

Noah looked at him, puzzled.

"Whoever left it, left it for a reason. You don't just use someone's blood to paint forest animals on a closet door without a reason behind it."

"I think we should leave that to the police."

"Says the one who opened the door in the first place. Come on, throw me a bone and kill my boredom. I mean, I did just buy you breakfast."

Noah rolled his eyes as he sent the photos.

FOUR

Noah's weekend passed as a forty-eight hour chunk of intoxication with brief, intermittent slivers of sobriety. He woke Monday morning to his cell phone vibrating off the top of his nightstand and clunking to the hardwood floor. He reached it just as it went to voicemail.

His room was dark, courtesy of blackout curtains. He laid his head back and rubbed his palms against his eyes until the pressure caused yellow and green spots to pop in and out. Pain wrapped itself around his knee and traveled down his shin. He reached for the orange bottle on his nightstand and shook a pill out. There were only four left inside. He choked down the Percocet with no water and looked through his missed calls: *work, Rob, work.*

An invisible hand gripped his stomach. The letter. Someone had found it in the glove box. Son-of-a-bitch. Feet on the floor, elbows on his knees, he dialed his voicemail and swallowed.

But it wasn't a harsh message; it had nothing to do with his letter of resignation at all. Someone had called in sick for their shift and they were looking for afternoon coverage. Relieved, Noah recalled what had happened the last time he had offered to cover a callout. Reminded of it every time he stretched his leg or tried to walk. He took another pill, just out of spite.

Empty bags of microwave popcorn littered the coffee table. Beer bottles stood like skyscrapers next to open, overdue Redbox cases. He pulled a glass from the sink, ignored the smudged fingerprints, and cranked the faucet. With his other thumb, he deleted his missed calls, pulled up his contacts, and dialed a different number.

A bubbly voice on the other end answered. "Thank you for calling Dr. Linden's office. This is Trish. Can I help you?"

Noah cleared his throat, phlegm catching in his chest. "Yeah, hi, this is Noah McKeen. I was calling to see if my prescription was ready. I'm going to be in the area this afternoon and was wondering if I could come in and get it."

"What's the prescription for?"

"Percocet." He was sober, and because so, there was a touch of shame in his request.

"Just one second."

He heard the clack of the phone being put on the counter, followed by the rifling of papers and the typing on a keyboard. Seconds passed. Noah refilled his glass of water and began to drink when the girl's voice returned on the line.

"I'm sorry Mr. McKeen, but you're not due for a refill on that medication until the fifteenth."

He felt himself physically recoil. Like a fist had connected with his chest.

"No," he said with feigned confusion. "I haven't picked up a new prescription in almost a month."

"I'm sorry. According to what I have, you last filled this medication on August 15, which would put you at three weeks next Thursday."

"That really can't be. I only have two left."

The line went silent. After a second he could hear the sounds of her fingers on a keyboard. "Really, I'm sorry Mr. McKeen, but there's nothing we can do until you're due for a refill. If you'd like to come in and talk to Dr. Linden, I can schedule you an appointment."

He scratched the side of his face and paced the apartment's small kitchen, separated from the main living room by a cheap black counter made of the same material they used for desks in high school science labs. There was a small, circular table near the wall of the kitchen with two chairs and a pile of mail on it.

"Mr. McKeen?"

"Yeah—yeah, I'll come in and see her. What's the closest she has?"

"I can get you in on Friday at one o'clock."

There were only two pills left in the bottle on his nightstand. A lonely little duo.

"She doesn't have anything today?"

The receptionist clicked her tongue. "No. Nothing today. I'm sorry. And she will be out of the office tomorrow and Wednesday for a conference. Would you like the Friday appointment?"

Deflated, he leaned back against the counter. "Yeah. Yeah, that's fine."

When he hung up, he fought the urge to throw his phone. But another, internal voice countered his anger. *Have you really been taking that much?*

It was true. He had been. But the pain had been severe enough. Hadn't it? Back-to-back calls killed him. And every time he bent down, he felt the muscles constrict like a python just waiting for the joint to pop and the bones to turn to dust. And now, he was running out of the only thing that kept them solidified.

There was something else he could do. Someone else he could call. But that was supposed to be a favor for a rainy day. Part of him—the part of him that wanted relief from pain—believed that it was, in fact, a rainy day, and if he didn't do something, the week would be a thunderstorm. Withdrawing from opioids was not something he wanted to do. Nothing that would kill him—or at least that's what every medical professional said—but watch someone go through it, and that point could be argued.

Fuck it. He dialed the number and resumed pacing.

"What's up, Noah?"

"Hey, Mick. You working?"

"Will be in a bit. Eleven-to-eleven. Why? What do you need?"

Noah was nodding in his kitchen, though Mick couldn't see that. Without warning his nerve left him.

"Nothing," he said.

"Then why'd you call?"

"Nothing," he repeated. "Really, not a big deal. I'll swing in later."

"Alright."

Eighteen months ago, he would have woken and gone for a two-mile run, came back and found Amber cooking breakfast in her underwear. It would take seconds before there would be flour handprints on her chest and ass. But rather than hoisting a beautiful woman onto his counter, her legs wrapped around his waist, pulling him farther into her, he was standing in his kitchen alone, debating the validity and need for prescription strength pain medication.

And in his mind it was justified. As it always was. With an exhale, he shuffled back to bed where cotton sheets swallowed him and his apathy.

***

Noah punched 9-1-1-* on the keypad of the ambulance entrance to Caligan General. The universal code. The doors slid into the wall with the *whhhnnntth* of plastic wheels on guided tracks. The emergency room was laid out in a U with the nurses and physician workstations at its center. He nodded, wrinkled his nose at the smell. Where nursing homes had the scent of death, hospitals stayed on the line of the dying.

As Noah walked, he passed a scraggly-looking woman sitting on a stretcher in the hall. An intravenous line had been inserted into her left arm, with a bag of fluid hanging from a pole on the bed. She clutched a basin. White, foamy spit pooled inside it.

"Hey, Noah." A nurse smiled and waved as she bent over to look at a computer screen, her stethoscope around her neck, each end a separate pendulum. She looked back up, a sudden look of remembrance on her face. "Hey, were you really on the other night?"

Noah cleared his throat. "Yeah. Sara's Point call?"

There was a slight, yet noticeable, widening of her eyes. "What happened?"

The woman on the stretcher was doubled over with spit hanging on her lips. A fake groan in her throat. The nurse didn't wait for his answer. "Was it really a murder?"

Now that she had said it, Noah felt he didn't have to. He shrugged his shoulders and offered her nothing extra. Though there was a gnawing in the back of his head. It had been a murder. Had Robert found anything in relation to the door? There had been such enthusiasm, though that was Noah's brother. Always obsessed with the macabre. If Robert had read Poe a hundred times growing up, it would be a low guess.

"Wow," the nurse said quietly. "I'll bet it was her husband. I watch those shows, and it's always the husband. They should check to see if he had life insurance on her. I don't get how people think they can get away with something like that."

A second nurse appeared behind the counter. Her curls framed her face, bouncing off her shoulders as she walked. Freckles dotted each cheek, and when she spoke, she had the faintest hint of an Irish accent. "Noah, what are you doing here?"

"Just looking for Mick."

She nodded over her shoulder. "Prompt Care."

"Thanks."

A patient groaned from behind a curtain. Seconds later a male voice said, "Almost done. Just don't move."

Noah followed the back hall of the ER into a separate area divided into six minimalistic rooms equipped with chairs rather than stretchers. No cardiac monitors, no cabinets filled with supplies in case a patient coded, because a patient would never code in Prompt Care. It was a fast-track area for minor orthopedic incidents and other ailments that didn't require the full attention of an emergency room. It held the bare essentials: walls lined with short counters, sinks, bandages, and splints.

Glorified Band-Aid stations inside rooms meant to patch up boo-boos. Around the corner was a small work area. Noah nodded at the nurse, a young Spanish woman he didn't recognize. Just another day-shifter. Another one that could tolerate the damn light. Dr. Mick Hens looked up from an iPad, his feet resting on the counter.

"You don't normally work Monday, do you?" Noah asked.

Mick put down his tablet. "Pick-up. Natasha's on vacation. Day 11-of-13 for me."

"Ouch."

"No kidding. So, what's up?"

Noah looked over his shoulder at a nurse he didn't know. If it had been night, when the ER was staffed by people he had worked with, delivered codes and broken bones to, there would be no need to avoid candid words.

"Maria," Mick called. The nurse looked up from her phone. "Can you give us a second?"

She pulled a pack of cigarettes and a lighter from her purse. When she was out the door and into the waiting room, Noah spoke. He was careful to make frequent eye contact and strain his expression when he could.

"The knee's no better, Mick. One back-to-back, and I'm laid up for days."

"Yeah, I heard about you taking the triage job." The doctor *tsked* and folded his arms across his chest. "That fly car is sought after, Noah. You give that up, and you'll never get it back. They'll have no problem replacing you."

Noah looked at the ground, a pit in his stomach. "Yeah, I know. I don't have a choice."

"It's really that bad?" Mick waved his arm in the direction of the main emergency room. "You'll waste away in this shit-hole. You work hospital as a medic and you won't hang meds, you won't even hang fluids. You'll take histories and start IVs. You're way too good for that. What you should be doing is going to medical school, if you honestly want off that fly car."

"Right," Noah furrowed his brow. "And where am I going to get the money for that?" He pointed to his knee. "I'm still paying for this."

"I get it. I just don't want to see you fuck up your life because you've given up on fixing it."

Noah's face burned. A corrosive mixture of anger and disgust. His heart hammered against his chest. Mouth dry. Lights. Day shifts. The smell of the place.

Mick leaned back in his chair. "It mean's you'll have to work with Amber, you know."

Noah's head snapped up. "Wait—what?"

The doc nodded. "She transferred down from ICU about a month ago. She said it was to get off of nights, but I think she just missed it. She's doing three twelves— mid-shift I think."

Noah's mouth twitched. The muscles in his cheeks went slack. If he took the job, then he would work three twelves too; it was the way of the hospital world. All fine except it meant that the best case scenario had him working with her once a week, while the likelihood—because God was bored it seemed—meant they would work the same weekends and the same shift during the week. He closed his fists to hide his shaking hands.

"So, Mick, what do I do? Stay on pain killers for the rest of my life?"

The doctor shrugged. "I don't do chronic pain management, but I can refer you to someone who does. I mean, it's not the right way to go, but if that's what you think will do it. What happened when you tried physical therapy?"

"Nothing."

Mick leaned forward and grabbed his knee. Noah recoiled as the doctor rolled his thumbs over the top of the joint, pressing down and squeezing.

"What are you taking for it again?"

Noah looked over Mick's head into the Prompt Care waiting room.

"I *was* taking Percocet, but I've been out for about a week, and ibuprofen isn't doing a damn thing. Is there anyway you can help me out? I hate asking, but I'm frustrated and tired and to be honest, about to throw my fucking career away."

Mick spun in his chair and reached for his bag. The door to the waiting area opened as the nurse came back in, her attention on her phone. She took a seat back at her computer and her scrub top crawled up, revealing the tail of a pick thong. Noah couldn't help but stare. Her skin seemed smooth. Soft. And the curve of her hips was—

"Look." Mick handed him two pieces of paper. "One pill every eight hours. This is the strong stuff, the 7.5-325. I wrote it for you to take every four. Don't. This way it'll last a little longer than 30-days. The second one is for cyclobenzaprine, the muscle relaxer. Take it at night; it'll help you sleep. Don't take them at the same time unless you want to be out cold for half-a-day."

Noah smacked the scripts against his open palm. He knew this. He was a medic that carried narcs more powerful than either of these in his bag. Meds under such scrutiny they required daily audits and two-person accountability when refilling. But addicts are stupid. And he was playing the stupidest one. "Thanks, Mick. I really appreciate this."

He shook his head. "Don't thank me yet. There's a stipulation to these, Noah. Meet with Catalina. She's a new physical therapist."

Noah opened his mouth, but the doc raised his hand. "I know; PT didn't work the first time. I want you to give it a second try, okay? Do that, and I won't call the pharmacy and tell them you stole my script pad. Got it?"

He stared at the scribbled writing. A full bottle and muscle relaxers to boot. "Okay," he said. "What's her number?"

Mick wrote it on a sticky note and handed it over before picking his iPad back up and shooing Noah out with a grin.

At the door, Noah turned. "Hey—" he did his best to ignore the nurse sitting like an awkward buoy between a pirate and the Coast Guard. "How is she anyway?"

Mick lowered his tablet. "The truth?"

Don't ask a question if you don't want to know the answer. It, like most good advice, was never followed. With his hand on the doorframe, Noah nodded. He caught Maria looking at him from the corner of his eye.

"She's good."

"That's good." Despite his attempts to stop, Noah kept nodding. "She seeing anyone?"

"Yup," Maria blurted.

She sucked her cheeks back and immediately focused on her phone. Noah squeezed his hand against the door handle.

"Do you know who?" Noah asked.

Maria said, "She's been seeing an ortho PA. Name's Neil something. I can never remember. The skinny one with glasses."

"Noah," Mick said. "Go call that physical therapist."

He whacked the scripts against the wall. "Right— Right. Thanks again, Mick."

FIVE

Noah left the drugstore and pulled into the parking lot of Hardy's Liquors across the street. There was a guy behind the counter cutting ads or coupons from a newspaper spread near the register.

Signs plastered the walls: **Sale! 30-Pack $20.99!**

Drinking had never really been his thing. When Amber was around, they got drunk together. They got drunk and did crazy shit while they were out and crazy shit while they were in. The woman was fire, and she erupted with just a little gasoline. A touch of liquor, a song on the radio that spoke to her body, and it was game over. Primal.

He stopped in the whiskey section. Paused to look at the different bottles. Then he moved to the next aisle where the shelves were lined with vodka. He reached for one, his hand on its neck, when he let it go and continued walking.

"Need help finding anything?" the clerk asked.

Noah just shook his head. He inhaled deeply and let himself relax. Forced the badness down and gave in, letting an unseen force guide him as he kept walking. Down one aisle and back up another. He would find something. Sooner or later, he would find something.

Before Noah could, though, his phone rang. He thought of ignoring the call, but when he saw it was Robert, his interest was piqued.

"Hey," Noah said as soon as the call connected.

"Hey, can you talk?" Robert asked.

Noah looked over his shoulder. The clerk was busy at the counter, fiddling with something. But that was an odd thing to check. What did it matter if the clerk was busy or if he was standing two feet away?

"Noah?" Robert said.

"Yeah, sorry. I'm at the store."

"I'll make it quick. Have you heard from the detective? Did they find anything else on scene? Any fingerprints or evidence or anything?"

Noah furrowed his brow. "No. Not that I know of, anyway. I'm not really involved."

"So they haven't found anything?" Robert asked quickly.

"No. Why was there something in the pictures? Did you figure something out?"

There was a pause on the line. A muffled sound like a hand being dragged across the mic or the cell being fumbled.

"Robert? You there?"

His voice came fast and furious. "Hey, I have to go; Claudia's coming."

The call disconnected, leaving Noah wondering why it was a big deal if Robert's wife found him on the phone. He puzzled for a second, then dismissed it as nothing more then an angry wife—something Claudia was no stranger to being.

Noah's hand came to rest on a bottle of rum as he thought: *I could be a pirate.* He pictured the white sand beneath his feet and the turquoise water as it lapped the shore. With a bottle of cola from a cooler in the back, he was set. *Yeah, I could definitely be a pirate.*

He parked outside his apartment building and stretched like a dog lying in the sun. The bag holding the bottle of rum and soda was a plastic treasure chest clutched tight against his body as he walked inside and avoided the stairs. With a final lurch, the elevator stopped its ascent and the doors dinged open. Happy, his mind on the first drink that would send him to a tropical location filled with pale sands and teal waters, Noah didn't see Detective Madsen until he rounded a corner and they collided.

The rum hit the floor with a clunk but thankfully didn't shatter. Noah chased the soda bottle across the hall, the inside of the bottle filling with bubbles. When he turned back, Detective Madsen held out a pill bottle, her eyes on the label. He snatched the medication back and shoved it into his pocket.

"Hello, Mr. McKeen," she said.

Her voice was smooth. A mellow track playing in the background of a restaurant where you can't get a table without a reservation. Noah fumbled with his keys, trying to shrug away apprehension and nerves.

"What can I help you with?" he asked.

"Just hoping to ask you a few questions about the other night. Trying to piece some things together."

He chuckled. "My brother—" and then immediately remembered he had violated every patient privacy law by showing Robert those pictures.

"Your brother what, Mr. McKeen?" Madsen asked.

"Thinks I need some sleep," Noah said quickly, praying Madsen would let it go.

As the lock turned, he remembered the state of the place: dirty dishes in the sink, crumpled clothes on the floor. He half muttered, "Ignore the mess."

With the bags on the counter, he quickly put the bottle of rum in a cabinet and the bottle of soda in the fridge. He shoved the pills into the silverware drawer and asked if he could get her something to drink. She waved her decline as she kept walking, stepping from the kitchen into the living room, her head constantly moving, looking this way and that.

"You shouldn't drink with those," she said without looking in his direction.

"I'm sorry?"

"If you're hurt," she nodded her chin slightly. "Mixing those pain pills with alcohol isn't a good idea."

That irked him. Made his skin crawl. She was law enforcement, and he was medical. A thin, decisive line.

"So," Noah said in an attempt to pull her attention back to the kitchen. He poured himself a glass of water. "I'm not sure what else I can help you with. Has there been any development or anything?"

"Do you live alone, Mr. McKeen?" she asked.

Noah nodded slowly. "I do."

It was her turn to nod. She leaned against the wall just next to his kitchen table, keeping the ability to see the living room and kitchen all at once.

"Her name was Marisa Ann Newton. Does that sound familiar to you at all?"

Noah shook his head. "Should it?"

"So you don't recognize the name?"

"No."

"Did you have any other calls that night? Prior to that one?"

He pursed his lips. Hadn't this question been asked already? He tried to replay the conversation—the borderline interrogation—from last week. "I think so. Yeah, there was a chest pain earlier in the evening and then a dizziness a little later on."

"Do you remember what time?"

Noah leaned over his counter. With two fingers he pinched the bridge of his nose. Why couldn't he remember? Truth be told, he could barely remember the calls themselves, let alone what time they went out. Hadn't there been a third one? A motor vehicle accident? No. Not that night. But he couldn't be sure what times the others were dispatched. Everything was fogged over. Like silhouettes in a morning mist.

"I'm sorry," he said.

The detective pushed herself off the wall. "Do you mind if I use your bathroom? One too many cups of coffee."

"No—not at all, just down the hall on the left."

He was happy to be rid of her, if only for a moment. Why couldn't he remember the other night? Had he really taken that many pills? Was it the pills? There were never any memory problems before. Not that there were any now. He could remember the calls. He could recall everything about the murder scene: the state of the body, the closet door.

"Are you religious, Mr. McKeen?" Detective Madsen asked as she reentered the kitchen.

Had he heard the toilet flush? He gave her a quizzical look.

"The crucifixion on your wall."

"Oh," Noah said. "I was at one point. Trying to get back to it."

"Faith is difficult. Anyway, thank you for your time. If you think of anything, please give me a call. Okay?"

Noah nodded as she slid a business card into his palm. When the door clicked shut, he almost fell to the floor in relief. Half celebrating, half-panicking, he swallowed another pill with a stiff rum and coke. The tang of the liquor made his lips curl back.

SIX

Despite the fact that there was surely only one, Noah saw two stoplights rock back and forth. Little red orbs that swayed in the middle of the night, pushed by a sudden breeze.

He rubbed his hand down his face and tried to clear away some of the high he was riding. As if that was possible. An unfortunate outcome of taking one too many, just a little too quickly. Judgment barred. An hour-or-so overlap before the effect of the first (or second) pill dissipated and the third (or fourth) latched on.

The radio on his dashboard crackled to life. Alive with the sound of beeping tones that signaled he was needed.

"CN dispatch to Sara's Point respond with the Alpha-One medic: 201 Maple Hill Drive, 82-year old male, lifeline activation. Feeling faint, general weakness."

The light turned green and Noah groaned. "Alpha-One responding."

"Alpha-One responding, 23:17."

His head felt heavy, and he fought to keep his eyes open, when he realized he had never turned his lights or sirens on. With a quick flick, the sides of the road flashed to life in oscillating reflections of blue and red.

The house was a raised ranch at the end of a quarter-mile dirt driveway. A shell of a rusted truck was parked at the edge of the woods, vines and small trees smothering the life out of it. The ambulance hadn't arrived, and the only other car was a sedan with blue volunteer lights flashing in the rear window.

Noah hopped out. Steadied himself against the side of the Explorer and took a deep breath of cool air.

He knocked on the front door. Several seconds passed without an answer, so he tried the handle and elbowed the door open.

"EMS. Hello?"

There was no answer from inside the house. Like most raised ranches, the door opened to two sets of stairs. He peered down into the lower level where a light glowed, only to hear shuffling from a room on the first floor.

"Hello, it's the paramedic." With him announcing himself, where the hell was the first responder? The car was outside in the driveway, blue light flashing and all.

At the top of the stairs were a kitchen and living room. There were dishes in the sink. A pile of them. Newspapers and magazines littered the counter and tucked to the back, half-hidden under the mess, was a weekly pill container.

"Noah."

He turned quick, jumped back half-a-step. It was a volunteer EMT, dressed in a jumpsuit with the Sara's Point patch worn off. No money in the budget for new gear. The man's face, his sharp jaw line covered in stubble, was familiar. Sober Noah could have placed him.

"He's back here; come on."

Noah adjusted his pack and monitor and followed the man down a short hall to a bedroom. There was an old man on the ground slumped against the bottom of a bed, chest slowly rising and falling.

Noah dropped to the man's side, gripped his wrist for a pulse.

"Signs?" he asked without looking up. The EMT didn't respond. Noah counted the beats in the man's wrists. Faint but there. "Was anyone here?"

"N—no. Not when I got here. I just got here. The door was unlocked. Kind of different than the other night, right?"

Noah looked up and then it clicked. The DOA—murder victim. This guy was the EMT Noah had passed heading into the house, the one getting undressed by his car.

"No kidding," Noah said. "Get a blood pressure for me."

The man fumbled. Noah heard patting. Was he looking for a cuff or a stethoscope?

"For God's sakes, man. Just go check his bathroom; find out what meds he's on."

The EMT rushed from the room, and Noah shook his head. He'd have to talk to the chief at some point. Mention the quality individuals Sara's Point had resorted to recruiting.

There was no orange Do Not Resuscitate bracelet on the old man's wrist.

"What's your name?" Noah asked as he unbuttoned the man's flannel shirt and placed square cardiac stickers on loose, pale skin. Stray hairs curled around the edges.

There was a faint siren in the distance, and Noah hoped there would be some form of competence on the ambulance. A rhythm appeared on his monitor, and he slapped the automated blood pressure cuff on the other arm, reaching for the man's hand in order to look at his fingers. Calloused and hard.

"Yep," he said quietly.

He dropped the man's hand and reached in his bag for a portable glucometer and an IV kit. The EMT came back with six pill bottles cradled in his hands, ready to spill over like a winning pot from a Vegas casino.

"What's he got?" Noah asked. "Anything for diabetes?"

"Um. I think—hold on."

Noah rolled his eyes and grumbled while he tied the tourniquet around the patient's arm.

"Metop—metoprolol?" the EMT said.

"Nope. That's blood pressure. What else?" Noah flicked his finger against the inside crook of the man's elbow, before pushing the needle inside. Blood flashed. The small chamber filled red. "Get that."

The EMT didn't move. Noah pointed. "The glucometer—get it."

"Right. Right, sorry." Pill bottles hit the floor. Scattered and rolled.

"Watch it," Noah snapped.

"Sorry."

"It's fine; just pay attention, okay?"

The EMT laughed—not an awkward, nervous laugh. Noah paused. Looked up, but the EMT was fiddling with the glucometer, a smile on his face that stretched from ear-to-ear.

The patient groaned. A guttural sound from deep in the man's chest. Noah pulled a pen from his pocket. He pushed the tip of the ballpoint into the end of the withdrawn needle, forcing a small amount of blood to drip onto a test strip. Lines floated across the glucometer's screen as Noah taped the intravenous line to the man's skin. The monitored beeped. Displayed a blood pressure of 88 / 56.

"Shit," Noah hissed. "Okay, in my bag. Grab a liter of fluid."

"Right." The EMT fumbled over the zipper on the edge of Noah's bag. "You're so good at this. It's unbelievable to watch."

The man's comment caught Noah off guard, but before he could answer, the glucometer chimed.

"36," Noah said. No surprise. He was already drawing up an amp of dextrose, ready to give the man an injection of pure sugar. The front door opened and Noah locked eyes with the other EMT. "Go get them in here."

The first responder lingered, just for a second, before nodding, and heading out of the bedroom.

Noah exhaled as he pushed the medication. Seconds later, as the ambulance crew entered the room, the bumbling EMT no longer with them, the old man on the floor groaned, groggy and disoriented. Noah attached a bag of saline to the IV line and handed it to one of the standing EMTs as he began to tell them about the patient. A small kernel inside of him popped, sending out a faint, airy feeling of success and happiness. For the briefest, minute part of a second, the feeling was better than that of the drugs.

***

Noah's supervisor caught him Tuesday morning at the end of his shift. He was a short, overweight man named Paul whose only remaining strip of hair ran like a buffer between his ears and the top of his head.

"You wanted to see me the other day?" Paul asked.

Noah opened his mouth slightly. The envelope was in his bag, safely retrieved, none the wiser. His Tacoma sat twenty feet away. Freedom, just barely unattainable.

Paul adjusted his belt and Noah noted the overhang of the older man's gut. He was on his way to a similar body structure. The first hint of it already appearing in key areas: cheeks, chin, a little in the chest. The thought was repulsive. Amber was perfect. Toned, slim, and athletic. The way he used to be when they went for runs together in the early morning, passing children who were still waiting for the bus, relishing the burn in muscle tissue and the inside of their lungs.

Pushed by adrenaline, they would devour each other, the taste of sweat on his tongue as he peeled her tank top strap down and licked her shoulder. Against the fridge. Against the wall. On the couch. The bed.

If he grew a gut, that would be the final nail.

"The other day," Paul prodded. "Before all that shit happened with the murder call, you said you needed to talk to me at the end of your shift. Everything good?"

"Yeah, yeah," Noah said. He waved the man away. Tried to buy an extra second before blurting out the first thing that popped into his head. "Explorer was running a little rough. Seems fine now, though. Forget I said anything."

Bullet dodged. He had reached his truck when his supervisor called after him.

"Noah," Paul waited until he was at the truck to continue. "Do you need to talk to anyone?"

Noah's face contorted, the muscles in his forehead scrunching together. "What?"

Paul raised his palms. "Between me and you. No tough guy act, nothing. If you need to talk to someone, you have to let me know. There's no shame in it, and you know that."

An awkward silence passed between them. Noah's stomach grumbled. "I'm good, Paul. Thank you though."

Paul nodded as Noah climbed into the driver's seat of his truck, hand resting guiltily on the center console.

***

Eight.

Eight was the number of times Noah had entered Catalina's number into his phone, and also the number of times he had deleted it without calling. In between each one, he had dialed Robert's number and, like with the physical therapist, decided not to call. Though Noah wanted to. God, did he want to. He had questions, more than he thought he would, but the fact was that Noah had responded to an actual DOA murder call, the first in his tenure as a medic.

What had the deer meant? Noah walked to his bedroom, pulled his laptop from the floor, and brought it into the kitchen. As the computer booted up, he glanced to the counter and saw the unfinished rum and coke. Noah grabbed the glass and slugged it down, finishing it just as the laptop dinged.

Noah Googled 'deer' and the results were as expected: hunting, animal emojis, news articles about overpopulation in New England woods.

He tried 'bloody deer,' but erased it before he pressed search, the environmentalist in him wanting to avoid pictures of shot animals and gored hunting trophies.

Noah thought out-loud. "How about *deer as symbology.*" Then remembered Willem Dafoe's character from *The Boondock Saints. I'm sure the word you were looking for was symbolism. What is the symbolism?* Noah typed 'deer as symbolism.'

In the split second it took for the page to load, Noah decided he wanted another drink. He returned to the computer, glass in hand, to find articles about spirit animals, regeneration in the case of antlers falling off and growing again. Nothing, not a single page, about murders.

What a way to spend a Tuesday night. Noah stretched; he didn't have to work, and he felt good. He smiled at the thought of the feeling. Feeling. *Feeeeeeling.* His lips were numb as he mouthed the word. He grabbed his keys and headed for the door, stopping with his hand above the handle. One more for good measure. The pill went down nice and smooth.

Noah drove out to Sawyer Ridge in Buckland. A curved road that overlooked the Sawyer River. He pulled over at a scenic lookout known best for its view of the sunset across the valley below. Two other cars were parked in the dirt wedge of a lot. In his center console was a pint of vodka. He unscrewed the top and sipped as the sun went down. Rays of yellow, orange, and gold colored the horizon.

Another car pulled in and parked just ahead of him. He shifted slightly and shoved the pint of liquor between his seat and the center console. It was a young couple. College aged. Probably students at Northern. Maybe students in one of Robert's classes even. They held hands and sat on the guardrail observing the final few minutes of daylight. Noah watched the girl lean her head on the guy's shoulder. In return, he kissed the top of it.

Noah pressed his thumb and finger into his eyes and pinched the top of his nose. Green spots vanished when the pressure released. Instead of the college couple sitting on the guardrail, he saw himself and Amber. He saw her laughing at a joke he had made and playfully shoving him. He saw her kiss his neck and nuzzle her forehead into his shoulder. He saw—

Noah was out of the truck, the noise startling the young couple. The guy rose, his hand out to guide the girl behind him.

"Whoa," the guy said. "What's up, buddy?"

Noah spit. Stopped behind the guy's car, raised his foot, and drove his heel into the bumper.

"Hey—what the fuck are you doing?"

The guy scrambled toward him, but Noah stomped forward. "Get out of here."

They stared in disbelief. A car drove past, headlights cutting across the darkening scene, and in them Noah could see that the girl was scared. Not a single bit of him cared.

"That whore will break you, kid."

"Excuse me," she yelled.

"The hell did you just call her?" The kid came forward, but Noah took one clean swing.

His knuckles connected with the kid's jaw and the kid fell back, hand slapping against the side of his car. Noah lunged forward, causing the girl to scream.

"Get off him," she shouted and pushed. Noah raised a hand to fend her off, and the kid took the opportunity, curled his legs, and pushed Noah off with both feet.

Noah stumbled, the momentum causing him to fall. His head hit a rock. Sharp pain exploded behind his eyes, and the world flashed black. He crab-crawled backward before pulling himself to his feet. The girl cried while the guy stood ready, fists waiting.

"I—" Noah stumbled. "I'm—I'm so sorry. I—Jesus Christ."

The toe of his shoe caught something, and he tumbled, hitting the ground again. Car doors slammed. Tiny rocks hit his body as they sped away. The sun was gone and so were they.

He slammed the driver's door of his truck and took another swig. A trooper drove by, causing a lump to form in Noah's throat. Fresh off an assault. Open vodka bottle in his hand. But the officer didn't stop. The cruiser followed the curve of the road out of sight, and Noah exhaled, resting his forehead on the bottom of the steering wheel.

He pulled out of the parking area, leaving the other two cars and whoever had remained inside them during the altercation. Sawyer Ridge was black at night. No street lights. Just the moon, the stars, and the shadows. Several miles down the road Noah pulled over and stepped out of his truck. He stretched his arms out, reaching farther, farther, until taunt muscles tingled. The air had chilled in the half-hour since sunset. Each breath pulled a crisp cleanse into his lungs. Good in; evil out.

Noah stood alone. To his left, across the street, the river rushed below. Standing stone still, there was the sound of water rushing like wind in the trees. On his right, past a guardrail that hadn't been present two years ago, was another embankment. Noah hopped over, the tip of his foot catching on the metal lip, causing him to fall face first, tumbling downward until his body collided with a tree, slamming his hip against the trunk.

He gasped. Pain wrapped around his waist but dissipated, unable to hold against the chemicals in his system. Pain pills fought misery, and they did a damn good job.

"Hell," he groaned.

Rolling, using the base of the tree to step against, Noah attempted to orient himself. Street up, pain below. He could barely see in the dark, but there wasn't really a need. A thousand visits had burned the layout of the woods into his brain.

Noah shuffled several yards and rested between a large rock and a tree. Just above him, right below the first branch, was a deep gouge that dug into the bark.

This was where the driver side had come down. Where the side-mirror had dug into the wood in a mashing of human engineering and nature. In the end, everything returned to the Earth.

"It rested against that," Noah said to no one.

Intoxication pulled at him. Grubby fingers that clung to each eyelid in an effort to pull them shut. Not a yank; a slow fall of utter completeness. Fog crept inside the narrow slits that remained open. Blurred lines. Turned trees into people. Rocks and shrubs swirled, molded together to form a damaged car with shattered windows and caved in doors and frames.

Lights flashed from the road: red, blue, red, blue. A narrow blob—no, not a blob—Buckland's assistant chief, stood at the very top of the embankment shouting down orders like a general.

"Stabilize both sides," he shouted. His voice echoed. Reverb effect on an electric guitar. "Tie off the rear to the second tree down there. Engine crew, get those fucking lights set up. Let's go!"

The car creaked as one of the emergency medical technicians tried to pull open the driver door.

"Easy," the chief called. "Use a wedge and block under the rear fender. And Anderson, what are you doing? Get in that car now!"

A firefighter tossed his helmet over. Anderson smashed the rear window of the car before hoisting himself inside, radioing back to the chief. "One patient, Chief. Unconscious. We need ALS or something, and I need a second set of hands."

When spoken, the chief's words were everywhere. Dissipated the air and flowed into Noah's ears on invisible waves.

"Dispatch, need ALS to Sawyer's Ridge and find out if the helicopter's flying."

"ALS and request for MED-Flight." Dispatch echoed over the radio.

ALS. ALS. ALS became Noah. They were calling. Noah looked up, searched for his voice under tired, heavy eyelids, and saw his SUV, a bright addition to the flashing array of lights, at the top of the embankment. He crawled up and toward the road in an attempt to warn himself. Push the uninjured version away from the scene. He had to warn himself. Push away from the scene and prevent the injury that still caused him torment. That stole a year of his life in a physical therapy program that didn't work. An injury that tore Amber away from him in the six months that followed. And continued to torment him almost two years later.

He clawed his way to the guardrail and back onto the road, determined. Red and blue orbs illuminating the night in brief, almost violent flashes. The chief was there. Then gone. Trees that were people in the darkness were nothing but wood in the reflection of emergency lights. Only the lights at the top of the hill weren't coming from the fly car; they were coming from a light bar on top of a cruiser.

But the police had been up the road on the night of the incident; why was a cruiser parked. . . behind Noah's truck? Because the lights weren't flashing from some memory. Some vision brought on by the fog of narcotics. They belonged to a police officer. One that was standing on the side of the road, flashlight in hand.

Noah did his best to make slow, steady movements over the guardrail. "Oh—um—hello? Officer. Sorry. I—ugh—went to take a piss and dropped my phone. Pretty steep drop." He forced a laugh and brushed his hands against his thighs.

"It is," the officer said. She was older than him, mid-forties with tired eyes. "Been drinking tonight?"

"No—ma'am. Well, actually, yes, earlier—not now. I'm not drunk. I had a drink, but that was earlier."

"Right. Have some ID on you?"

He fumbled for his wallet, repeating *of course* like a mantra. She studied the picture. A faint hint of recognition on her face. They had undoubtedly been on some call together. A psych or drug overdose. Maybe he had picked up a chest pain at the station for her. Someone suffering from a sudden case of incarceritis. Either way, he smiled, thinking he was golden, when she reached for something on the rear of her belt.

"I want you to blow on this for me." She held out a hand-held breathalyzer and attached a little plastic mouthpiece to one side.

He pursed his lips. His palms became sweaty as his heart rate quickened.

"Officer, I haven't had a drink since dinner. I only stopped because I was making a phone call—don't want to drive while talking, right? I was in the middle of the conversation, and I realized I had to piss. I shouldn't have done that in a public place, but I did, and I'm sorry."

She nodded. "No, that's good that you got out to talk on the phone. Long conversation?"

"Just finished a second or two ago."

She stepped toward him. "Funny, seeing as your phone is in your cup holder. Now blow."

Noah took a deep breath. There were more opioids in his system than there was alcohol. One blow wouldn't put him behind bars.

Dead wrong.

A tow-truck came to pick up his Tacoma, and he rode to the station in the back of her cruiser. He didn't say a word, just leaned his head against the window and watched the world flash by, his life among the branches and the trees.

***

The cell door opened, and Amber stood there in teal scrubs and a brown fall jacket. She was slender and stood five-six. Her hair was dark auburn, tied in a ponytail. She wore minimal make-up, just a light layer of black mascara and a spot of foundation on the right side of her forehead to cover a burn that had scarred her when she was seven years old. Her eyes were deep blue, and against the color of her hair, they provided a lustful contradiction. Fire and water in the flesh.

He followed her in silence until they were on the front steps of Buckland's Police Station. The door shut behind them.

"So," Noah said cautiously. "What do I owe you for bail?"

"Neil knows the chief." Amber answered.

"Of course." With that revelation came a bitter taste in the back of his mouth. It rolled across his tongue like choked-back vomit.

"Would you rather I have left you there? Because that was my first thought."

"No—no. Sorry. Thanks." He tried to smile. A sole corner of his mouth rose. "You know where my truck is?"

"Impound," she said and walked past him. Her silhouette threatened to disappear in the night. "They said you could get it in the morning."

He paused and then hurried after her. His knee ached with each step. "Wait, Amber, can I at least catch a ride with you?"

"No," she said flatly.

"How am I going to get home?"

She spun on her heels and they nearly collided. "Not my problem, Noah. Now get your shit together so you can move on with your life and stop fucking up mine."

"Wait," he grabbed her hand. "Sorry. I just didn't know who else to call."

"Exactly. You have no one else. Next time, call your brother. Maybe his disappointment will weigh a little heavier than mine. God knows everything else he said always did."

"Amber, that's not true."

"Yes it is. You hang on Robert's every word, no matter how important or relevant it is. Yet I'm standing in front of you practically screaming, and you still don't hear me. How is that—no. I'm not doing this. Goodbye, Noah."

"Amber," he called but she didn't stop.

Noah ran through the parking lot and stopped in front of her car. She laid on the horn, but he didn't move.

"Will you get out of the way?" she yelled through the open driver window.

He opened his mouth to shout back but stopped. He dropped his hands in defeat and stepped aside. To his surprise, though, the car didn't rush forward. Its engine hummed, idling. Amber tossed her phone to the passenger seat and scratched the top of her head, causing hair to tangle between her fingers.

"You need to sober up, Noah."

She spoke without looking at him. He was grateful for that.

"Robert might not see it. You might not see it. But I spent enough time lying next to you to know it. It's one thing when you're fucking your life up, Noah, but you keep going like this, and you're going to slip up, and someone's going to die because of it. And that? That's not something I think you could live with. Not anymore, anyway."

Noah looked up from the ground, biting into his bottom lip. His mouth pulsed with pain from his own teeth. "I'm sorry."

"Stop apologizing!" She slapped at her steering wheel until the sound of her palms on leather were the only thing he could hear. "It's all you ever do anymore. It's pathetic. Do you remember when we met? You were a rock. You hadn't let anything dig into you, and now you're practically cut open. You've become a baby, Noah."

"Jesus, Amber." He stumbled over his own words. "Maybe this is ten years of being tough finally breaking."

She shook her head. The engine hummed louder and then died back down. "No. That's nothing more than an easy way out. You were fine the other night, weren't you?"

Head tilted to the side, Noah stared.

"The DOA in Sara's Point," Amber said. "Elle told me you were on. Said it was brutal."

Noah didn't want to talk about the DOA in Sara's Point. He didn't want to talk about anything related to work. "Amber, I never meant for this—any of this—to happen."

She huffed. "Noah, none of us mean for bad shit to happen, but it happens none-the-less. It's how we deal with it that matters."

Another blow. He could do nothing but nod until he heard her door locks click.

"Get in, and I'll drive you home."

SEVEN

Noah threw two Percocet into his mouth and took a swig of coffee before returning the mug to the cup holder. The taste of Bailey's and Jameson lingered. He should have stayed home and slept. Called the physical therapy department, asked for Catalina, and set up an actual appointment. But anger had been his alarm clock and justified an impromptu visit. It was, after all, something that so many people wanted him to do. Robert, Mick, Amber.

Amber.

The ride home from the police station had been silent. Not even an attempt at small talk. They arrived at his apartment without a word spoken. Come inside. Have coffee. Words that bounced inside his skull that couldn't be spoken because, if they were, they would be met with a resounding no.

Then Amber broke the silence. "This is the last time I'm helping you, Noah."

He focused his eyes on the dashboard. The clock that read 03:32. Staring until the edges of the little green digits began to blur.

"You've said that before," he finally muttered.

"Yeah. Yeah, I did."

"I get it, though. You have your new life. Neil." He said the man's name with a sneer. "Don't worry. I'll be fine on my own."

"The old you would have been. Without a doubt. And don't be so melodramatic to think that I want nothing to do with you because of Neil. I want nothing to do with you because you're killing yourself, and the sad part is, you won't be lucky enough to actually die. You'll spend the rest of your life in this abyss of misery you've created, until you finally do make a mistake and inadvertently kill a patient. When that happens, maybe then you'll actually end it. I don't know. I really don't know anything about you anymore."

"That's such bullshit," he spat. "First off: you know more about me than anyone else on this planet."

Amber looked out her window. She began bouncing her leg, just slightly, but Noah saw it, and in that second, he became furious. How dare she act like she was bored? This was them. The two of them, and she was jittering like the conversation couldn't end quickly enough. He whipped off his seatbelt and grabbed her by the chin. He could feel the edges of her teeth through the skin of her cheeks. Like a mutt when you're forcing it to drop a toy. She slapped at him, gasping in shock.

"Listen to me, Amber: there isn't another medic anywhere that can stand next to me. I've been in this twice as long as you have, so fuck off with your condescending bullshit. Go through what I've been through, and then try and lecture me. But you wouldn't last. You'd start crying, unable to handle *anything* without someone picking you up like I did when we first met. You want to know why I'm a rock? Because of people like you. Because someone has to be able to put up with the shit you can't handle." With a thrust he shoved her head back into the seat and let go.

"Thanks for the ride," he snarled and slammed the door.

***

Sitting in the hospital parking lot, hand above the mug of Irish coffee, Noah wondered how it had gotten that bad that quickly. It had been a fifteen-minute ride from the police station to his apartment, and in that time, there had been silence, a brief spat, and an assault. A job well done.

Noah chomped on several mints and threw a piece of gum in his mouth before heading inside. Walking, he felt his blood burn. Just the recollection of the night before caused him to squeeze his fingers into his palms. The front doors slid open. Several people stood talking in the corner of the atrium. Dress clothes. Business casual. Folders and laptops under their arms.

"Fucking place sucks during the day," he muttered.

Passing by the radiology waiting area, his eyes caught a familiar sight on the front page of a newspaper. Noah paused, picked up the paper, and found himself looking at the house in Sara's Point.

MURDER ON THE LAKE—THE WATER TURNS RED.

. . . woman found dead in her bedroom. . . first murder in Sara's Point in over 80 years. . . multiple stab wounds. . . cause of death found to be blood loss. . . throat slit. . . no leads. . . deer drawn on the inside of a closet door. . . woman's daughter stated in lieu of flowers.

Noah flipped the paper upside down and headed for the elevator, his head reeling. It had been a murder, that much was obvious when he'd arrived on scene. But there were no leads? Sara's Point police couldn't find any kind of evidence in the house? That drawing had been done with someone's finger, and they couldn't pull a print? Unless whoever did it had been wearing gloves at the time.

The elevator dinged and the doors slid open. Physical therapy was down the hall and to the right. Noah passed a nurse's station, careful to keep his head down and avoid eye contact. It was too early; he was too buzzed.

Taking a breath, he pushed open the door to the physical therapy suite. A large, open area greeted him. There were three beds on each side of the room, one occupied with an overweight man attempting to stand with the assistance of two aides. Two treadmills against the far wall, and twin rows of obstacles—rails to hold patients up as they tried to walk, box steps to gain muscle mass in the lower body, mats for stretching and yoga—lined the center of the room.

"Need something?" a woman said quickly. Her tone was nice, with just enough *don't waste my time* hidden underneath. She had a fake tan, freckles, and a ponytail of dark hair streaked with near-white highlights.

Noah fumbled in his pocket. Pretended to reach for something. "I'm looking for Catalina? Mick—Dr. Hens— referred me."

"That's me." She smirked. "Call me Cat. And you must be Nate?"

"Noah," he said.

"Normally," she said. "I'd ask you to make an appointment and come back. But it's a slow day, and I owe Dr. Hens a favor, so follow me."

He trailed behind. Her hips swayed underneath dark blue scrubs. Noah could feel the euphoria of the pills he had taken begin to radiate from the center of his body. The warmth. The numbness.

"Sit." Cat pointed to a mat on the floor. There was no ring on her hand.

"So, if I remember right, Dr. Hens said you were injured in a car accident?"

"Kind of."

She stood over him, arms across her chest. "Well?"

He nodded. Vigorously.

"No. What happened?"

A dawning. Light breaking through the haze of drugs and alcohol. "Oh—I uh—I broke my knee. Shattered it actually. Tore the muscles. Everything. It's alright, definitely gotten better, but after a couple of calls back-to-back, it starts aching and then that's it."

"Ouch," she whistled. "How long ago?"

"Ugh—about seven months?" he lied, though he wasn't sure why. If she talked to Mick, he could easily tell her that it was more like twenty.

Cat rocked her head from side to side. Wheels turning. Studying. "You try PT before?"

He nodded.

"Not with me." She smiled and squatted down.

Her hands were on his shin. Noah's eyes went straight to the v-cut in her scrub top. Nothing but a white bra underneath. She applied pressure, forcing his knee to bend. He clenched his jaw. Fake. Grimaced in pain. Good. There was no pain with the magic he was feeling, but that didn't matter. She didn't feel the magic. It was only for him. She looked up, met his eyes, and shook her head.

"What?" he asked. Had she caught him looking down her shirt? No, he had only looked once. Like a minute ago. And even if she had, did he really care? At the bedrock of it? God, her hands feel good.

She extended his leg, rested it on the mat and let go. Her fingers wrapped around his knee, the tips of them touching the bottom of his thigh. Her lips were small, perfectly proportionate for her face. He leaned his head to the side. Followed her neck with his eyes. He thought of kissing the crook of her shoulder, trailing upward with the tip of his tongue until he reached the bottom of her ear. She squeezed. Noah jerked backward, yanked his leg away from her and scrambled to his feet. His face felt hot. "Sorry."

"You alright?"

"Yeah." He brushed his hands on his pants and turned, watched the fat man in bed. One. Two. Three. Four. He exhaled and turned back around. He wouldn't look up from the floor. "Sorry, anyway."

Cat laughed, walked to her desk, and grabbed a business card. She tucked it in his front pocket, causing him to awkwardly shift his hips. He looked at her, confused.

"You need some work," she said. "But I can't do it when you're on so many pain pills, because I can't tell what you can really tolerate. Call me on a day you're off and your knee's not bothering you as bad."

As he nodded, she leaned closer and added, "And next time, forget the gum and mints. I'd rather smell the alcohol."

She winked, leaving him speechless.

On his way out of the hospital, Noah stopped in the emergency room. He hit the plate on the wall, and the doors that read 'closed unit' swung open. Sounds and smells rushed at him. The beeping of alarms. Fingers on keyboards. The low hum of conversations.

Amber stepped out from a side hall, and Noah became still. She carried a bag of IV fluid and a clipboard. He followed behind her and leaned against a wall as she began typing on a computer.

"Noah?" He turned at the sound of his name. A respiratory therapist stood behind him, a bag of supplies in her hand.

"Mia," he half-smiled. "How are you?"

He couldn't bring himself to look over his shoulder and see if Amber was looking, but she had to have heard his name. Damn it, Mia. A warm sensation spread across his cheeks at the thought of being caught, forcing an inevitable conflict.

"Good, good. What are you doing here during the day?"

He shifted on his feet. "Checking in with someone. Just bullshit stuff. I really gotta get going though; sorry."

"No problem. It was good to see you."

Noah waited a few seconds after she left and then turned, but Amber was gone. He exhaled, felt a wave of relief, and decided to get out before luck turned against him. Three steps toward the door and the tide shifted;

Amber stepped out from a supply room, her arms folded across her chest.

"Noah, what are you doing here?"

His mouth was suddenly dry. He could feel the cracks in his lips.

"Are you—" She stepped closer. Squinted as she stared. "Are you high? Noah, what the fuck is wrong with you? How can you think walking in here on drugs is a good idea?"

"No—no, I'm not." He immediately went to apologize and then stopped. Who was she that he needed to apologize for anything? She had made it perfectly clear the night before that what he did was no longer her problem.

Amber threw her hands up and pushed past him. He snagged her wrist and spun her around, stronger than he intended, and her body wound up against his. She pulled back immediately, but he squeezed, holding her there.

Her smell. The warmth coming from her. The anger was gone. Stabbed by longing. No. He shook his head. Bury it.

"I was up in physical therapy," he hissed. "Don't tell anyone. I'm getting everything taken care of."

"Noah, let go of my wrist." She pulled.

But he held her.

"Noah." She clenched her teeth.

They were in bed. Her hands above her head, one wrist over the other with his grip pinning them there while she squirmed and bit her lower lip.

"Noah," she snapped.

He came to and dropped her arm.

"Jesus Christ." She rubbed her wrist. "Get some help."

The images were overlaid in his head: her walking away in the ER and her walking away from bed to get a glass of water. He stood there and stared at the empty hall.

EIGHT

Noah answered his phone on the second ring. Rain pounded against the windshield of his Tacoma as he drove to the ambulance headquarters. His brother's voice was in his ear, amplified by the lingering traces of a hangover.

"Where are you?"

"Driving to work?" he half-asked, half-answered.

"When you get there, stay there. Don't sign on."

He looked at his dashboard. 18:46. "Rob, I've had a shit couple of days, and my shift starts in fourteen minutes."

"Good. It'll only take me ten to get there," Robert said.

"I haven't heard from you in I don't know how long. I don't have time for this now."

A stoplight turned red. The reflection of it blurred in the smear of rain as his windshield wipers *thwu-thwunked* across the glass. His phone clicked and buzzed in his ear.

"Robert?"

Call ended. The light turned green, and Noah whipped his phone at the passenger door, denting the plastic above the handle and spidering a corner of the screen.

***

17 West Main Street. Unresponsive. Noah hadn't even started the SUV.

A set of headlights cut across the parking lot. Robert pulled next to him as Noah was beginning to leave. They rolled down their windows, Robert shouting before they were all the way down. "Where are you going?"

"Unresponsive in the center of town."

"Okay, hold up one second."

"I don't have time for this right now."

Robert pulled his car from the center aisle and into a parking spot before jumping into the passenger seat of the Explorer. Noah clenched his fists. He wanted sleep. He had gotten none after he'd left the hospital, unable to stop pacing, rehashing his argument with Amber over and over and over. The lingering feeling of her skin on his fingertips.

"What is happening?" Noah asked, exasperated.

"Just drive," Robert said. "I'll explain."

He pulled out of the lot. His speedometer climbed to seventy as his lights flashed and his sirens wailed. The radio was alive with call signs and responding units. Each transmission repeated by the woman working dispatch.

"Alright," Noah said as he slowed for an intersection, hammered on the siren, and sped through. He felt the SUV twist slightly, the strain of the engine on its already abused chassis, and he relished in that fact. He wanted it to break. He wanted everything to break. "What's the deal?"

"I know when the next murder's going to happen."

"What? What murder?"

Robert squeezed the passenger handle as Noah took a corner, hammering on the accelerator at its apex. The radio crackled. "Ambulance 370 on scene."

"The Ripper guy," Robert said. "Jesus, Noah, slow down."

"The Ripper guy?" Noah asked. "Rob, this isn't one of your classes. What are you talking about?"

"My God, you're dense. The call you were on last week—the woman who was murdered with the deer on her closet door."

Emergency lights flashed ahead. Vehicles parked outside of a three story Victorian squeezed tightly between two others just like it. Old mill towns—the shittiest locations always had the nicest houses.

"Yeah," Noah said. "I saw the article. It said the police had no leads or anything."

Robert was laughing. "I'm not surprised. They don't know where to look."

"And you do? I searched online but couldn't find anything. How did you?"

"You sound like a freshman."

Two cruisers and an ambulance were on scene. Noah's eyes darted to the front yard as an EMT ran into the house. His mind analyzed. How many people lived there? One family or a multi? Had he been there before? Overdose meant borderline respiratory arrest and if someone was already running—

"Noah?" Robert hit his shoulder.

"What?"

"Did you hear me?"

"No, a little busy." He braked and threw the SUV in park.

"Noah, the guy's mimicking Jack the Ripper. He's going to kill another person."

Half out of the driver's side, Noah froze. "Wait—what? How do you know that?"

"The deer." Robert's face was glowing. "The deer on the closet door that *you* found. It was symbol referring to Buck's Row in Whitechapel, London. It was where the first body was found. There were five total, which means there's going to be five here."

"Noah!" Someone shouted from the front yard. A police officer was waving a hand in the air. "We need some damn help here."

Noah hesitated. Looked back at his brother. "Just stay here, okay?"

The house opened to a stairway and narrow hall leading to a kitchen. A large woman was screaming, trying to force herself past a police officer and into the living room. Noah saw the toddler on her hip. His wails as loud as hers. Behind them stood an older guy with a gray beard and grease stains on his shirt. He was skinny. His mouth hung open and three of his front teeth—two top and one bottom—were missing. Black, rectangular holes.

"He's barely breathing!" A female EMT yelled to his right.

Noah rushed into a cramped room with too much furniture. A glass pipe with burnt remnants of marijuana sat on the mantle. Dozens of magazines cluttered the end table. Dirt and dog hair had been pushed into the corners, clumped together in gray piles. No guns that he could see. No knives. On the floor next to the couch was a man. Noah put him at 5'11, a rough 250-pounds. The guy's chest moved up and down. Slow.

An EMT looked up from the floor. Brown eyes. Coffee-stains on her teeth. She pulled her hand from the man's neck with a look of alarm in her eyes.

"Pulse is thready."

She reached behind her for a portable oxygen tank and clear plastic mask. Noah tossed a saline bag to another EMT. An older kid named Matt who he knew from a few shitty accidents. He could handle his own. "Spike that and grab the monitor leads."

Noah put on a pair of gloves and pushed up the man's right sleeve. Track marks. A constellation of scars nowhere near the same elegance as those in the sky. He shook his head, tied a band around the fat-man's arm and found a vein. Thin and hard to feel. "When was the last time he used?" he called.

It was no use. The woman just screamed. Blubbering sobs of nothing. The officer radioed for backup and tried to get her to hand over the kid. Social services would be there in the morning. If it even took that long.

 The IV flashed red, signaling positive blood return. He withdrew the needle, connected a line. Matt reached over with the bag of fluid, but Noah shook it away and instead shifted through his meds. He drew up a dose of naloxone, marketed under the name Narcan, detached the needle, and screwed the syringe into the IV line.

He pushed the drug and seconds later the man gasped for air. His hands clawed at the oxygen mask as his eyes shot open, jaundice and bloodshot. The EMT rocked back on her heels and gave a nervous laugh. Noah smiled at her. Gave her a pat on the shoulder before he connected the bag of fluid and helped them get the guy on a back-board and then onto the stretcher.

They loaded the man into the back of the ambulance, and Noah called to his brother who was leaning against the side of the SUV. "Follow us to St. Vincent's."

Rather than reply, Robert unfolded his arms and held up a small plastic cylinder. Even in the dim light from the lamp post Noah recognized it. He stopped, hand on the back door of the ambulance and felt himself deflate. His shoulders slumped.

"Rob," he called, but his brother was already behind the wheel of the Explorer.

***

"You're a fucking idiot," Robert said the second Noah opened the driver's door and sat behind the wheel. The lights of St Vincent's ambulance bay glared in the wind-shield. Robert had parked the SUV next to an ambulance and returned to the passenger seat. "Can you even drive right now? When was the last time you took one of these?"

"Rob, I'm fine."

"Obviously not. Get out; let me drive."

Noah slammed his palm against the wheel causing Robert to pause. "I'm fine. If I get a call, you can't be driving."

Robert grumbled something under his breath and shut the passenger door. "You see this every day—you incessantly bitch about addicts and seekers, and yet here you are. You're one of them. I get what happened to you was bad, but for fuck's sake Noah, it was almost two years ago. This prescription was written all of five days ago, and it's almost half gone!"

"Rob—"

"No. Shut up. You don't get to defend yourself in this, so just drive."

The ride back to Caligan was silent. No radio chatter. No calls. Even the rain had ceased.

When Robert finally spoke, despite Noah's attention, there was no eye contact. Not even a glance. "Two years into my doctoral program, I almost quit. I never told anyone this, but I was having a hard time. I thought I was just weak and couldn't hack it. The rest of my group was dealing with the same workload perfectly fine, and yet I was drowning. I was overwhelmed, and I couldn't sleep worth a damn thing."

He forced a laugh. "There was one week where I think I may have caught all of fifteen hours, if that. I started seeing things: little spots in the corner of my eyes that I knew weren't there, but they made me look back anyway. And I kept thinking...how? How is no one else struggling?"

Noah slowed to a stop underneath a red light. Robert looked over at him.

"They were on drugs: Adderall. Vyvanse. Some of them were even doing lines in the library, cutting them and lining them against mouse pads. I couldn't believe it, but then again, it made sense. That's how they were all getting by. So, I bought some—I think it was Adderall— the girl I bought it from told me to crush it, snort it, and I would be good to focus for an entire night. She swore up and down it would let me catch up on everything so that I could finally get some sleep."

Tones came over both the radio and Noah's pager. It was going to be that kind of night. "Dispatch to Sara's Point, respond with the Alpha Medic—17 Middle Road: 86-year old female, chest pain radiating to the abdomen."

Noah hesitated, his hand over the radio, staring at his brother.

"I ended up throwing them out," Robert finally said.

After a second of silence Noah asked, "How come?"

Robert exhaled and shook his head. "Because I thought: *what would Noah do?*"

The muscles in Noah's face let go. As if their tenacity had vanished and with it their hold on the bones of his skull.

"You already had your life figured out. You had aced anatomy and physiology; you blew through your paramedic program. You had saved lives, Noah. And I needed drugs to write a history dissertation? How pathetic is that? So, I threw them out and suffered through it because that's what I thought you would have done."

Noah opened his mouth but nothing came out. Words tangled together, jumbling into an inaudible blob. He squeezed the radio. His throat scratchy as he notified dispatch, "Alpha Medic responding."

***

Noah parked the SUV on the side of Middle Road. A small ranch, two large trees and a gravel drive. There was a single volunteer on scene, his car parked farther down the road, its blue light flashing. Noah grabbed his stuff as he heard dispatch speaking to the ambulance. The rig was still two minutes out.

A door banged across the street. A mom, dad, and son on the front steps of a colonial, their television on and visible in the window. Noah nodded but doubted that they saw.

He paused outside the front door of the ranch. Light crept from between curtains in the bay window. Shouldering his bag, he stepped inside and to the right.

"I just—I just found her like this." The first responder spat.

He was a younger kid, an MRT maybe, not yet through the emergency medical technician program. He should have hung back and waited for an officer to get on scene or hit the station and waited for the rig to roll, but he probably lived close. He was shaking, his hands raised. "I didn't touch anything. I didn't move anything."

Noah dropped his bag to the floor. The woman was not 86. She was all of 36. Maybe. And she was dead. Plain and bloody simple. Red saturated the patterned rug beneath her body. Her stomach had been torn open like the previous victim. Her intestines had been pulled out, and placed across her shoulder as if someone was trying to dig in deeper. There was a strange familiarity to her and Noah hated that he couldn't place it. He knew her. This was someone who he had seen before, had maybe even talked to and yet he couldn't recall who. Before his accident—who was he kidding—before the drugs, Noah could have said where and when the last time he spoke to this woman had been. He felt nauseous as he spoke into his radio.

"Alpha Medic to dispatch."

"Go, Alpha Medic."

He took a sharp inhale. Scanned the room quick. No weapon. No footsteps. No noises from the other parts of the house. His eyes came to rest on the coffee table, pushed at an angle toward a brick fireplace. On top of the table was a two-foot tall fake Christmas tree. Several ornaments hung from the branches, and a tiny gold star topped the false pine. Four tiny liquor bottles—nips of rum—led away from the tree in a short line, ending at a small gold ring.

"What do we do?" The EMT's voice pulled him from the trashy Christmas scene.

"Right," Noah said and grabbed his radio. "Patient DOA. Start PD. No further medical units required."

"Roger, Alpha One. Patient reported DOA. Starting PD to scene. Cancel responding units."

Noah lowered his radio and stared at the bloodied body, when he heard his brother's voice behind him. "Jesus Christ."

"Robert." Noah spun.

A board creaked as his brother walked forward and squatted in the living room. The woman's left arm had been placed across her chest while her legs were cocked outwards, bent at the knees. Noah circled the body, stopped at the head. His stomach gurgled as acid rose in the back of his mouth.

"It's remarkable," Robert whispered.

Noah glared. His brother pointed. "She was strangled, just like Annie Chapman was. Her face is swollen. Her lips, her tongue."

"What are you talking about?" he hissed.

Robert looked up at him with a gleam in his eyes. "This." He waved his hand. "It's been done before."

Noah spoke through clenched teeth. "Robert, her intestines have been ripped out."

Robert nodded. "And draped over her shoulder."

"Stop that. Stop finding joy out of this."

"I'm not! I'm sorry. I didn't mean any disrespect to her or anything, but can't you see what's going on here? I mean, look at what's scattered next to her: the two combs, one in a paper case. Who carries a comb in a paper case? No one. And that? A piece of an envelope?" Robert reached over and snagged the paper.

"Don't touch—"

Scrawled on the front of the envelope was *London, M2S.*

Noah felt a chill in the room. The sweat on his brow had vanished. He stared at the woman's empty eyes. Hollow brown irises coated over with death and all its finality.

"Jesus Christ," Robert gawked at the coffee table display. "This is something."

"Robert, come here," Noah said. But rather than listen, his brother took out his phone and started snapping pictures. No better than Rogers at the Sara's Point call. "Robert!"

"Noah," he snapped. "This is something. This means something, and the police will be here in minutes. If I don't have pictures, then I can't figure out what it is."

Before Noah could argue, sirens could be heard in the distance. The wails became louder.

"There will be three more of these," Robert said.

The EMT took a step towards him. "What do you mean?"

"This is only number two. There will be three more before whoever this is, is done."

Noah scoffed. "How can you possibly know that?"

Robert shook his head. "Just like a freshman."

"Fuck you, Rob. How do you know there will be another three bodies?"

"Like I told you before: five bodies. Five women. Jack the Ripper. That's who this guy is trying to be."

NINE

The next morning, Noah once again found himself staring at the soft, defined face of Detective Alyssa Madsen. She tapped a pen against the metal table while a bald uniformed officer stood behind her. "I'm not going to lie to you, Mr. McKeen."

Robert and Noah both looked at her.

"Noah," she added slowly, offering his brother a *sorry, better luck next time* smirk. "This is the second murder scene that you have been at in the span of a week."

Noah felt his breath catch in his chest. "I wasn't the first on scene. There was another responder there, plus I was with Robert. We had just left St. Vincent's. You can call any of the staff there. I can give you the name of the nurse I talked to."

She raised her palms. "Calm down. I didn't say you had anything to do with it. We checked with the hospital, spoke to the nurses on staff."

While that gave him a momentary feeling of relief, it soon faded. Replaced by hesitancy. If they had already checked with the hospital staff, then they had thought, at least at some point, that he was responsible. It hadn't even been an hour and officers had already dug into his story, searching, analyzing each part of it for any cracks or weak points.

"Regardless," Madsen said. "It still doesn't bode well. That and the little incident in Buckland a few days ago—you weren't drinking last night were you?"

From the corner of his eye, he saw Robert lean forward and stare.

"No, I wasn't drinking last night." Though without sleep in the next few hours, he may as well be on his way to getting shit faced.

Madsen continued. "Can you think of anyone you know who would want to torment you or follow you? Anyone who knows your schedule? A person in your life with a history of mental illness?"

He whistled, ran his palms down the tops of his thighs. "I don't think I've ever had a stalker. At least one that I know of."

"So," she shifted, leaned on the opposite arm. "Do *you* have any ideas about what is going on? Or are you chalking it up to bad luck? Wrong place, wrong time?"

"I have nothing," Noah said. "But my brother does."

A small flash of elation on her face. "And?"

Robert's arms shot forward, his palms on the table. The uniformed officer took a step toward them, but Madsen held her hand up. A funny sight: a woman half his size telling him what to do. Robert's words came out in rapid fire.

"Detective, if you look at both crime scenes, everything from the state of the bodies—particularly the specifics of how they were left—along with the items left behind, the mural on the inside of the first closet door…"

"And you know about all of that how?" she interrupted. "I didn't think the paper went into that great of detail."

Noah looked at the floor and wedged his hands between his legs. The detective nodded as if to say *of course*. She hadn't bothered hiding the annoyance in her voice. "What about them?"

"Right. Anyway. If you look at all of that, not to mention the coinciding dates, these two murders are nearly identical to the first two murders committed in Whitechapel by Jack the Ripper."

The uniformed officer laughed. Madsen glared at him.

"That's a stretch: see a dead body and your first thought is the striking similarities between it and a murder victim from a hundred years ago?"

"Actually, it was a hundred-and-twenty-nine years ago."

Noah closed his eyes as his brother continued.

"I teach history at Northern University. One of my classes is *Addicted to Tragedy: An Analysis of History's Darker Times.* Jack the Ripper is usually where I start or where I end, depending on the semester."

"Sounds interesting," she said.

"It is. Jack gets a lot of the attention, but the plague is also big—oh and Dante is pretty popular among college kids. Have you ever read it? Fascinating take on Purgatory and Hell, along with the trials a person has to go through in order to redeem themselves, either in the eyes of the Lord or in their own eyes."

"Robert," Noah hissed.

Robert ignored him and spoke faster. "I used to do a lecture on its similarities with Jihadists, religious extremists, and cult followers in the modern age to show how, despite the years that have gone by, our beliefs on right and wrong and the morality behind both can be quite complicated."

"Robert," Noah hit his brother's shoulder. "Stop."

He slumped bàck. "Sorry."

Detective Madsen smiled. "It's an interesting theory. How did you come up with it?"

"The deer. Well, everything. But the deer were the big thing."

"How so?"

He leaned forward again, his fingertips touching. No-ah shifted his weight, praying it wouldn't launch another lecture.

"Mary Ann Nichols was murdered on August 31, 1888. The first call that Noah responded to was on August 31. Before I even realized the coinciding dates—wait, can I ask something?"

Detective Madsen shrugged.

"Who called 9-1-1?"

"A woman—we believe the victim."

"Fascinating. I'd really like to hear it if that would be possible."

"Why don't you just finish your explanation first?"

Robert cleared his throat. "Of course. So, if you are correct, and it was in fact the victim that called 9-1-1, that means whoever perpetrated this crime took the time to not only kill her, but also arrange everything on the floor like it needed to be, and then draw that mural on the closet door. All of this before any officers or medical personnel arrived on scene. He would have had to have known the response times of the local agencies, and he would have had to have a damn good reason to paint that mural, or else why risk getting caught?

So I focused on the mural first. And it just clicked. It was a painting of deer, specifically bucks, lined up in a row." Robert held his palms out and looked from person-to-person, but no one bit. He lowered his head slightly. When he spoke his voice was deflated. "The name of the street that Nichols was murdered on was Buck's Row."

Detective Madsen raised her eyebrows.

"After that," Robert went on, "I just looked at the picture in more detail: the pocket mirror, the white handkerchief, the cut across the throat. It was Mary Ann Nichols exactly."

"So," she said. "You thought whoever did it was masquerading as Jack the Ripper?"

"I did. And tonight proved it."

"How so?"

"Because," Robert said. "Noah, what time did tonight's call go out?"

"I don't know? Why?"

"Best guess."

"Just after midnight?"

Robert smiled. "Annie Chapman was murdered on September 8. Anyone want to guess what today's date is?"

When no one answered, Robert continued, though sounding slightly discouraged. "Jack the Ripper killed five women. They're called the canonical five, in order to separate them from other homicides in that area during that time. I swear, Detective, that if we don't do something, there are going to be three more."

***

"Well," Robert said as they walked down the front steps of the station. "That was riveting." Noah cocked his head to the side, doing his best to ignore the ache in his knee. His brother added, "Whether they listen or not, at least it was an interesting way to spend the night! I have to figure out the Christmas tree, though. It has to be a tie to Annie Chapman, but I'm not sure how or why."

Noah grabbed his brother's collar and whipped him around, shoving him backward. "Two people are dead, Robert. Nothing about this is interesting. Let the police do their job and stay out of it."

"I know," Robert said with his hands up like a hostage. "But you can't argue that this is intense. We're tracking a killer, Noah. This is the stuff they make television shows out of."

"Are you—Rob, how are you finding joy in this?"

Robert's face contorted in an uncomfortable, confused expression. "I'm not? I just think..."

But Noah stalked off, ignoring what his brother thought in favor of distance.

Robert trailed after him. "Are you really not going to pursue this?"

"Pursue what? A killer? No, I'm not."

"How can you just let it be? This could be the most important thing you ever do. Think of the lives you could save. There are three more out there that he's going to kill."

Noah snapped. "I do save lives. I don't need to act like a detective to validate *my* life. And besides, you have a family at home waiting for you. You have a son and a daughter. What's Claudia going to say about this? How's she feel about you out gallivanting with me at night? Because she was never too thrilled about it before."

"What happened to you, Noah?"

The question caught him off guard. He stepped back, grabbed his belt with both hands, and adjusted his stance. "Nothing. I'm being rational."

"Bullshit," his brother spat. "You should be all over this. It's the drugs, isn't it? Those pain pills. God damn it, Noah, get rid of them."

"Nothing is different about me. I take medication to treat pain from an injury."

Robert shouted over him. "An injury you got almost two years ago. What is wrong with you? It's no wonder Amber left you."

Noah lunged forward, but Robert shoved him back, and his fingers slid off his older brother's shoulders, his grip coming up empty. Silence fell between them. Birds chirped from the woods to welcome the coming dawn, while white steam rose in waves from the wet pavement.

"Noah, I'm—"

Noah waved his hand in the air and headed for his truck. He kicked the tire with as much force as he could bring forward. A burst of pain shot through his toes providing reassurance that he could still feel.

He turned back to throw the fact in Robert's face, only his brother was gone, replaced by Detective Madsen. She hugged her overcoat tight against her small frame. "He's got an interesting theory, to say the least."

Noah exhaled. The sudden desire to do nothing but sleep overwhelming, crashing down on him with the force of every ocean. He needed to figure out what he was going to do about the triage job. And resigning from the fly car. And Amber. And his physical therapy. Every additional thing piling on top of one another until the tower threatened to fall. He didn't need another thing to top it off.

"Don't agree?" she asked.

"Detective," Noah pulled open the driver's side door and turned back before getting inside. "I don't give a fuck."

She smiled as if she had expected that answer and nothing but that answer. There was something in her eyes that made him uncomfortable. She didn't blink. He looked out his window as he pulled onto the road. She was still standing in the lot, hands in the pockets of her coat, watching him drive away.

TEN

Saturday afternoon, Noah decided he wasn't going to work that night. He reached for his phone but remembered it wasn't next to his bed, but in his kitchen. He got up and went to fetch it, but he paused at the end of the hallway, just before the living room and kitchen. Something was off. A feeling that made the hair on his neck stand up.

Noah stared at the room. The blanket that was normally across the couch back had been bunched in the corner. And had he left the remote on the floor? Why would he put it there?

He couldn't remember sleeping on the couch. Though he must have. How else would the blanket have gotten there and the remote wound up on the floor? He shrugged off the questions and the unsettled sensation, finding his phone on the kitchen counter.

A fraction of him felt remorse for calling out sick. Only a fraction. The vast majority of him was furious. Furious at the idea they had checked his alibi before he had finished giving it to them. Furious at the fact that Robert was trying to drag him into a whirlwind of shit that he just did not need right now. If he could fix one thing, he would be able to work on the rest.

The idea was baffling. He had spent the majority of the last decade working twelve-hour shifts, missing weekends, parties, birthdays, and holidays; reunions, funerals, marriages, all in an effort to help people, and here he was, at the feet of Sara's Point Police attempting to convince them he was a good person. And Amber. The little bitch. Thinking he was slipping to the point where he was going to kill someone.

But worst of all was Robert. How dare he throw Amber back in his face? Bring up the past and rub it in. Robert knew the story. Robert knew everything that had happened. Not just the accident that had destroyed Noah's right knee, but everything else.

He thought of going to church. Of visiting Mary's Cathedral and asking Father Michaels what was going through God's head. When exactly was the omnipotent one going to let up?

Maybe when he did something good again.

Noah ripped open his laptop. Punched in 'Jack the Ripper' and pressed search. He had heard of the notorious killer before, but aside from name recognition, Noah knew next to nothing about the London murderer.

Robert had been right: there were five known victims. Five women who had been mutilated, the last of which almost beyond recognition. Mary Ann Nichols, she had been first. Found on Buck's Row with her throat slit and abdomen mutilated. Then came Annie Chapman, followed by Elizabeth Stride and Catherine Eddowes.

Stride and Eddowes had been found the same night. Something that would be called 'the double event.' Noah clicked on a thumbnail of Mary Jane Kelly, the last of the Ripper victims. Her body had been. . . destroyed. Even in grainy black and white, the grotesque brutality of it was evident. Noah pushed his chair from the table, stood, and paced the kitchen.

Robert said someone was mimicking this maniac? So much for church. What would be the point? The idea of balance was lost amongst a high tide of evil, hell bent on drowning out all the good in the world. And if the world didn't care, then why the fuck should he?

Noah downed a shot of rum and pulled out his phone. His vision swayed. Swiping through his contacts, he fidgeted with the cap of the pill bottle. He leaned forward, slipped, and caused the bottle to pop out of his hand, rattling pills across the counter and onto the floor.

"God damn it."

On his hands and knees, he picked at each pill until he was sure he had retrieved them all and put them back into the bottle—save for one—and screwed the lid on tight. Pill in his mouth, tucked between cheek and teeth, Noah drank down another shot. The liquor burned, but it did the job. His attention was back on his phone. Scrolling through, looking for her number.

The highlighted bar rested on Amber's name, causing Noah to pause. He stared at the screen, glared at it in contempt. In the peripherals of his vision, the room rocked back and forth. With a swipe of his thumb he scrolled down.

"Where is her number?"

Then it dawned on him. He walked to the other side of the kitchen and flipped through envelopes, receipts, the entire pocket-refuse pile, until he found Catalina's business card. He held it up, triumphant.

"Okay." He swayed. "Do I text or do I call?"

He stood for a full two minutes before he finally began typing out a message.

Hey it's Noah from the other day. Need to set up another appointment ;)

Reading it made his stomach turn. "Nope."

Hey it's Noah. What are you up to?

Not awful. But something kept him from hitting send. It was innocent enough, not cringe-worthy, and yet it seemed wrong. All he wanted was someone to hang out with. Someone to meet up with for a beer. But that was a lie, and he knew it. He wanted to fuck. A half hour where nothing mattered and everything felt good. A fraction in life where two people forgot about their shitty existences.

She had definitely come on to him; that much he was sure of. But it was also several days ago, and he'd never contacted her, which meant she had probably lost interest.

Then he said to hell with it and decided to call, figuring she probably wouldn't pick up because it would be a number she didn't have saved, and if it went to voicemail, hey, he could leave something harmless.

She answered on the third ring.

"Hello?"

"Hey, Cat; it's Noah."

An awkward silence on the line. His heart thumped. The sensation odd and fuzzy beneath layers of drugs and liquor.

"The paramedic with the busted knee."

"Oh." She laughed. "Mick's friend. 'Bout time you called. How's it going?"

Noah smirked. At that point, anything beat being alone.

* * *

They met at a bar in Buckland. A small place with two pool tables and a corner devoted to karaoke on Thursday nights. She wore a black dress and heels. Her hair was curled, falling strategically around her eyes. They took a seat at a round pub table, a beer in front of him and a margarita on her side. Deep shadowy lakes covered the skin underneath her tank top straps. At first they looked odd. Caused Noah to squint in the dim light, but as he studied her, tried to focus and really take her in, it became obvious that they were shadows from lack of muscle and fat. The woman was barely more than skin and bones.

"How long have you been at CG?" Noah forced himself to ask.

Cat laughed, took a sip of her margarita, and said, "Please. Do you really want to talk about that place?"

"Not really. No." He wanted to order food, if only just for her.

"Good," she declared. "Because when you're not at work, you are not at work. You know what I mean? Especially with everything else going on."

"What—everything else?" Noah questioned.

"The murders," she said quietly. "Didn't you hear?"

Noah clenched his jaw, teeth grinding. "I—"

"There's been two of them in the past week, or well, just over a week, but still. I mean, I could get it if we lived in the city, but this isn't Hartford. People don't get stabbed and stuff out here. Especially not in Sara's Point."

"Yeah," Noah said. "You're right about that."

"What do you think is going on?"

Noah shrugged.

"At first I thought it was the husband—for the first one, anyways—but then, after this most recent one, the paper said she didn't have a husband or a boyfriend even, just a kid that she adopted. How sad is that?"

Noah's chest shrunk as he involuntarily exhaled. An adopted kid? Seriously? Wait—that meant—where had the kid been when his mother was killed? Had he been in the house when Noah and Robert and the other EMT were there? Why hadn't he checked the rest of the house?

"Noah?" Cat touched his arm.

"Yeah—yeah. Sorry."

"You alright? You're zoning out over there."

The radio shifted to something upbeat. Pulling at his arm, Cat hopped out of her chair. Noah resisted.

"I don't dance."

"Everybody dances," she said. "Just depends if you're good or not."

"Then by that logic, I am not."

Rather than tug harder, she pushed forward. Wedged her hip between his knees until she was pressing against him. Her smell was intoxicating. Tropical.

"You dance with me now, and maybe I'll dance with you later."

She pressed her lips against his and lingered. Just as Noah opened his mouth to slide his tongue forward, she pulled away and laughed. The tug was at his arm again, and she was pulling him to his feet and into the small crowd that had begun moving to the music.

He was at that point: the tip of the iceberg, where a perfect buzz lingered. One false move, one extra sip, and it would teeter, falling into a state of too drunk, leading to nothing but a headache and vomiting.

They swayed. Surprising him with mobility and grace, Cat rocked her hips to each side as people around them did the same. Body heat joined together, producing sweat. A collective smell of human lust. Fingers touched bare skin. Her body pressed against his, as waves of euphoric pleasure washed over him, retreated, and crashed down harder, making his back shiver. With each thump of the bass, he felt her hips move in flawless rhythm.

When the song was over, the connection broke, but moments later, a new beat pulsed through the speakers. She laced her fingers with his, holding him on the dance floor until they both needed water and a step outside for a quick breath of fresh air.

Back inside the bar she laughed, giggled as they sat, and Noah couldn't help but do the same. God, it felt good. How long had it been since he had let go? Since he had actually had a good time? They talked about music, and while he was more into country and classic rock, Cat liked hip-hop and dance, even touching a little into dubstep and techno.

"It all depends on the mood," she said. "Anything I can move to."

Noah offered another round and slipped to the bar to grab their drinks. Contemplated ordering a plate of nachos. Feeling good, he raised his arms and danced back to the table, beverages in hand.

"You move pretty well for someone with a bad knee," she said.

He froze on the barstool. "Yeah well, miracle of modern medicine."

"Ah, got the good stuff, do you?"

He smiled like a bragging little boy and gambled on her sense of humor. "Damn right."

A few seconds passed, then with a gleam in her eye, she asked, "Have any on you?"

That was unexpected. He arched an eyebrow and contemplated. How many did he have? Could he afford to give her one? Of course he could. Except—except it was crazy. She was a physical therapist asking for drugs. Not only that, he hadn't figured out how to get another script after this one. His stock was vital.

She lowered her eyes. "It's fine if you don't. Sorry for asking. I hope that doesn't make me a horrible person."

"No, no, no—give me one second. I'll be right back."

While Noah walked to his truck, he attempted to wrap his head around what was happening. None of it made sense. Then again, some things in life made no sense. Before heading back inside, he stole a look at his phone. One missed call. He bit his lip and pulled up the list to find Amber's name at the top. He raised his hand in frustration and shook the phone in his fist. *Call her,* a voice in his head uttered, and for a moment, he actually contemplated doing it. Wait—what was he even thinking? Noah tossed his phone back into the truck, paying no mind to where it landed, and locked it inside.

Passing Cat's side of the table, Noah dropped the pill on her cocktail napkin. As he sat down, he had a strange, gut-wrenching feeling. He watched her pop the drug and immediately felt regret. This was wrong. This was the dumbest thing he could ever do. How did it get to the point where he was trading pills against the insinuation of sex?

"Tell me what happened," she said.

When he didn't answer, she said his name, snapping his attention back to the bar.

He fumbled with his beer. Picked at the label. "Sorry. Tell you what happened?"

"Yeah, with the accident. How'd it happen?"

Someone in the crowd *whooed* as the song changed. Three girls began jumping up and down as the guys they were with (or so he assumed) leaned against the bar grinning. Pool balls clacked together. Conversation drifted from the next table. Everything rumbled inside his ears.

"Actually, you care if we get going?"

Cat pursed her lips. "Uh—yeah. Is everything alright?"

"Yeah, yeah. Just let's go back to my place and have drinks. We can talk there."

"Okay."

Fogged by the noise, the booze, and the drugs, Noah laid a twenty under his beer, forgetting that he had already paid, and followed her out to his truck.

***

Cat drove Noah's truck back to his apartment. The world was a blur outside the passenger window. Trees. Light poles. Funny little reflectors on guardrails. Everything seemed in its place.

They laughed. Their hands on each other as they climbed the stairs. His knee absent of any pain. Her fingertips touched the back of his neck, pulled him to her. Their lips touched, and he fell on top of her against the stairs. They kept laughing as he rolled off her, steadying himself.

With one hand on the railing, Cat pulled herself to her feet and reached for his hand before leading him the rest of the way. The skin of her thigh was soft as he slid his fingers up. She playfully smacked his hand, turned at the top of the stairs, and grabbed both sides of his face, forcing her tongue into his mouth and pulling away as soon as he reciprocated.

Inside his apartment, they settled over two glasses of rum and coke, nearly finishing the bottle in the process. Noah fumbled with his phone, trying to slide it into the dock of a speaker. With success came a cheer.

"So," Cat said, leaning over his counter. "Tell me."

Noah hesitated, momentum stolen from his step. With a heavy exhale, he pulled a chair from his kitchen table, spun it backward, and sat. He spoke without looking at her.

"I, uh—" This was it; he just had to say it. "I responded to an accident out on Sawyer Ridge. It was a rollover down an embankment. The car was on its side, propped between two trees and this massive rock."

He stopped, took a sip from his drink. "So I climb down, the guys on scene already had wedges in and the car tied off, and I see the driver inside. She was young, early twenties, and she was fucked. I'm talking barely conscious, broken bones, the whole deal. There was glass everywhere. So I crawl in, nearly on top of this MRT holding c-spine, do a quick airway assessment and trauma feel down, when one of the trees bucks and the car slides."

Cat put her glass down and looked at him, eyes wide. He waved her concern away.

"It held, but we had to get her out. By this time, the helicopter was in the air and her breathing had started getting really shallow."

"Shock?"

"Getting close." Noah took a breath. "Anyway, to get her out, we needed the Jaws of Life, you know? And I had to reposition myself to get a better hold to try and shield her. Well, they get the lines run down the embankment and the tools hooked up."

He looked up at Cat. "No one disconnected the battery, and by some shit luck, there was still power in the system when they started cutting. They cut right into the airbag. The thing blew; the tool shot away from the post and drove down onto my knee, completely shattering it, tore the ligaments and tendons, everything was just…"

His voice trailed off. He felt her hand rest softly on top of his, and they stayed there for a moment, frozen with no other sound than the dance music playing from the speaker.

Noah finally shrugged, took a sip from his drink, and said, "Shit happens, right?"

Cat nodded. "I bet the girl was grateful."

"Wouldn't know. She died before they got her out of the car."

She lowered her forehead to the countertop. Noah just nodded. A strange mixture curled inside his chest: relief that the story was out, not that people hadn't heard it—it had been the talk of the three towns, even the city, for weeks following the incident—but because it felt good to vocalize it to another human being. And there came the second emotion: the regret. It shouldn't have been this woman he was talking to; it was something that had been shared with someone already, and that intimate moment, that confession-like connection, should have remained between only them.

He patted the top of Cat's hand and pushed himself from the chair, heading for the bathroom. His fingers found the bottom of the crucifix as he passed, though he couldn't bring himself to look Christ in the eyes. Not quite yet.

His reflection in the bathroom mirror looked steady, but he felt the counter move under his hands. The world around him rocked as he reached for the bottle of muscle relaxers and twisted the cover off. The bathroom door opened and Cat stood there. In a second she was on him, her lips against his, before pulling away just as abruptly.

"You want to forget about all that?"

He shook the pills like a rattle, but before he could get one into his mouth, she took the bottle and said, "One second." Before leaving the bathroom and sifting through drawers in the kitchen, only to return a minute later with a plastic sandwich bag.

With two pills inside the bag, Cat sealed it, and crushed them underneath the orange bottle until she could pour a pile of powder from the bag. Using the edge of Noah's tweezers, she made two lines, bent forward, and snorted one of them. She came up quick with a growl-like noise, followed by quick inhales through her nose.

Noah stared in disbelief as she rubbed residual powder from under her nose.

"Trust me," Cat said. "It works much faster than taking them, and it hits you differently. It'll help you forget."

Overwhelmed, Noah tried to stumble out of the bathroom, but she stepped in front of him, slender fingers on the sides of his face. Warmth radiated from her, and for a brief second, the world wasn't cold.

Cat stepped back, blocking the doorway. "*I'll* help you forget."

She hooked a finger under each strap of her dress and pulled them from her shoulders. The dress hit the floor, and when he looked back at her, Noah saw two of her in his vision. He tried to uncross his eyes, only they weren't crossed.

A smile crept onto her face as she watched him stare. He exhaled. Bit his bottom lip and watched as she undid her strapless bra, adding that to the pile of clothes on the bathroom floor. Her hips rocked as she walked over, the bones jutting against her skin. Maybe pills weren't her first choice in powdered chemicals.

She moved her hands to his chest and pressed her mouth against his. Her tongue was warm. It touched his and twisted. She pulled away, nodded in an effort to appease his nerves and hesitation. A soft kiss on the lips, and she dropped to her knees, undoing his belt. Noah nearly recoiled at her touch. She looked up at him and motioned for the counter.

"Go ahead."

Again he hesitated. She squeezed him. His hips bucked at a feeling of pleasurable discomfort. With nowhere else to go, Noah leaned over the counter, lowered his nose to the edge of the line, and felt the warmest sensation at his waist. His legs shook. The feel of her mouth amplified by the drugs in his system. He looked down, forehead pressed against vanity, and felt a stab of shock in his stomach.

Her hair had become red. Dark red as it moved back and forth. She moaned slightly as she swirled her tongue around him. He stared at the freckles on her shoulders. Amber's freckles. He fought the urge to grab her hair, pull her up and kiss her. How did she get there? When did she get there? He closed his eyes in pleasure and remembered the line of powder on the counter.

He dropped a hand to the top of her head, twisting her hair between his fingers. Leaning forward, he took one swift inhale through his nose and the powder was gone.

ELEVEN

There was yelling in his ears. A woman's voice. Someone was rocking him, shaking his shoulders. A warm sensation lingered underneath the left side of his face. His eyes opened, but he could only see the outline of his own lashes against the blinding white of the world.

When he tried to sit, he couldn't move. His arms were pinned. A weight against his biceps held him down. *Why couldn't he move?* His chest rose and fell with increased urgency. Despite the rapidness of his breathing, there wasn't enough air going into his lungs. He was going to die here. He was going to suffocate.

Noah fought the restraints on his arm. Sweat pooled in the little dip where his neck met his chest. Each word he tried to speak was a muffled mumble filled with saliva and the acidic taste of bile. Something warm ran from his nose. He gave up pushing and let his head roll to the side. A dark silhouette formed in the glare, and he knew, he knew that was where he had to go.

***

It was the beeping that woke him. Rhythmic. A beat. *His* beat.

Noah stirred. His throat burned. His eyes shot open and he scrambled, whipped his head side-to-side, only to see the protective rails of a hospital bed. Blankets weighed heavy on his chest. A nasal cannula fed oxygen into his nose. He paused for a split second and then the dread came as the color of the walls, the layout of the room, the *smell* all funneled together into one realization: he was lying in a bed in the emergency room of Caligan General Hospital, and he was there because of an overdose.

His eyes rolled back and he welcomed darkness. Oblivion held sanctuary, but it wasn't time for him to be safe, not yet. Robert's voice pulled him back. Doubling his nausea. "There's some work for us to do. You know, if you're done trying to kill yourself, that is."

Noah's head pulsed.

"How—" His voice was hoarse, raspy like a concertgoer after a long show. "How did you know I was here?"

Robert sat in a chair in the corner of the room with one foot resting on the opposite knee. Noah didn't give him time to answer. He quickly rolled, heaved and vomited on the floor. Bile splattered as he continued to wretch. A tech rushed in. Tears burned the corners of Noah's eyes while his stomach did somersaults. The tech cleaned him up, pushed a towel across the floor followed by sanitary wipes, and rolled him back while eyeing the vital signs on the monitor.

"That's gonna happen," he said, and once he was sure Noah was done vomiting, he left the room. On to the next patient.

"Right then," Robert said and stood.

"Rob," Noah called. "If she's not working, don't tell Amber I'm here. Please."

Robert sucked at his bottom lip. "Yeah," he said and stepped toward the door of the exam room.

Amber appeared at Robert's side, a coffee in each hand. She wore a black coat with a fur-lined hood and a pair of dark jeans. Her hair was tied in a ponytail, as it always was, and angled to the side. "When did he wake up?"

"Only a few minutes ago. You want me to stay?" Robert asked.

"No," Amber said quietly. "Thanks."

"I'm surprised you're here," Noah coughed as Amber stepped next to the bed.

Each word burned like fire. Given the choice, he would rather swallow swords. She didn't say anything, only leaned against the railing of the stretcher and played with the coffee cup's lid. When she finally did look at him, Noah realized how bloodshot her eyes were and how deep and dark the bags beneath them were.

"When we decided to end things," she said. "Or rather, when I decided to end things, I told you it was because I couldn't watch you kill yourself. I meant it metaphorically. That was almost two years ago. Two years, Noah, and I gotta tell you, it hasn't gotten any easier. I mean, Jesus Christ, what are you doing? What is this? I was coming over. I was on my way. Why would you want me to find you dead?"

That didn't make any sense. He tried to think, to remember what had happened in all of its detail, but try as he might, there were only flashes: a bar, dancing, a missed call on his phone...Had he called her? What had happened? He went home, that much he knew, but what happened there? Wasn't it Cat who came with him?

He felt every muscle in his body tense. Had it been Amber? Had he called her and she came over? Wait—that didn't make sense either. She had just said she was on her way over, which meant he had gone home with Cat. . .

Noah's eyes closed slowly, and he silently begged God, pleaded with Jesus Christ himself. "Did—"

Amber cut him off, her voice flat. "She was frantically getting dressed when I walked in."

Lying there, in that moment, Noah wished he were dead. Amber tossed her full cup into the garbage, the *swoosh* and *thump* of the plastic grasped Noah's attention. She stood there, in the corner of the room, pressing both of her palms against her eyes.

"I didn't mean for you to find me like this," he said. "I—I really wanted your help. That was why I texted you."

She forced a laugh and sniffled. "You are far beyond my help, Noah."

He shook his head; sweat had soaked through the pillowcase. "You're the only one that can help me, Amber. I think about you—about us."

"Stop," she snapped.

"About where we'd be if you hadn't had a miscarriage. Or I hadn't taken that overtime shift. I mean, fuck, you asked me not to, remember? We were going to Camden the next day. You were going to surprise me with the news. And I stupidly didn't listen."

Noah listened to her exhale sharply. In and out like a runner trying to control her breathing. He pushed himself up, causing the monitor to beep. The muscles in his chest burned, and he collapsed back down, sucking in air.

"I have to go," she said.

"No," he called. He raised his head. The room spun and vomit threatened to rise. "Amber."

She turned and stood at the foot of the gurney. Black streaks of mascara ran from her eyes. Her exhaustion coated her. It had mutated from a state of being to, in fact, being her. Their eyes met.

"Please don't leave. I don't want to watch you walk away again."

He held her gaze. Saw her quiver through his blurry vision. Her lips parted slightly, and he fought to hold himself upward, but in the end she didn't speak. She only shook her head and left the room.

TWELVE

Noah was cleared by psych—the entire incident labeled an accidental overdose. Free to go. He pulled himself into Robert's car and sat in silence. Despite the anti-nausea medication, he fought the urge to gag and retch until his stomach and intestines were splayed onto the floor mat like a spilled smoothie.

In his head, he neither saw nor heard a thing. It was all muddled. A murky pool of water he couldn't see through, and try as he might, couldn't drown himself in. He just kept floating, no matter how many rocks he put into his pockets. He tried to think of Amber, of the fact that she had stuck around until he had woken up, but the thought barely came. He attempted instead to think of Cat, but the very idea of her made his stomach turn.

Robert continued to ramble about the murders while Noah's head threatened to splinter into a thousand shards, allowing his brain to ooze down over his neck and shoulders. For all he cared, it could join the rest of his insides on the passenger floor. Streetlights and shadows passed by his window as they wound the route toward his apartment complex.

"I'll give you a week," Robert said as he parked the car. "Amber said you can't die from opiate withdrawal, so you'll be fine. She said it's going to be awful, but that you'll be fine. Though I suppose you know that."

His older brother reached into the center console and pulled out an orange bottle of pills. "She said these would help with the nausea."

Noah reached for the bottle of Zofran, little pills that dissolve before they're swallowed in order to settle the worst of stomachs, but as his fingers graced the bottle, Robert tossed them back into the center console and slammed it shut.

"Oh, I don't think so." He smiled. He actually, sincerely smiled. "You don't get any help with this."

With the little energy he could muster, Noah stared at him with a half-open mouth. Robert just laughed.

"If you beat this with the help of any medication, then all you're doing is furthering your dependence on it. Amber assured me you didn't *need* them, that I'm not inadvertently killing you or making your problem worse."

"Oh, she told you that? She's okay with this?"

"Okay with it? It was her idea. Noah, there is some serious stuff going on out here. Stuff the police haven't figured out that we can help them with. You need to get clear of this so we can work. Now get out. Get your shit together and call me when you're back to normal."

Noah opened the car door and nearly fell onto the pavement. It took him fifteen minutes to climb the stairs to his floor and another five to fumble with his key and the lock.

***

It started with the sweating. Noah awoke midday on Monday, his body glistening. Saturated fabric surrounded him, clinging to his skin as he rolled back and forth in an effort to make it all go away.

He did his best to get up. His knee ached. Chills hit him in random shocks down his spine. He shuffled to the kitchen, fumbled with the sink, and took several sips until the glass slid from his hand, crashing to the floor and shattering into a dozen pieces. Water pooled under his feet, and when he moved, he cut open his heel and trailed blood into the living room.

He tried the television. He tried a movie on Netflix while sitting in the corner of the couch shaking. His body was freezing, but his insides were on fire. In his bathroom closet he knocked over several rolls of toilet paper, Q-tips, toothpaste, and fumbled with a bottle of melatonin until he choked down three of them. Back in his musty bed, sleep finally came.

***

It was the middle of the night. Though he didn't know exactly which night. He fumbled, slapped his palm against the mattress, then out and against the edge of his nightstand, but he couldn't feel his phone. He couldn't find anything. The room spun. He retched but nothing came. His nose ran like a dog's, and his eyes teared when they opened.

He prayed for it to stop. Begged like a next-day drunk. But there was no God to answer him, only silence. Crawling from the bathroom, his mouth filled with saliva and sour taste, he stared at the crucifix hanging on his wall until he couldn't take it. Forcing himself to his feet, Noah ripped it down and whipped it into the living room.

Spinning. Sweating. Crying. Groaning. He ripped at the sheets on his bed. Fuck Robert. Fuck Amber. Fuck everyone. This was their fault. If he had just been left alone, he would have been fine. He wouldn't be in agony, doubled over like his stomach was boiling, the acid inside eating himself from within. He squeezed his body together, bent in half like a child, but no relief came.

He thought of the little calm he would have gotten with the anti-nausea meds Robert had withheld from him. Withheld from him at Amber's direction. *Okay with it? It was her idea.*

Fuck her. The cunt. Thank God she had left him. If she had been there, he would have killed her. Noah opened his mouth and puked green bile on his bedroom floor.

***

When they were dating, Amber used to joke that she never wore heels so she could sneak up on Noah whenever she wanted.

"You know," she had said. "In case I want to surprise you with my hands over your eyes or jump on your back like all those sappy movies we never watch."

"Knowing me, I'll probably elbow you in the face." Had been his response.

That led to a playful push, a shove, a pull at his shirt, a tug at her shorts, and a fall back onto the bed where they rolled into each other and let go of the outside world.

Four days into his withdrawal, Amber snuck up on him, quietly stepping through broken glass, crumbs, and dirty rags until she found him curled on the corner of his couch wrapped in a blanket and sound asleep. She saw the bottle of melatonin on the coffee table and quietly sat on the opposite arm of the sofa wondering how it had gotten to this.

She had seen him in a state like this before, though never from pills. And being fair, she had been in a state such as this plenty of times. What was it about alcohol that was so appealing, despite the negative effects both during and after? She shook her head. A pros and cons list no one ever paid attention to.

She draped her coat over the back of a kitchen chair and started cleaning. First the shards of broken glass, then the rags that smelled of food and vomit. She stripped the bed and threw the sheets in a pile. When she reached for his pillows, she found the crucifix underneath them. She placed it on his nightstand and dragged the pile of bedding to the laundry closet opposite the bathroom. With the lid of the washing machine shut and the water pouring in, Amber put her face in her hands and cried.

They would be starting to talk about his second birthday. Assuming it had been a he. She knew, something inside her told her, it was going to be a boy.

She wiped her eyes on the back of her hands and her hands on her pants before leaving the laundry room and putting new sheets on his bed. On the couch, his chest rose and fell under the blanket in a deep rhythmic wave. It was Wednesday night; that made it what, four days? He should have been just about through. Although everyone was different. She wanted to think that he had not been *that* bad. She knew that it hadn't been solely the painkillers that had brought him into the emergency room. His alcohol level had been .326, and for someone who rarely drank, that alone should have brought him in nearly comatose. But let him think it had only been the drugs. Maybe it would give him the push he needed to straighten his life out.

If he turns to heroin, it's your fault. If you had left him alone, he would have stayed on the Percocet. It's when the meds are gone that the needles come out and play.

Amber shivered the thought away and grabbed her coat. She held a pen over a paper towel but decided against leaving a note. She slipped out of the door and responded to a text Neil had sent her while she had been making the bed.

Sorry. Was at my sister's, heading over now.

THIRTEEN

Sunlight poured through the open curtains of his bedroom window, and Noah felt uneasy on his feet. His sheets were no longer wet, and the smell of decay no longer filled the room. There was something else: the apartment was clean. Had he done that? There was no way he could have done that. His head pulsed, and when he stepped, he felt pain constrict not only his knee but his abdomen and chest as well.

He checked his phone, but it was dead. A few seconds of fumbling with the cord and he had it plugged into the wall next to his bed. It could charge while he was in the shower. He hesitated, swaying slightly in the bathroom while contemplating whether or not he would vomit. But when the feeling came to fruition, it was merely gas. Noah twisted the knob and just stood there, feeling the scalding hot streams burn away a layer of disgust. The first of many.

He remembered being brought home by his brother. He remembered pain and vomit and sweat and a clenched fist gripping his insides while they burned like a cauldron. But how long had he been alone in his apartment? His face had stubble, but he could go a week without shaving, so that fact was of little help.

Toweled off, he scrubbed his teeth and rinsed with mouthwash four times. The bitter taste still lingered. Enamel coated with fur. He would have to eat something to rid his mouth of it, but with the thought of food, there came that queasy feeling. He was on his knees in front of the toilet but after a steady rock back and forth, a couple of deep breaths, and the rapid shaking of his foot, it passed.

The voice in his head suddenly shouted: *Wednesday, September 21.*

"September 21," he said to no one. And then it him: work. His shifts. He had missed how many shifts? He paced back and forth while his phone powered up.

"Jesus," he hissed while the Verizon logo continued to glow red.

Had his screen turned to plasma? Did the image burn itself into a state of permanence? Why the hell wasn't it—the screen flashed: three missed calls and three voicemails.

"Noah, it's Paul. Where are you? No call, no show? This is grounds for termination. Call me immediately."

Delete. He swallowed hard.

"Noah, this isn't fucking funny. I offer to help you out if you need it, and you burn me two shifts in a row? You're done. The second you get this and get the guts to come face me, bring all your shit, because you're fired."

Delete. Noah hit the speaker button, tossed the phone on his dresser and gripped at his hair.

"Noah," Paul's voice was different.

His tone had shifted to something gentler. No under-current of anger.

"Amber filled me in on what happened. Jesus, I'm sorry. I checked with your brother to make sure every-thing was okay. He said you were doing all right, just still out of it. Look, ignore the last message I left you. I put you on sick leave effective immediately. I still can't let two no-calls go without something, so I might have to give you a few days of suspension. I'm sorry, but my hands are tied. But you have a job and don't worry about next week's shifts. We'll work it out. FMLA or whatever it is we have to do. Call me when you can, so we can figure everything out. Take care, okay."

He stared in confusion. What had Amber told him? No way it had been the truth. First of all: HIPPA. Second of all: he would have been fired three times over, not offered assistance and sick leave. *Oh hey, you have a drug problem? You overdosed? Eh, don't worry about it; just make sure you come in on Monday. Oh, and if you could be sober, cool, but if not, no worries.*

Noah replayed the message before deleting it. The phone beeped back: *end of new messages.*

Nothing from Amber or Robert? No texts?

He sat at the edge of his bed and stared down the hall into the living room. The emptiness of his apartment seemed overwhelming. Utterly alone. He wanted to call someone, to hear someone's voice that wasn't Paul's. But at that moment, his boss was the only person he had. Just, would Paul hear him out?

FOURTEEN

Behind the wheel of the fly car, parked in front of a Mobil with a coffee in his hands sans Baileys and Jameson, Noah silently thanked God that Paul had heard him out. Noah's supervisor was skeptical, but with a doctor's note, urine drug screen, and the fact that Noah had worked for the company for nearly a decade, well, Paul had little choice in letting the medic go back to work.

The first call of the night had been a difficulty breathing. An old woman who, as Noah asked her if she had an allergies, a breathing treatment in his hand and ready to go, shook her head no. The woman's oxygen level had climbed to 90%, still low but better than the 87% it had been when Noah had arrived on scene. He wanted to see 94%—the hospital could worry about getting it higher, though it would never be higher than 95 or 96; smoking did that to people.

Her daughter (or he assumed she was her daughter) rushed back into the kitchen, barely missing one of the EMTs as they entered. Noah grabbed his blood pressure cuff from his bag and looked at the ambulance crew. Tasha and Rick, both good people to work with. Seeing them cemented the feeling of his return.

"Tash, grab a history from the daughter would ya?"

She smiled, gave him a quick thumbs up, and pulled a pad from her pocket.

It took them another four minutes before they had the woman on the stretcher and loaded in the back of the rig. Tasha hopped in back with them and retook a set of vitals, while Noah attached more stickers to the woman's chest and took a more detailed image of the electrical waves of her heart.

"Rick," he called up front.

"Yeah, boss?"

"Patch me into Caligan."

"You got it."

Noah printed the strip and copied down the vitals Tasha had taken. She looked up at him and smiled. "Glad to see you're back. If you need anything."

He was grateful. No one really knew what had happened due to patient privacy. But the EMS community was small and everyone liked to talk. Noah had been at Caligan general and had a psych consult. Some people put it together. Others either didn't care or didn't say anything out of respect.

He winked at her. "We got this."

Rick hollered back, "Channel four, Noah."

"Caligan General, this is Alpha-One Medic requesting a patch."

A second passed and Noah recognized Mick's voice on the other side of the radio.

"Caligan Med Control, go with your patch."

"Three minutes out with an 80-year-old female presenting with shortness of breath. Original O2 sat was 87 on room-air, up to 93 now after a breathing treatment. No complaints. Vitals are within normal limits, and an IV's been started."

He could almost hear Mick laugh when he came back on. "Stellar work there, Alpha-One; see you on arrival."

Noah latched the radio onto its cradle but snatched it back, unable to fight the urge. "Aye, Captain."

Tasha looked up at him, and Rick laughed from the driver's seat.

"What?" Noah shrugged.

They pulled into the ambulance bay.

Tasha and Rick wheeled the stretcher inside while Noah took one last picture with his cardiac monitor and unplugged the wires from the box. He hoisted it on top of the nurses' station while they followed a short man in camouflage scrubs to room five. Noah looked up just in time to see Amber on the other side of the ER. She paused, held her gaze on him, head slightly tilted. Noah raised his eyebrows quick and flashed her an *untouchable* smile, before slapping Dr. Hens on the shoulder and following him into the exam room.

"Physical therapy work for you then?" the doc asked.

The honest answer: *No, Mick, not only did it not work, but the physical therapist you recommended is a druggie, who I watched crush a Percocet into two lines and then snort one of them.*

Afterward, when I attempted to do the other, I overdosed, causing her to steal the rest of my meds and run out of my apartment with her slutty little cocktail dress tucked under her arm. But it's okay; I'm heading down the path to getting my head on straight—oh, and speaking of head, she wasn't too bad when she was on her knees.

"Yeah, for better or worse," Noah said. "Is this your first night back?"

"Yup." The doc adjusted his tie. "Just got in twenty minutes ago. Nice string of time off after all those extra shifts."

Mick introduced himself to the patient just as Noah's pager sounded. "Catch you later, Mick. Take care, Victoria. Your daughter should be here any minute, okay?"

The older woman smiled at him as the oxygen hissed through the mask over her nose and mouth. He snatched his monitor from the counter and left the ER as dispatch came over his pager.

"CN dispatch to Sara's Point respond with American Response Medic: Aurora Lake Road, closest address 88, rollover with ejection."

He froze in the door. American Response was out of the city, which meant a ten-to-thirteen-minute response time to Caligan alone, never mind the extra seven to Sara's Point. Tasha came running up behind him.

"Gary's got your rig here," she said. "He's pulling in now."

Time to play, he thought and hurried toward the Explorer.

***

Noah blew past a cop doing radar on the median of the highway. He glanced down at his speedometer and saw it just under triple digits. Dangerous, reckless, and against the policies of the company, but neither he, nor the cop who noticed his flashing lights and sirens, cared.

"Dispatch," Noah said into his radio. "Status on MED-Flight auto-launch?"

"Alpha-One, be advised MED-Flight is unavailable due to weather."

He leaned forward and stared up at the sky. *What weather?*

"Check on Life-Air out of Worcester."

"Checking on Life-Air," dispatch repeated with a little annoyance in his voice.

At the accident scene, two cars were on the road, one on its roof, outlined by scattered shards of broken glass and a pool of what Noah assumed was gasoline. The other was angled onto the embankment as if it had skidded there, abruptly stopped when it attempted to drive into the small hill. A kid who looked barely old enough to drive was jumping and pacing in front of the parked car. An Audi. Noah grabbed his gear as four firefighters jumped from the heavy rescue, grabbing tools from side compartments.

He could hear the ambulance and at least one or two cops coming behind him. The kid was screaming. He heard the word race.

"Where is he?" Noah yelled.

The kid started frantically pointing to the side of the road a dozen yards down. Noah sprinted over. Another teen. He could already see the makeshift cross on the side of the road. Flowers and balloons. Candles that would stay on someone's front lawn, unable to be removed by the homeowners because, well, who would do that? How could they face anyone after removing a memorial?

A firefighter kneeled with a backboard and plastic collar for the kid's neck. Noah pulled on gloves as the lights from the heavy rescue suddenly illuminated the road.

"Dispatch to Alpha-One," his radio buzzed.

"Answer it," he called to the lieutenant on scene.

"Dispatch from Buckland Rescue: go with your transmission."

"Life-Air is not flying due to weather."

Noah looked up and shouted. "What fucking weather?"

"There's thunderstorms in the area," the firefighter said quickly as he pressed his hands to the sides of the kid's face in order to hold his head and neck straight.

"Jesus Christ," Noah spat with no remorse.

He cut open the kid's shirt and ripped it to the side. Bruising had started underneath the left shoulder. Noah pushed his knuckles into his sternum and rubbed. The kid groaned but barely moved. Noah gripped his body, darted down each extremity, feeling a bulge on the right shin and a deformity on his left wrist.

The kid coughed and his lips turned bright red as blood ran from the corner of his mouth.

"Time to go," Noah hissed.

With an IV in and a quick round of meds, they loaded him to the back of the ambulance.

"St. Vincent's," He called to the driver. "Lights and sirens the whole way. Go."

They took off, the jolt causing Noah to stumble forward, catching himself on one of the cabinets.

"Noah," the EMT yelled. A guy he didn't recognize. Short hair, glasses. There was panic in his voice. "Noah—shit, he stopped breathing."

Noah whipped around. There was no rise or fall in the kid's chest, and his eyes were slightly open with only white visible.

"Fuck."

He dove for his bag, ripped out the intubation kit, and snapped down the metal laryngoscope. He felt for a quick pulse. Thready, but there. He positioned himself at the kid's head, held in place by straps and foam blocks attached to the backboard on top of the stretcher.

"Get the bag ready," Noah said and checked quickly for broken teeth or anything that could obstruct his airway.

His hand shook as he lowered the blade to just above the kid's mouth. Stop. Breathe. He had this. A procedure done a million times. He curved the blade down and into the kid's throat, pulling back and up, the muscles in his arm tensing at the needed pressure for him to see the vocal cords before he could slide the tube down—there!

Noah stopped, pulled the blade out, slid the insert out of the tube and, holding it in place with one hand, nodded for the EMT to fix the ambu-bag to the top and squeeze, providing artificial ventilation. With his other hand, Noah reached for his stethoscope and pressed it against the kid's bloodstained chest and listened for air to travel in and out of his lungs.

Perfect. He strapped the tube down and counted with the EMT as he breathed for the patient, when his monitor suddenly erupted with a blaring noise. Looking up, Noah watched the lines go flat.

"You have got to be kidding me," he hissed. "Start CPR. Leave the bag there; I got it."

He whipped a med from his bag: epinephrine. The devil's jumpstart. In this instance, the medication would most likely have no effect. Traumatic arrests were simply that: cardiac arrests due to severe trauma. But, in the off chance that there was an underlying cause, a condition Noah didn't know about, it was worth giving the injection and seeing if the sudden dose of adrenaline would do anything.

The EMT continued to pump on the kid's chest. Sweat beaded on his nose, ready to drip.

"Pick it up," Noah said.

"Huh?" The EMT was out of breath, but that didn't matter at this point. He had to keep going, and that was that.

Noah screwed the med into the IV tubing, glanced at his watch, and pushed the drug through the tube. "Another One Bites the Dust; that's the rhythm. Go."

The EMT started pumping again, the speed of compressions increased, when the ambulance banked hard, nearly tossing Noah to the side.

"Jesus." He squeezed the bag and breathed for the kid once. . . twice. "Where are we?"

The driver yelled back, "Just got on the highway."

Noah cursed under his breath, looked at the fake rhythm on his monitor, visible only because of the EMT's compressions. He squeezed the bag again once. . . twice, then ripped the radio from its place on the wall of the ambulance.

"Dispatch from Alpha-One."

It was seconds before they answered. Seconds that felt like hours.

"Alpha-One, this is dispatch."

"Tell Caligan General we're coming in with a traumatic arrest, roughly seventeen, maybe eighteen, CPR in progress."

"Roger, Alpha-One."

Noah leaned into the cab, "You get that."

The driver replied, "Yup."

Noah clasped his hand on the grab bar in the ceiling and paused for a second as the ambulance banked again, pulling off the next ramp. The glaring screen of the monitor showed jagged jumps that weren't actual heartbeats.

"Hold," he told the EMT, who was more than happy to take a break. Noah pressed his fingers against the kid's groin but felt no trace of a femoral pulse.

"Breathe for him," he yelled as he put his hands, one on top of the other, over the center of the kid's chest and began pushing.

Up, down. Hard and fast. He sang the song in his head, did his best to keep to the beat while he felt the kid's ribs bend. Elasticity in youth preventing them from breaking.

Two minutes of CPR and he traded back with the EMT so he could start a second IV on the other arm. He looked at his bag, contemplated the I/O drill to put a line straight into bone. He knew, somewhere in his head, he knew this kid was dead. Even if he did respond to these interventions, which he wouldn't, his brain would be mush, and he would never be the same. Noah wondered if, earlier in the night when the kid left, if he had told his parents he loved them. Or if he even said goodbye.

The ambulance reversed, and Noah threw his gear onto the kid's lap, positioning the monitor between the still legs.

They pulled the stretcher from the back and rushed inside, Noah guiding it with one hand and doing CPR with the other.

"One," A nurse said. He looked up and saw Amber.

Right into the first room where respiratory therapy was waiting along with two other nurses, a technician, and Dr. Hens.

"Round of EPI given in the field. Roll over. Ejected probably about thirty feet. Unknown down time. Responsive to painful stimuli on scene. Stopped breathing in the ambulance, tubed him, and then lost pulses."

The hospital technician and the same camo-wearing nurse from before called out, "Slide on three."

Noah halted CPR as they slid the backboard to the stretcher and the hospital tech took over. Amber ran behind him and rushed to attach the wall-mounted monitor to the kid's chest. She strapped a blood pressure cuff to his arm and pressed go.

"Fluid bolus wide open," Mick said.

Another nurse tossed Amber a bag of IV fluid. She spiked it, connected it to Noah's IV, and hung it above the bed. A sudden spasm bucked the kid's body against the remaining straps of the backboard and caused everyone in the exam room to jump backward half-of-a-step.

The monitor suddenly beeped and the flat lines began bouncing into a readable rhythm.

Noah stood there, mollified. "You gotta be shitting me."

The kid groaned and tried to move his head, coughing at the tube in his throat. Mick slapped his hands together.

"Alright, let's get him sedated and get x-ray in here for a portable chest to determine tube placement." He looked up from the patient. "Nice, Noah."

Noah couldn't help it. Disbelief turned into relief. He smiled. He looked at Amber, met her gaze and she smiled too, nodding in approval. He was elated, but he was still in the way. Noah stepped out of the room and tossed his monitor on the counter to begin cleaning everything off. The driver and the other EMT high-fived.

Noah stopped them as they headed toward the ambulance and patted the EMT on the shoulder. "Nice job."

"Thanks, Noah."

He felt bad he didn't know the guy's name, but it was what it was. They had saved a life, and that was a miracle in and of itself. He still couldn't believe the kid had a pulse. Such a low probability—next to impossible—and yet it had happened. As they left the ER, Noah paused, monitor and gear in hand, and watched everyone work inside the exam room before his eyes came to rest on

Amber. She pulled a medication from the crash cart and filled a syringe, ready to inject it when the time was right.

It was the first time she had smiled at him in probably a year.

FIFTEEN

"Well," Paul said outside of his office on Saturday morning. "That was a hell of a first shift back, am I right?"

Noah laughed and looked at the ground with the faintest hint of bashfulness. He felt good. He was sober, and he felt good. Who would have thought?

"Does that mean I can come back tonight?" He said it with an attitude, but broke into laughter a few seconds after.

"Yeah," Paul nodded. "Yeah come on back tonight. But go home and get some rest, okay?"

"Mhm, thanks boss."

The sun was over the trees and morning rays warmed the air. The deep blue of the cloudless sky only echoed the fantastic mood that pulsed through him. He felt no pain, no ache, nothing. In his truck, he grabbed his phone and took a chance; Amber answered on the second ring.

"Hey, what's wrong?"

"Nothing." There was shame in the fact that Amber immediately thought something was wrong. "Take it you got out on time?"

Noah's phone beeped in his ear. There was an incoming call from his brother. He needed to take it. Find out what Robert knew and get his head back in the game, but this time around, Amber's voice would be number one. This was how he would get everything back to normal. Always put her first.

"Yeah," Amber said. "An increasing rarity. You sure you're good?"

"Yes," he said.

"Okay." There came a pause. "So, why are you calling?"

"Just was curious as to what happened with the kid after I left last night. Safe to say he made it?"

"Far as I know. We stabilized him as best we could, then sent him out to one of the trauma centers."

"I was on my way there; he should have gone there, but soon as he coded, it was closest facility."

"You did fine, Noah." Her voice trailed off. "You always do fine."

A lump caught in his throat, stretching the silence between them a few seconds too long. He began to ask her to coffee, but she spoke too quick.

"But I gotta go. I'm meeting Neil for breakfast and might actually make it this time. It was good to see you back at work. I mean that."

"Yeah," he said as her subtle resistance turned into a violent shove. One last-ditch effort: "You owe me a coffee though."

He regretted saying it as soon as the words left his mouth. There would have been another opportunity. Another chance.

"Really? Why's that?"

"Well, for starters, we had a good save last night, so we need to celebrate somehow."

"Oh, dear God," she laughed; it sounded forced. "I'll talk to you later, Noah."

"I mean it," he tried to keep her on the line, but she said goodbye and her voice was replaced by *beep-beep-beep.*

Driving toward his apartment, Noah pulled into the parking lot of Mary's Cathedral. The sun reflected off the building in a radiance of beauty. It was a truly remarkable piece of architecture, as so many churches and cathedrals were. Gothic structures—oddballs that stood out, though no one dared mock them for the uniqueness.

Despite the warm welcome the building offered, Noah couldn't bring himself to get out of his truck and go inside. Maybe if Amber had met him for coffee, knowing both his professional and personal lives were going back to normal, maybe then he would be able to step inside and thank God.

"I should have asked quicker."

Admitting this made it concrete. Fault rested on his shoulders. But the smile she had flashed had been genuine, Noah knew that much. He shifted his truck into reverse, pausing briefly for another look at the cathedral before pulling out of the lot and heading home.

Once at his apartment, he went straight for his bedroom and the crucifix he'd left on his nightstand, still unsure how it had gotten off the wall. He returned it where it belonged and crossed himself.

Taking his shirt off to head to bed, Noah paused at the edge of his bathroom door. The medicine cabinet above the sink was open. Not just ajar but fully open. He sifted through the contents, each of the three shelves. Nothing seemed out of place or missing, but why would he leave the door open?

Noah pressed the cabinet closed. The magnetic door stuck, meaning the fault was solely his, though he couldn't remember it at all.

***

Noah stepped out of the shower, stretched, and finished toweling off. His stomach was still full from breakfast with Robert, a thankfully uneventful meal.

Robert had insisted he follow Noah home, talk about the two murders and their blatant connection to Jack the Ripper in greater detail, but Noah stopped his brother before he could even explain the symbolism behind the fake Christmas tree and the little bottles of liquor. The woman had looked so familiar. But the fog of drugs and alcohol, anger and depression, coupled with the *carved* state of her face left a blank space in his mind that continued to bother him.

Noah had promised Robert he'd return to the Jack the Ripper theories once he had figured out what to do about the triage position he was supposed to start at Caligan General in the beginning of October. Less than a week away.

"I'll have to call and decline. Simple as that," he said to the fogged bathroom mirror.

His monologue was interrupted by three knocks on the front door. He quickly threw on a shirt and jeans, before greeting a postal worker. The slightly overweight man was dressed in a blue uniform and full mustache. He handed Noah a priority envelope and a data pad to sign without a single word.

"Thanks," Noah said and shut the door.

A typed address sticker showed his name and apartment number, with no return label fixed to the upper left corner. He tore open the top piece and pulled out a smaller white envelope.

"Jesus." He dropped the envelope on the counter and stared at the bottom corner saturated in red—the same thick, crimson that saturated bandages and gauze pads, hems of shirts and EMS jumpsuits.

From his bathroom closet, he pulled a box of exam gloves he'd stolen from Caligan General and hurried back into the kitchen. He slit the top of the envelope with a knife and immediately put the blade in the dishwasher. Inside the envelope was a piece of paper folded in three. The bloodstain formed a weird wave on the edge as he opened it.

Dear Boss,

I suppose I shall count myself lucky that it was you on call when I did the first one in. I thought at best I would have an incompetent detective nipping at my heels, never able to discern anything I left into something useful. Imagine my surprise when you arrived. Or was it something more than that?

I know Robert has explained to you what I'm doing and I will be forthcoming (call it good faith or sportsmanship it matters not to me). Dear Old Jack was never caught, which means neither will I be or this entire enterprise was for naught. No, I can't let that happen I'm afraid.

This letter is a warning, my friend. Heed it and maybe next time I'll clip a little something just for you. I admire you and Robert for figuring this all out so quickly, it's only fitting I show my appreciation. Leave me be, let me finish what I started and you will never know my name or see my face. Though you will see the handiwork. I'll make sure of it. Such a sharp blade makes such clean cuts, wouldn't you say? I bet you saw that woman's spine. Or blood-stained bones at the very least. Anatomy and physiology, so much more invigorating in flesh and blood, don't you agree?

Don't and, well, I know you're smarter than that. I'm glad that you're feeling better, Noah. Our demons can be such hurtful little things.

Yours truly,
Jack

Noah stumbled backward, staring at the cursive letters and the red drops the page was leaving on his countertop. He broke from the trance, eyes stinging as he ran and lunged for his cell phone.

"Robert," he yelled when the call connected. "Get over here. Now."

SIXTEEN

"I told you," Robert said. "I was right. I mean, are you seeing this, Noah? I was right. I knew it from the beginning."

Noah watched his brother read the letter a third time. His phone sat idle. 9-1-1 on the screen but *send* never pressed. His apartment was silent save for the hum of the baseboard heat.

"Do you have the detective's number?" Noah asked.

Robert shook his head, then patted his back pocket. "Actually," he pulled out his wallet, "I do."

Noah dialed the number and put the phone to his ear, only to have Robert jump at him. "Wait, wait. Don't call her yet."

Noah fumbled with the phone and hung up mid-ring. "Why?"

"If he wanted the police involved, he would have sent this to the police. The original Dear Boss letter from Jack the Ripper was sent to the Central News Agency, who then forwarded it on to Scotland Yard. As far as I know, you are *not* a reporter, nor are you part of any kind of news agency, which means he skipped that step. There has to be a reason he only sent it to you. You're not "

"He's a murderer," Noah said with disbelief. "Of course he doesn't want the police involved."

"Not true. If he sent this to the police, then he would be taunting them. Right now, he's only taunting us."

"Who would do that?"

"Taunt the police?" Robert snorted. "Don't you remember the DC sniper? The tarot card that said *'Dear Policeman, I am God'*? Or the Zodiac letters? Hell, I think even the BTK killer sent letters or something to the police, but I can't remember exactly what. I think it was a poem, or maybe it was that he wrote—"

"Robert! Come on." Noah shoved him. "Let's focus on what the Ripper did, alright?"

"Alright. Except no one really knows for sure."

"What are you talking about?"

"Well, it's actually highly disputed whether any of the letters were real or if they were all rubbish. Dozens of them were sent, but only three are considered *real*. Nonbelievers argue that the media sent them as a hoax to stir up public attention and get people in a panic. Killer on the loose in Whitechapel and all that."

His brother's words swirled inside his head. Spinning around and jumbling until Noah could no longer sort them into coherent ideas.

"So, scholarly arguments aside, talk to me. What does the average person believe about Jack the Ripper?"

Robert looked at him, almost annoyed that his research and education were being dismissed for a common ideology. "The common consensus is yes, there were three actual correspondences from the real ripper."

"So, he sent the police three letters?"

"Yes—well, no—not exactly. I told you, he sent the first one to the papers and they forwarded it to Scotland Yard. But we don't have to! We could solve this ourselves. I mean, come on, we're doing it so far, aren't we? He even says right here that we're doing better than the police. He wants us to."

Noah could only stare, his mouth hanging slightly open. Lips dry and cracked. "Are you mad? That's withholding evidence, and I'm pretty sure it's a felony. Not to mention the fact that we don't have any actual evidence, and he explicitly states in the letter that he doesn't want to be caught."

"First of all," Robert said. "Like you just mentioned: he's a murderer. Of course he doesn't want to be caught. And while you're right, we don't have any *actual* evidence, we do have pictures from both crime scenes. And the brainpower. You know, now that you're back in action and all. You never asked what I figured out about the second murder."

Noah grumbled. "What did you find?"

Robert's face glowed. "Right, so the first woman who died was a metaphor for Mary Ann Nichols—the first victim of the real Jack the Ripper. The second, the woman we found—well, the EMT found—was a metaphor for Annie Chapman."

"And you know this for sure?" Noah asked.

Robert pinched the bridge of his nose. "Let's pretend for a minute that we don't have a confession letter right here. Even without that, yes, I know for sure. See, Chapman was a heavy drinker. Liked the taste of rum, according to reports."

Robert raised his eyebrows, but when Noah only continued to stare, he went on. "Her husband and her split at some point, I forget the actual date, but that's not important. Anyways, her husband paid her an allowance every few weeks, kind of like old-school alimony. But that dried up when her husband died. Want to know when he died?"

"Does it matter?" Noah asked.

"It does. He died on Christmas day in 1886."

"I thought the Ripper murders were in 1888? What's it matter if he died two years before?"

"Jesus Christ, Noah." Robert flicked the corner of the letter making Noah wince at the thought of microscopic blood spatter. "When we got into the house and found that woman, what was on the coffee table?"

Noah thought for a minute. "A fake Christmas tree and nips?" His eyes widened. A dawning of realization. "The real Chapman liked rum and her husband died on Christmas day."

"Well," Robert said. "You're not an idiot. But see? We *can* solve this; we don't need the police to be involved."

Noah hesitated, phone still in hand.

"No. No, I'm calling her."

The call connected and Detective Madsen's voice came across. "Mr. McKeen, you're not calling just to hang up on me again, are you?"

"Uh—no, no, ma'am."

"Good. What can I do for you?"

"Actually, I think there's something that I can do for you."

* * *

Detective Madsen arrived with two uniformed officers: a short, portly man and a masculine-looking woman Noah recognized from a psychiatric call several months back.

He and Robert sat in the kitchen, reiterating the events of the morning for the third time. The male officer took notes while the woman whose name he couldn't remember wandered around his living room, eyes darting to each corner.

Noah tossed his cell phone back and forth, hoping Amber would return his call. He'd left her a voicemail— he wasn't sure why, as this had nothing to do with her— because when he'd hung up with the detective, it seemed like the only logical thing to do.

"The only thing that bothers me, Mr. McKeen, is why you called your brother before you called us."

"Because…" He tried to think of a believable answer, but the truth was, he didn't have one. Mainly because there was none. "I don't know. I just did."

Her eye contact lingered. Three curls of brunette hair hung in front of her face. She scribbled something in her pad and rose. "I'd like it if the two of you could come down to the station for me."

"How come?" Robert asked.

"How about because you've both been referenced in a letter by someone claiming to have murdered two people in the last month. All in a manner, might I add, that was originally pointed out by you."

She stepped toward them, face hovering above Noah. "But if that's not enough, how about the fact that a letter dipped in blood allegedly arrived at your door, and rather than call us, you called your brother. Does that work, or should I come up with something better?"

Robert slapped his palms against his legs. "Nope, that's good with me."

The detective smiled and moved to step around the counter when her foot crunched something. Stepping back, she bent down, only to return a second later fishing for a napkin. She picked at the floor, held the napkin over the counter, and let little bits of broken pill rattle free. Robert glared at him.

"No—no, Rob, it's not—no."

The detective arched her eyebrows and waited, but neither of them said anything more. After a moment she said, "Harris, grab a bag for this, along with the envelope and the letter, then get down to the post office and see who would have been the delivery person for this area. Gentlemen, do you want to lock up before we leave?"

They drove in Noah's truck, opting to carpool rather than take separate vehicles. The impression was that they were going to be there for a while.

In the time it had taken for the detective and her lackeys to arrive, to the brothers heading down to the station, Noah had begun to regret calling Madsen. He remembered times when he had ignored medical control and made calls based on his own judgment that had turned out to be correct. Why couldn't he do that now? He had the basic information he had pulled from the web in addition to what Robert knew and yet. . .

"Amber still hasn't called you back?" Robert asked.

Noah stopped tapping the top of his phone and put both hands on the wheel. "Probably never will."

"No, she will."

"What makes you say that?"

"How do you think your apartment got so clean?" Robert asked.

"She came over? When?"

"We both did, actually, just so you know; don't hesitate to throw a little gratitude my way."

Noah stared. Thought of the little things out of place. The oddities that made his hair stand on end. "You were coming into my apartment without me knowing?"

"I was checking on things," Robert said. "Just making sure."

"Making sure what?"

"That there wasn't a dead girl in your closet, Jesus. I was checking in to make sure you were okay. Sorry for caring."

"Rob," Noah snipped.

Ahead of them, the detective stopped at a light. Noah eased on the brakes and stopped a few yards behind her.

"Amber cares about you," Robert said. "She just doesn't want to watch you kill yourself, you know?"

"Not an issue anymore."

"No, I know, I'm just saying."

"Thanks," Noah offered. He forced himself to smile until a new question popped into his head. "Should we get lawyers?"

"Lawyers?" His brother snorted. "If we were under arrest or being charged, they wouldn't have let us drive on our own. We haven't done anything but try and help them. Frankly, they should be thanking us rather than dragging us down here. But, if I'm being honest, I rather enjoy it."

"I don't know how you find this enjoyable."

"Come on, Noah. There isn't the least bit of you that thinks this is somewhat fun? What else do you have going on right now?"

He turned right. Passed two kids on bicycles. "Nothing, except trying to get my life back on track."

"True," Robert said.

"Are you really that bored at work?"

There was a deep exhale from the passenger seat. "It's not work. Work is actually the best part of my day, even the freshman class."

"Claudia?" Noah guessed. Out of the corner of his eye, he saw Robert nod.

"It's been a rough few months, and it's gotten a lot worse with Emma up at school."

"She's only going to Northern. You guys could carpool for God sakes."

"She's dorming there."

"Oh."

They were half-a-mile from the police station, nowhere near enough time to finish the conversation, but it would have to be finished at some point.

He parked the car and looked over. Robert answered without him having to ask a second time. "We don't need lawyers."

They trailed behind Detective Madsen until reaching the same narrow corridor Noah had been led down before. A uniformed officer exited from a metal door and stood behind the detective.

"Noah, I'm going to have you sit with Officer Keene here for a few minutes. He's just going to ask you a couple questions about your employment."

Noah furrowed his brow. Madsen instructed Robert to follow her to an adjacent room. The officer's face was stern in the fluorescent ceiling lights, and the questions, as Noah suspected, were asinine. How long have you been a paramedic? Have you ever had to attend grief counseling? Are you thinking of advancing your career?

The door finally opened, interrupting Noah's one-word answers, and Detective Madsen came in, taking the seat across from him. The uniformed officer rapped his knuckles on the table and left.

"What is this?" Noah asked. He leaned his elbows against the metal table. "Are you interrogating us?"

"No," she said calmly. "Mr. McKeen, you have been the only constant in a series of very brutal events in a very quiet town. We just have questions for you. Would you like for me to interrogate you? Because I could. I could arrest you right now and turn this into a very unpleasant conversation."

She held his eyes and, for the life of him, he couldn't tell if she was bluffing. There was no sign of faltering. No twitch in the muscles above either of her eyes, at either corner of her mouth. Nothing. Detective Madsen was stone.

"Just ask your questions, okay?"

Madsen nodded, her face remaining void of any expression.

From a manila folder, she pulled paper-sized photographs of both bodies and the bloody areas around them. "It's fair to say you remember both of these scenes, correct?"

Noah nodded, noting when he did so, that there was no tape-recorder or prod to respond verbally. Unless he was on film. An unsettling thought.

"Let's start with the first scene: Marisa Newton." She slid another picture on top of the murder scene, this one taken in a yard with a child on a rope swing and a grill in the background. The woman was smiling at the camera, happy.

"Do you recognize her from anywhere?" Madsen asked.

Noah shook his head and had the faint recollection of being asked that before.

"You never took her in before? Insulin was found at the scene. If she was a diabetic, there's a good chance she's been to the emergency room."

"With all due respect, detective, over half of this country is diabetic."

"How did you get into her house that night?"

It took a second to remember the particulars, as if the night in question had happened a year ago rather than a month.

"The front door? I wasn't the first on scene."

"No, Sara's Point ambulance was there several minutes before you."

"If you know that, then why are you asking me?"

Fake oozed from her smile. "Just like to hear everything from you."

"Alright, well, now you have. So what else do you want to know?"

"You heard no other footsteps in the house when you went in, correct? Other than those from the ambulance members on scene?"

"Not that I know of? I mean if I had heard anything, I would've assumed it came from the crew on scene, you know? Up until the point where I actually saw her body, I assumed it was a routine call, so I wasn't exactly looking for anything out of the ordinary. There was nothing disturbed downstairs that I could tell. I think some food on the table?"

"Pretty impressive you can remember that," she said and her tone made him shift in his seat.

"Habit, I guess."

"Mhm. Let's jump to Alexia Cay." She slid the second woman's picture forward.

Noah could just see the edge of the fake Christmas tree. The row of little nips of rum leading away like Santa's footprints in the snow. But Noah wasn't focusing on the tree or the liquor or anything else in the scene, because at the second Alexia's name had been uttered,

Noah realized where he recognized her from. His chest felt like hands of ice had wrapped around it.

Detective Madsen slid a second, normal picture, on top of the first. Alexia was holding a small dog, trying to get it to look at the camera while it insisted on licking her face. Locks of brunette hair curled around slightly chubby cheeks. She wore thick, clear-framed glasses. "Do you recognize her?"

"Yeah," he said, his voice cracking. "Yeah, I do."

"Where from?" Detective Madsen asked.

"What do you know about her?" Noah countered.

"Mr. McKeen, where do you—"

Noah slammed his hand on top of the picture. "Where's her son?"

"How do you know she had a son? Mr. McKeen, how do you know her?"

Tides rose in his throat. Choking them down, Noah forced his composure to remain somewhat in tact. "It's not really her son. She adopted him when her sister died."

Detective Madsen clicked her tongue. "I highly advise you tell me how you know all this."

"Because I was there," Noah snapped. He took a second. Inhaled a deep breath. "I was there when her sister died. She died almost two years ago in a car accident out on Sawyer Ridge."

SEVENTEEN

The early-afternoon air hit him like a humid barrier. The thickness of it dragged against his shirt as he ran down the steps of the police station toward his truck, desperately hoping that by some grace of God, there would be a stray Percocet rattling around in his cup holder. His brother called after him, but Noah kept moving.

Two receipts and loose change. Noah slammed his door, re-opened it, gripped it until his knuckles turned white, and slammed it again. But it wasn't enough. The fury. The rage. For a second time, the same child had been left motherless, and now Noah was tied to both. An accident that killed her, and may as well have killed him, too.

"Noah," Robert yelled. "What the hell happened?"

"I'm done," Noah finally said. Madsen had come out of the police station. Stood a dozen yards behind Robert.

"Did you know?" Noah yelled. He stalked toward her, hand in the air. She remained perfectly still, arms at her side. "Did you know I responded to that call? That, that crash left me permanently injured?"

"You don't appear to be injured any longer, Mr. McKeen."

He could have hit her, cracked her stone expression, and watched her face shatter like a marble sculpture toppling to the ground. She was waiting for it. If he launched himself, even snarled at her, it would give her ammunition to use against him.

His nails dug into his palms, forming half-moons in his skin. The humid air weighed down against him, pressing his clothes to his skin, his sweat causing the fabric to stick, adding to the feeling of claustrophobia.

Rather than engage her, either verbally or sealing his fate physically, Noah dropped his hands. "You're going to have to talk to the others who were on scene, because I'm done."

"Noah," Robert said.

Noah got into his truck and didn't stop until he had reached his apartment.

***

The unseasonable heat broke just before midnight. Bright flashes of lightning illuminated the night sky before giving way to sudden claps of thunder. Rain pounded against his apartment's sliding glass door. Noah had remained on his patio when the first drops came spurting down. They hit his skin like ice. Like cold rain in late September should have felt.

When he slept, he found himself on Sawyer's Ridge, his hands cradling Michelle Cay's neck as he repositioned himself inside the car. There was no EMT in the back seat; it was only the two of them. Lightning flashed. His skin buzzed, hairs standing on end. It felt wrong. There had been no storm that night.

Everywhere around him people yelled. Michelle groaned; he could feel the vibrations of her vocal chords in his hands. Thick, warm liquid oozed across his knuckles, and Noah realized he wasn't wearing gloves.

The car rocked, as if hit by a tumbling boulder, snapping the girl's head to the side and nearly sending him into the rear windshield. He struggled to hold his grip, his fingers touching the cloth of the headrest as he clawed his way back to her, but it was too late. Her neck twisted at the wrong angle. He knew it was broken, but there was still life in her eyes—there had to still be life in her eyes.

Lightning flashed. Thunder exploded. The car rattled in the aftermath. When it ceased, so did the noises coming from the first responders. Shouts replaced by the low hum of organ music.

Noah opened his eyes and found himself sitting in a pew, staring at an altar. He slowly looked around, swallowing saliva like a rock, when he realized that everyone was dressed in black. Everyone except for him. Lanterns swung on chains above him, and candlelight flickered from the altar. On top was a casket with the upper portion of the lid propped open.

"You have to go up now," the woman next to him said.

She was older with a thick southern accent. He tried to respond, to say this was a mistake, and he shouldn't be there, but each time his mouth opened, he could only say, "Of course."

Eyes. Everywhere eyes were on him. The congregation stared as a collective mass, and Noah knew there was no way out. He rose quietly, slowly, and shuffled to the center aisle. Shadows darted in the recesses behind the altar as a breeze pushed the flames of the candles.

At the altar, a young woman stood wearing a black strapless dress and matching veil.

"You have to go up now," she echoed the southerner's words.

Though she looked nothing like her, her voice was Amber's. It stabbed Noah like a knife.

Expecting 'of course,' Noah was shocked when he instead said, "but she's already gone."

The woman put her hand on his cheek. Her fingertips soft. "She still has one song left to sing."

He wanted nothing more than to keep the woman's hand there. There was comfort in it. A gentle guidance.

He turned and stepped toward the coffin, when he heard a child laugh behind him.

Noah whipped back, scanned the sea of nameless faces, until his eyes rested on a young boy sitting on the corner of the second row, his legs not long enough for his feet to hit the floor. He giggled again, and Noah took a step toward him.

The woman appeared at the bottom of the steps with her hands up. "You can't."

"I have to." His attention remained focused on the child.

Something was wrong. The black of the boy's clothes was wafting away, drifting upward, and curling like smoke. He felt the woman's hands on his chest, and when he squeezed them to move her, they were no longer soft. Hard and rigid, her flesh felt like scales. She hissed and he jumped back, crashing backward into the altar, sending the candles tumbling to the floor.

Darkness descended on the cathedral. The organs ceased playing, their harmony quickly replaced by a communal humming. When he looked up, the congregation was stepping toward him. Between their legs, he saw the child being led away by the scale-hand woman.

Scrambling to his feet, Noah called after him. The wall of people pushed him backward, toward the altar.

"No." He fought against them.

Their shoulders pushed against his chest as he tried to reach over them. Jumping, fighting, trying to swim in a sea of solid mass. They drove him up each step while the woman led the child farther away. When the backs of his legs rubbed against the coffin, he looked over his shoulder. The wooden box was empty. In lieu of a body was an empty void of black.

"Sing, Noah," the woman's voice, Amber's voice, whispered in his ear. "Sing."

He opened his mouth and screamed.

* * *

Noah slapped at his cellphone as it rattled across the glass coffee table.

"Hello?" He half-yawned.

"Hey," Amber said.

Noah bolted upright. In his mind he saw her: the veiled woman with her voice. The solemn humming of the congregation filled his ears.

"Noah?"

"Yeah—yeah, sorry. What's up?" He stumbled off the couch, slamming his shin into the coffee table and cursing into the phone.

"Are you alright?"

"Yeah, just hit the damn table with my shin."

He heard her nervous laughter. "I was just returning your call from yesterday morning. You sounded kind of. . . panicked. Everything alright?"

Gulping down the last of a glass of water, he backhanded his lips dry and recalled the letter he had opened three feet from where he was standing and the absurd morning it had led to. But that was yesterday. That was pre-storm, pre-cleanse. This was today, and it was all over. Everything from the past was done and gone. Including. . .

"Yeah—no, I'm good. Sorry about that. Weird morning."

She didn't respond for several seconds. "Noah?"

"Hmm?"

"You sure you're good? You can tell me if you're not."

Really? Could I? He wondered what that would legitimately get him. Sympathy? Doubtful. Pity? More than likely. Because that's what he had become: the pity case. The abused puppy everyone felt bad for yet no one adopted.

"I'm good, Amber. Shouldn't have bothered you. Are you good?" Why had he asked that? Of course she was fine, but when an answer failed to come, he was glad he did. "Amber?"

"Honestly, slightly freaked out with everything going on. How are you not?"

"You mean the scenes?" There was almost disappointment in his voice.

"What else would I mean? Two women were murdered, Noah. I saw the news headlines; one of them was Alexia."

"I know," he said. "I was on."

"Are you kidding me? Why didn't you tell me?"

"I didn't think you'd care. It was just—"

"Jesus Christ, Noah. Where are you?"

He looked around his apartment as if he needed reassurance. "At home?"

"I'm taking you up on that coffee. Meet me in fifteen minutes."

EIGHTEEN

Amber tilted her head. Her lips had molded into a thin pressed line. He had seen this look twice before: once when he told her he had wanted to go back to community college, complete his prerequisites, and take the MCATs; the second time when he had told her he wanted to try and have a child.

"Where are the pills?" she asked finally.

"What?"

He lowered his voice. "I'm not high, Amber."

"Then why didn't you call me?"

Noah's phone sat idly between them, the screen dim but not yet dark. He stumbled over his words.

"I didn't think to. With everything else going on, this kind of took a back seat."

"How does this take a back seat?" She demanded. "Noah, two people have been killed, and you've responded to both of them. And now you tell me that the person doing this sent you a *fucking* letter about it? If this is in the back seat, who the fuck is driving the car?"

A waiter appeared with a pot of coffee and refilled their mugs while Amber casually hovered her palm over the phone screen. When the man left, she picked up the device again and pinched the edges of the screen to zoom.

"I don't believe this," she said. "This is insane."

He held his palms up. "That's why I'm done."

"What do you mean?"

He exhaled and rubbed the back of his neck. "For the second time in his life, Adrian lost a mother."

Amber frowned. "I know. It's awful."

"It's the second time I've been involved, and he doesn't have a mother."

"What? Wait—Noah."

"No, not wait Noah. There is no wait Noah. If I hadn't destroyed my knee, if I had been more careful about watching that cut and where I stuck my foot, then Michelle would still be alive. If I didn't get involved with this shit, then Alexia would still be alive. That family has had enough of me and I don't need to check with them on that."

"God damn it, Noah," Amber hissed. A head turned from the next booth. "We have had this conversation a hundred fucking times. You had nothing to do with Michelle—with either of them—dying."

"Say it all you want, but it is what it is." Noah picked up his coffee, felt the warmth wafting off the liquid as it neared his lips.

Amber raised her hand. The waiter came over and she asked for the check, sliding a twenty into his hand before he could finish tallying it up.

"What are you doing?" Noah asked.

"I can't exactly yell at you in a crowded coffee shop. Let's go."

* * *

Amber followed him to his apartment where he made another pot of coffee and began mixing pancake batter. He wasn't hungry, but Amber hadn't started yelling, and Noah was afraid if he kept eye contact for more than a few seconds, her nerve would return.

"Do they have any idea who's doing this?" Amber asked.

"No idea," Noah said, his voice flat. "I'm sure they'll figure it out."

She snorted. "Yeah, once you and Robert tell them who it is. You alone are smart enough, but the two of you together...Why, I never stood a chance."

"You always stood a chance. Robert had nothing to do with it."

"No, I know; not like that. I just meant in conversations and everything."

He paused mid-stir, shook his head and continued mixing the batter.

"What happens next?" Amber asked.

Noah froze. "With us? I don't know."

"No," she said. "With the Ripper case. If Robert's right about this, what happens next?"

Noah clenched his teeth. Stupid mistake. "Um, well, there's been what? Two? That would mean the double is next."

"The double?" Amber asked.

"Yeah," Noah said. "I guess murders three and four happened in the same night. The third one was a woman named Elizabeth Straw—no Stride, Elizabeth Stride. She was killed like the others, throat slit, but there was something different about her. I guess, from what I've read anyway, is that the Ripper was interrupted in that one."

"What do you mean? Like they almost caught him?"

Noah shrugged. "No clue. But, while her throat was slit like the others, she had no other injuries anywhere. So, I guess he must have been interrupted or something."

"Who do you think it is?"

"I don't know." Noah placed the bowl on the counter, done with the effort, and turned to face her.

"You have to have some idea. I mean, kinda seems like this guy has a thing for you." She held her hand out, ticking off her points on each finger. "He makes sure you're on when he kills these two people, the second one just happens to be Alexia Cay, and then he postmarks a letter where he directly mentions you and Robert? Come on, Noah, really? You have to have some clue who would be doing this."

"I have no fucking idea, Amber. Sorry."

She waved him away, ignoring the curse. The coffee pot made a gurgling noise. Noah pointed to a cabinet near the fridge. "Cups are up there."

She put her hands on her hips. "I did live here at one point."

He shrugged. "Yeah, well, been a while."

Noah tried to read the lines in her face, the tiny space between her parted lips. His gaze drifted upward, and she was staring at him. He unfolded his arms just as she pressed her lips against his.

Her hands found the back of his neck. Their bodies against each other like puzzle pieces. She backed away, pulling him with her until she was against the refrigerator. The taste of her lips. Her tongue. His hands went from her cheeks to the sides of her neck, before dropping to her chest and pushing her breasts together.

Amber raised her leg, the inner part of her thigh against the outside of his jeans. Noah dropped his hands to her butt, lifted her off the floor, and carried her to his bedroom while the coffee pot sat idle on the counter.

When they were done, lying next to each other, the top sheet of his bed wrapped awkwardly around his arm and half of her leg, Noah stroked the hair from Amber's face and hooked it behind her ear.

"You're still just as beautiful as the day I met you," he said.

She held his gaze before forcing a little laugh and looking to the ceiling. "I was crying the day you met me."

"Eh, there's beauty in sadness."

"Mhmmm. Gothic romanticism. How sweet."

Amber rolled to the edge of the bed, fingers shuffling about her jeans until they found her phone.

"Shit," she said. "I gotta go."

"Wait." He rolled to the edge of the bed as she tugged her pants on. "We never even ate."

Amber grabbed her shirt from the floor and pulled it on.

"Like that was your intention," she said.

"Hey, you were the one who suggested coming back here."

"Yeah, because I felt bad for you." Her mouth twisted. "I didn't mean it like that."

He forced a laugh, eyes downcast and focused on the top of his bed. "It's fine."

"Noah…" She sat back down, one leg tucked under herself. Her lips parted for several seconds, but she didn't say anything.

"It's good, really." He got up and got dressed. "Tell Neil I said hi."

"Noah, don't do that. There is so much damaged shit between us; do you have any idea how long it would take to fix it all?"

"I'm not going anywhere." He was speaking louder, raising and dropping his arms. "I've been in the same spot for over two years."

"Exactly. You need to move on, or anything between us is just going to revert right back to where we were, and I'm sorry, but I am not doing that again."

He grumbled and grabbed his phone from the nightstand. Of course there were no missed calls or text messages, but looking at the screen prevented him from having to look at her. A technological buffer as she walked out of the room.

Her voice called from the hall, "Did you start going to church again?"

"No."

"Maybe you should. Might be what helps you."

In the kitchen, He followed her to the kitchen, yelling out of desperation. "What if you're what helps me?"

She shook her head. "I'm not. Not anymore. Noah, we've done this. We've been here, and we've done this time and time and time again, and I'm not going back to it. I love you. I always have, and I always will."

She stepped closer to him, gazes locked as she pressed her finger softly against his chest. "But there are demons in there that no one: not me, not Robert, not even God will fight for you. But we can lead you in the right direction, and that's what I'm trying to do, what I've always tried to do. There's a reason you were brought to Michelle's sister, and I'm sorry, but I don't buy that it was the master plan of some murderous psychopath. I think it was a coincidence—and a necessary one—because now you have a purpose, a personal reason to help that detective and catch this guy. Please, for every other woman that lives around here."

The air of the apartment was still. No sounds from the hall and no noise from beyond the slider door. Amber opened the door, pausing with a somber half-grin on her face. "I'm sorry."

Noah shook his head as she shut the door and left.

NINETEEN

When Noah rang Robert's doorbell, his niece Emma answered. Her hair was straightened to her shoulders and dyed black. Her ears stuck out slightly, adding a layer of goofiness to her.

"Hey Uncle N." Her lips curled slightly upward. "Now's not really a good time."

A feeling of instant remembrance. That wave of *damn it* when you recall the one thing you left at home on vacation. He and Robert hadn't had the chance to finish their conversation from the other day. On cue, shouting rang from the second floor, followed by the click clack of heels walking above them.

"Thanks, kiddo." He wedged his way inside, leaving Emma to shut the door. "Where's your brother?"

"I don't know. Playing his Game Boy somewhere."

"Game Boy?"

She shrugged. "He's got like every video game ever made, and he sits around playing one from a hundred years ago."

"Okay, Okay, it's not that old. Let's not get carried away or anything."

She chuckled, and he remembered that, according to Robert, she wasn't supposed to be there. Had he lied about Emma dorming at Northern for sympathy?

"Em, I thought you were up at school?"

Robert's wife Claudia shouted at the top the stairs. "And how the fuck do you expect that to happen, Robert? If you opened your fucking ears and didn't act like such an asshole all the time, it wouldn't be a God damn issue, would it?"

"S'posed to be," Emma said. She folded her arms across her chest. "I came down to have Dad look at my car. The stupid check engine light keeps coming on, and then all this shit happened, and he still hasn't fixed it. Now it's freaking Saturday, and I'm stuck here."

A door slammed above them and something hit the floor before the shouting resumed.

"Is Mikey?"

"He wears his headphones when they fight. Besides, he's probably in the bonus room."

"Alright, let's look at your car."

"Really?" Her face glowed. She rushed toward him and threw her arms around his shoulders. "Thank you, Uncle Noah."

He found Robert's code reader on the toolbox in the garage and plugged it into the port under her steering wheel.

"So, school going good? Are you taking your Dad's class?"

"God, no. I would die. Could you imagine him? He'd probably tell shitty stories like: ha-ha this reminds me of the time little Emmy here sliced her leg open when she first tried shaving."

Noah laughed but couldn't argue with the girl. The display in his hand beeped and flashed a set of numbers. Using his phone, he Googled the make, model, and error code and came up with the painfully simple and excruciatingly annoying answer.

"It's your gas cap."

"What?"

"Yeah, this happens all the time. It's something to do with the sensor that tells the car the cap is on or something like that. Your car's fine though, so don't worry about it."

"Wait, so how do you fix it?"

He placed the reader back on his brother's toolbox. "You wait until you have to get emissions done and then spend twenty bucks on a new one."

"Oh," she said. "Awesome! Thanks, Uncle Noah. I owe ya one."

"Don't mention it. Wait—aren't you going to say bye to your parents?"

She paused, one leg in the car. "In that house? Nope. Bye!"

Back in the front yard, he found Robert sitting on the top step. There was a red mark on his cheek, and though he was years older than Noah, it felt like he was just a child, staring up and looking for answers in the late afternoon sky.

"I don't blame her," he finally said. "I wouldn't want to say goodbye either."

"Rob," Noah's voice trailed off.

"It's fine. This has been a long time coming. We probably should have split up way back when, but of course, I got her pregnant. And don't get me wrong, I love Emma to death, and we had a nice run of good years after she was born, but I don't know, maybe things would've been better, you know? God, listen to me. How awful for a father to say that."

"It's not awful to wonder about choices you made; everyone does. We're an opportunistic species, just sometimes we don't always see the right answer the first time around."

Robert looked at him with a raised eyebrow. "The hell are you talking about?"

"I think we should go talk to that detective."

"Really?"

Noah nodded as a breeze stirred orange and red leaves on otherwise bare branches. Their color echoed the setting sun as it began its descent toward the horizon. In several hours, twilight would lead to darkness, and the noise of the world would become quiet against the overwhelming weight of the night sky. Darkness was a bed, and it could either provide a calm reprieve or a place for chaos to fuck in.

Noah told him what had happened with Amber. All of it. It seemed mean in a way, to talk about something good that had happened to him while his brother was suffering. But he had been in a bad place for so long, it felt remarkable to say something positive about his own life.

Robert stood and Noah instantly regretted saying anything. How could he have been so inconsiderate? Once down the steps, Robert turned back, "Well? Are you coming?"

***

"You know," Noah said as he pulled into the police station. "I think this is the first time I've come here semiwillingly."

Robert laughed. "We are making a habit out of this, aren't we?"

"Doesn't matter. We're going to end this."

"Nice."

Once inside, they asked for Detective Madsen and were told to have a seat on one of the two benches in the foyer of the station. Chirps came from a PA system embedded in the ceiling. Noah tried to decipher any recognizable addresses or complaints as they sat and waited.

Leaning back, he looked across the room to a triangular wooden box with an American flag folded inside. Several medals hung in a frame above the box. They must have belonged to the sergeant killed on the highway last year. His name escaped him, but Noah remembered the incident. It hit the department hard. A decorated officer and a war hero struck down by a drunk driver? No

wonder the cop had given him such a hard time on Sawyer Ridge. Despite what people say, grudges never truly
go away.

His mouth suddenly bubbled with disgust at his own
behavior. What had been wrong with him? How had he
let himself act that way? He held a desire to crawl inside
a cave and die. Everyone who looked at him, regardless
of the fact that they were strangers, silently judged him.
He could see it in their eyes.

"Alright." A uniformed officer waved them toward a
door.

He led them to the same hallway they'd been in the
day before. This time, however, there were two chairs
beside each other in the same room. They slid them out,
the piercing sound of metal dragging against the ground,
and several minutes later Detective Madsen walked in.

The uniformed officer remained standing in the corner of the room until she waved him away.

"Well," she said plainly. "There won't be another letter for a few days, so I know that's not why you're both
here."

Robert smiled. "You actually looked into it?"

"Does that surprise you?"

"Well, yeah, a little."

"Why's that?" she asked. "You think it's a sound theory, don't you? Not just a wild goose chase to occupy our
attention?"

Noah swallowed hard as Robert slumped back in his
seat and muttered.

"Look," Noah leaned forward. Despite his effort, he
couldn't bring any conviction to his voice. It sounded
weak. Right then, a child had more stones than him. "We
just want to help. Obviously, there's a reason we're still
involved right?"

"Mr. McKeen, the only reason you're still involved is
because you choose to be. We checked your alibis for the
nights of the murders, and they are both solid. There's
nothing else we really need from you."

"Maybe there's something I can do that will—wait," he paused, lips pursed. "I didn't give you an alibi for the first night. I was at the firehouse in Caligan. I know I told you that much, but there was no one there who could verify that—all of the guys were sleeping."

"Are you saying you weren't at the station, Mr. McKeen?"

"Yeah, Noah, what are you saying?" Robert echoed the detective.

"No, I was at the station. But how did you verify it?"

There was a pause between them. Ticks coming from the caged-clock. Detective Madsen dragged her teeth across her bottom lip. "The dash cam footage from your vehicle."

Noah sat back. "Son-of-a-bitch."

"You have a dash cam?" his brother asked.

"Yeah, I forgot all about those. We put 'em in after the string of racial shootings that had happened. Company put them in all the vehicles. Just in case."

"The warrant for the footage came through," Detective Madsen said. "And we were able to verify your location that night. Surprised your supervisor failed to mention anything."

Noah thought of Paul. Overworked. Exhausted. The skin underneath his eyes the deep purple of fresh bruises. The added stress of Noah's absence. No surprise, Paul didn't say anything.

"Can we see it?" Robert asked. "The dash cam? I'd really like to get a glimpse of the house, if that's okay."

"It's not. You are not a detective, Mr. McKeen, and quite frankly, your constant enthusiasm for this entire ordeal doesn't sit well with me. Even though you've been vetted as well, don't think for one second that I won't look into every aspect of your life until I can say without a doubt that *I* have faith in you."

"Detective," Robert said. "This man sent a bloody letter to my brother's door."

"That's besides the point, Mr. McKeen."

Noah rested his fingers on the edge of the table, wrestling with what he wanted to say. The cards had been thrown down face up. The police had no use for either of them anymore. But Noah, in his own way, needed to be part of ending the ordeal.

"Again," he said softly, his voice as earnest as he could make it. "We just want to help. So please, just push Robert's enthusiasm out of your head. Maybe there's something on the tape that you missed—nothing against you, please, believe me on that—but, I've been a paramedic for ten years. I can read scenes, and maybe now that things have slowed down a little, I might be able to pick something out that I or you or anyone would have missed the first time around."

Madsen held her gaze firm. Seconds passed until she finally slid her chair backward and left the room. Noah turned to his brother and, through clenched teeth, said, "Cool your jets."

Robert nodded.

Detective Madsen returned several minutes later with a laptop. The uniformed officer stepped inside, backed toward the corner, and hooked his fingers into his belt. The muscles of his tree-trunk arms pushed veins against his skin. Noah eyed the gun on his waist.

Madsen spun the laptop toward them, angling it so each of them could view it simultaneously.

On the screen was a blurred image of the road, taken from the center of the windshield. In the near distance was a blue light, refracted in the rear windshield of a car and the house. 137 Oak Street, where the first of the canonical five recreations lay inside.

She slapped the spacebar in a plastic *clack* that initiated the video loop.

The SUV parks, lurches forward, and then rests. Noah gets out. He walks across the field of view, nods to an EMT donning his civilian clothes, and heads up the stairs of the house. The man shuts his trunk, pulls out a phone, types something, and leaves. Minutes pass. A woman

EMT can be seen standing by the ambulance. More flashing lights appear, and two officers park curbside before heading into the house. After a few minutes, Noah reappears along with a third EMT and stands next to the woman from the ambulance. They talk amongst themselves until the officers exit the house and approach them. A cop points to something over the woman's shoulder. Noah nods. Grabs his bag and heads back to the SUV.

"Well that didn't really show us anything," Robert said, disappointment evident in his tone.

Noah remained quiet, internally replaying the footage in an effort to differentiate between what the camera showed and actual memory. He recognized the first EMT's face. The one putting his street clothes back on. Whoever it was had been at the diabetic call a while back; a bumbling idiot that couldn't keep medications straight. The screen blurred. Madsen rewound the footage until the image stopped frozen at the Oak Street sign.

Noah asked. "You've talked to everybody else who was on scene that night?"

She pulled a manila folder from underneath the laptop. Both brothers stared in slight surprise, neither of them noticing it had been there.

"We were able to speak with Rogers and Miranda, yes. However, Mr. Lechmere has been out of state on business for the past several weeks. We spoke with him briefly over the phone but have yet to bring him in for a more thorough questioning."

Noah shifted in his seat, wedging his hands underneath his thighs. "You don't think that's odd?"

"Yes. We did. Which is why we verified his purchase of a plane ticket from almost three weeks before the murder and then watched him on airport security footage."

Noah felt as if her tone had kicked him in the groin. Robert's laughter broke the tense silence.

"You guys are idiots."

"Excuse me?" Madsen snapped.

The uniformed officer took a step toward them.

"Mr. Lechmere's first name wouldn't be Charles, would it?" Robert asked, his words laced with sarcasm.

"No," Madsen said. "But I assume you have a point."

He straightened, his tone less mocking and slightly nervous. "What—um—what is his name?"

"His first name is Connor."

"And his middle name?"

Madsen's eyes flashed with anger. It burned, twirled in each iris like flames. "Clarence."

Robert rocked back and started laughing again. Noah was going to be sick. He would spend the night in jail. Just when he was getting things back to normal, he would be arrested because of his dipshit brother.

"C. C. Lechmere. Ha. Alright, so you didn't *really* look into anything." Robert leaned toward the detective. "And I actually believed you for a second there."

"For fuck's sake, Rob." Noah said.

"Relax Noah, we just caught a killer."

"Five seconds," Madsen said, her hands visibly shaking. "And then I arrest you for obstruction."

"Okay, so Mary Ann Nichols was the first woman that Jack the Ripper killed. The first of the canonical five victims. Her body was discovered on Buck's Row in Whitechapel, London. Hence the deer painted on the closet door of our first little lady. Nichols's body was found by a man named Charles Allen Lechmere; a man who also went by Charles Cross or C.C. Lechmere."

Noah's eyes went wide as Detective Madsen's narrowed.

"Detective," Robert said. "This man is leaving heavy symbolism at each crime scene, not only identifying who the woman is supposed to represent but who he is trying to be. The canonical five murders that happened in Whitechapel will happen again here in Sara's point. Jack the Ripper killed five women and this man." Robert pointed to the screen. "Will kill five women here. There will be three more bodies if we don't stop this. The next? The next you will find with her throat slit just like the others, but aside from that, there will be no injuries. No abdominal mutilations. No missing organs, nothing. And then, a few hours later, you'll find another. For God's sake, all you have to do is Google 'the double event' and you'll get a basis of what I'm trying to prevent."

Madsen scratched the back of her head. "*Are* you trying to prevent it, Mr. McKeen?"

And with the question asked, Noah realized he wanted to know the answer just as bad as the detective.

Noah stared at the image on the screen. The man he had nodded at, passed by within feet of. But unease settled over him. Not by the man on the computer, but by his brother sitting next to him. Robert had insisted on going with him. Insisted on being involved from the beginning.

Throw me a bone. Help me kill my boredom.

TWENTY

"They're going to move on him," Robert said as they walked back to Noah's truck. "They're going to swarm his place tonight, and we're going to miss it."

"Yeah, well, you're lucky they didn't move on you." Noah was already dialing Amber's number. His thumb hovered above the send button when Robert snagged it away from him.

"What's that supposed to mean?" Robert demanded.

Noah felt his muscles twitch. "Nothing. Just cut back on the enthusiasm, okay?"

"I teach this for a living. Now I get to live it. How can I not be excited?"

"Yeah, well, it's unsettling. Now give me back my phone."

"Not yet. We have to see this through. Finish this, and then you can run back to her.

Think about it: if you call Amber and this guy escapes, it's always going to be in the back of your head that he got away. Can you live with that gnawing your brain into mush? He's got three more women to kill and we have a leg up on him. Noah, we know the dates of when he's going to kill them. You won't get a second chance at this. When he hits his target, that's it, he's done."

"Rob, can I just have my phone please?"

Robert held Noah's phone like a middle school bully. "Come with me first."

"Come with you where?"

"We're going to wait and follow them when they go. When we watch them make an arrest, then I'll give you your phone back."

Noah thought about punching his brother in the stomach. A blow hard enough to make him drop the cell and force a spat of dry heaving. Then there was the other side, the tiny side of him, which was addicted to chaos. After all, he had seen it this far through, what were another few hours. Would it be a few hours, though? If they needed a warrant, could they get one almost immediately? He tried to think of how it worked on television.

"You're going to get us arrested," Noah said.

"Eh," Robert waved the notion away and tossed his phone back.

"Wait, why are you giving me this?"

"Because," he said as he ripped the keys from Noah's other hand. "Like it or not, you're already hooked."

***

It was 8:07 at night. They had spent several hours sitting in a gas station parking lot three buildings down from the police station, and there was still no mass exodus of officers leaving to apprehend Lechmere. Noah sat in the passenger seat. He shifted his weight for the third time in under a minute and tried to dig the last crumbs out of a potato chip bag, but his fingertips came out all grease and no score.

"Maybe they couldn't get a warrant or whatever," Noah said.

"I don't think they need one. Probable cause, right?"

Noah shrugged. "I don't know. I still don't think it was a good idea that we walked in there without talking to a lawyer first."

"Why?" His brother sounded genuinely surprised. "We pretty much solved the case for them."

"Yeah, but you've watched *48 Hours* and stuff. Sometimes they could have the guy all figured out, and it turns out a tiny bit of evidence points in a different direction, and then, bam."

Robert gave him an incredulous look. "Don't tell me you believe in all that wrongly accused bullshit."

Noah sensed that there wasn't a right answer to this. "I'm just saying that I don't want to go to jail for the rest of my life because I messed up and opened my mouth too soon or something."

Robert gave him a quick slap on the leg. "Toughen up, Shirley."

Noah rolled his eyes and looked out the passenger window, his elbow against the door, fingers across his mouth. Twilight had passed and only a fading glow remained behind the trees. The days were getting shorter. Something that would become more noticeable in October.

If the year were divided into night and day, Noah imagined October would be a month long twilight. Everyone preparing to rest. The coming months reserved for sleep.

Restfulness aside, there would always be the others; the people that schemed when the sun went down. Noah had encountered plenty of them during his tenure. Meeting them at their worst, when their grand plans—hustle, stack bills, git money—had inevitably failed.

"Can we at least drive? I can't sit here and stare at nothing all night. Come on, just around the lake or something."

Robert shook his head. "We won't know if they go after him, so what would be the point?"

Noah pointed to the scanner screwed into the underside of his dashboard, like a little box that controlled trailer brakes. "I can pick up their dispatch."

His brother pursed his lips. "Alright, fine."

Noah leaned over and twisted the dial as Robert turned the ignition. Adjusting the volume, Noah switched the radio to auxiliary, so they could hear the transmissions through the truck's speakers. He set the program to bounce back and forth between the EMS channels and the separate one Sara's Point police used.

"What if he hits someone in a different town?" Robert asked.

"I don't think he will. I mean, do you? The other two were in Sara's Point; why would he move?"

His brother contemplated but couldn't answer.

Noah asked, "Did Jack move around?"

"No, the canonical five were all in Whitechapel."

"Did he kill more than those five women?"

"Depends on who you ask. Personally? I don't think he did. But, there are some researchers out there—Riperrologists, actually—who believe several other women killed around the same time could be attributed to him as well."

"Why do most people accept the five, though?"

"Style they were killed in. Type of woman they were. The five are definitely relatable. That much, I won't argue with."

"Hmm." Noah thought about this while the trees blurred past, as they drove away from the center of town and began the long wrap around Aurora Lake.

An abyss at night. Pure darkness above the water. Stars played hide and seek with passing clouds. Square panes of light illuminated the opposite shore—windows of cabins and houses where people lived normal lives. Because that's what the lake was: a constant state of normalcy. No matter what happened in life, the water remained the same. Rocking back and forth. Existing in a perpetual state of waiting. Waiting for people to visit and fish, or wakeboard, or simply lounge on a boat under the warm afternoon sun.

In the reflection of the window, he saw Amber in her bikini standing on the bow of his boat. He missed that boat. A ski boat made for the modest-sized lake that signaled a time when everything had gone according to plan. Of course when that plan shifted, it was one of the first things to go.

Amber laughed that sweet summer laugh of hers. Big sunglasses covered half her face—dark lenses rimmed with white plastic. Her hair tied back. He could almost see her look over her shoulder and giggle, making sure no one was watching before she rocked her hips, bent her knees, and dipped slightly. With her tongue slightly out, she squeezed her chest, forcing water from the wet fabric. Noah raised a beer while thinking: *this is it for me; I've won.*

His scanner buzzed. "Dispatch-to-Sara's Point: Intersection of East Street and Arnold Drive: vehicle fire."

Seconds later, units began responding. Volunteer firefighters with hard-ons and wet lips at the thought of flames. The scanner jumped over to the police frequency in time to catch a request for traffic control.

Robert pulled the truck to the side of the road. They had a clear view through a space between two trees. In the distance, the dark of the lake melded into the abyss that was the night sky, blending air and land. Water and sky.

"You should call her," Robert said. "You want to."

It was true—beyond true. Noah wanted nothing more than to dial her number, meet her for a quick bite before jumping in his truck, explaining everything that had happened in rapid fire. If he couldn't get it out in the ride over, it wasn't coming out, because when they got to his place, he would throw her back onto his bed and jump on top of her.

But he didn't call her. Nor did he move to pull his phone from his pocket. He continued to stare out at the lake, listening to the hum of the truck's motor. The radio jumped to the police frequency and dispatch requested a unit to the hardware store in the center of town. Reports of a burglary. Suspect still in the area.

"I will," Noah finally said. "Just not now."

He didn't look, but he knew Robert was smiling. "Told you that you were hooked."

"Whatever," he grumbled. "Rob, what's going on with you and Claudia?"

His brother leaned back. Suddenly tense. "It's just the usual stuff. If you ever get married, you'll see."

Noah looked over. "I don't believe that. Not every married couple argues and fights all the time. If they did, by this point people would stop saying I do."

Robert started to respond when the scanner buzzed back to life: "Dispatch-to-Sara's Point: second call. Respond with Alpha Medic: 713 Grey Road, 84-year old female, epistaxis and chest pain."

Noah scrunched his nose. Tried to remember who was on.

"What's epistaxis?" his brother asked.

"An acute hemorrhage in the nasopharynx."

"Try again."

Noah put his fingertips to the sides of his nose and mimed a waterfall. "Uncontrollable bleeding from the nose."

Robert nodded. "Just lean back, right?"

"Eh, now-a-days you actually lean forward."

"Why?"

"Prevent the blood from going down your throat and impeding your airway. Imagine how bad that would be? Choking to death on your own blood?"

No sooner had he said it did their eyes meet. Robert's face flashed panic. "What day is it?"

"I don't know." Noah reached into his pocket for his phone.

Robert pressed his head against the steering wheel. Mumbled. "Okay, after Chapman, Jack killed Elizabeth Stride. Think. They found her early in the morning, but what day was it? It was a Saturday. Saturday."

Noah reading from his phone and Robert speaking from recollection, both spoke at the same time. "September 30."

Robert threw the truck in reverse. Rubber chirped as he cut the wheel. Noah's stomach rolled. Noah began dialing the detective's number.

"What are you doing?" Robert demanded.

"Really?" Noah nearly shouted back. "You're really asking me that right now?" When Robert didn't respond, Noah said. "I'm calling Madsen."

Robert smacked the phone from his hand.

"You need to stop doing that," Noah snapped.

The truck banked sharp. Tires on the yellow line. Robert straightened the wheel and followed the lake. The ever-tranquil lake.

"That call is right on the other side of the lake. We are two minutes away. He won't be expecting us. We surprise him, and that's it, it's over."

Noah stared, jaw open in disbelief. "You're delusional. First, you have no way of knowing if this is him. It could very easily be just another call. Second, let's say it is him. He's probably crazy, like certifiably crazy. Maybe even has a gun. Have you thought about that? Rob? Rob, watch the road!"

The bed of the truck swung around as Robert overcorrected a turn. He threw the blinker on and cut left, away from the water. The engine roared as he hammered his foot on the gas.

Acid rose in Noah's throat. He burped, tasted vomit and swallowed it back like an awful shot of cheap liquor. Voices inside his head screamed for him to pick up his phone and dial Detective Madsen. Robert slowed at an intersection, stopping as the front end of the truck hung just past the white painted line. The engine ticked as it cooled back to a safe idle, ready and waiting to be abused again.

"Robert?"

His brother replied without looking. "I saw something."

Noah shot forward in his seat, the belt across his chest sliding up and catching against his throat. He tugged the annoyance down and repositioned himself, straining to see in the darkness. Three houses down was a horseshoe shaped driveway with an SUV and a sedan. Lights were on inside the house. Noah could see some-one—an outline in the light above the front door.

"Robert, you don't know if that's him," Noah said. "It could be a family member waiting to flag down the ambulance."

"Well, if it is, then driving by will do no harm."

For the first time in years, Noah felt the internal struggle over fight or flight. His choice was always the first. Dive in. Sear your skin against the fray. But here, in the truck, Noah couldn't be so sure that was his response.

"He's leaving," Robert said, his voice barely above a whisper.

Noah fumbled for his phone. Over the scanner, Sara's Point ambulance requested mutual aid from Buckland. They were still on scene of the car fire, and it had sapped the small town's resources.

Taillights illuminated the horseshoe gravel drive, red then white as the sedan shifted from park to reverse and began rolling backward onto the street.

"Noah, that's not someone waiting for the ambu-lance."

"Maybe it's not the address of the call," Noah said.

But he couldn't even convince himself of that. Robert turned the wheel, eased on the gas, and took the turn.

"Rob," Noah hissed.

Was he really doing this? Were *they* really doing this? Part of him screamed, but whether it was a scream of pure adrenaline-fueled excitement or trepidation, he couldn't tell.

Robert said nothing. Drove slowly down the road. Noah could hear the tires on the pavement through his cracked window. The sedan was coming toward them. Oblivious to who they were. Or so Noah had to assume. They were fifty yards apart when he repeated Robert's name.

Thirty yards. There were no other cars on the road. No headlights aside from the two vehicles. No taillights in the distance. Just them. A jousting match with no lances. Twenty yards. Noah swallowed hard. Gripped the door. Ten yards.

The sedan began to pass, their two front-ends parallel. Noah exhaled and then braced himself as Robert suddenly cut the wheel and hammered on the gas. The truck barreled into the side of the sedan. The car skidded; the back end swung out. Rob cut the wheel the opposite way to prevent a full circle spin and drove the car off the road and down a slight embankment. The man in the driver seat had his hands up shouting words Noah couldn't hear.

"Jesus Christ, Rob!"

But his brother was out of the car. Standing in the angled headlights of the sedan as it teetered on two wheels.

"Detective Madsen," Noah yelled into his phone. "We got him. We got the guy. We—shit. Grey Road. Hurry."

Two gunshots rang out.

"Rob!" Noah shouted. He ducked against the side of the truck. He saw Robert fall clutching his shoulder. Noah called out, tore around the back end of the truck. The man stood next to the front-end of the sedan with a handgun raised. White smoke whistled from the car's bent hood. Robert groaned. Twisted. Clawed at the ground to pull himself to safety underneath the truck.

"Stop," the man shouted.

Noah froze with his hands up. His heart pounding. Robert's outline rolled back and forth, struggling to stay still against the pain in his shoulder? His upper body? Where had his brother been shot? Fuck, his brother was shot.

Was it the chest? Did it matter? How long would it take for him to bleed out? This man could stand here until he was sure Robert was dead, or he could easily put another bullet in each of them. Had anyone heard the gunshot?

Airway. Breathing. Circulation. Medical knowledge flew through Noah's head like rapid-fire bullets. He took a tentative step forward. Wherever the wound was, he had to apply pressure. Blood loss could lead to shock and the closest facility—Jesus-fucking-Christ, it was Robert. It was his brother, not just another patient lying on the ground. *No. Detach yourself; it's the only way to make clear decisions. Biases lose lives.*

Another small step forward. His eyes had adjusted slightly. Their growing ability to see in the dark allowed him to spot the blood seeping into the fabric of Robert's shirt.

Noah looked up, met eyes with a man holding a gun pointed directly at him. If he was going to die, he was going to die doing what he was put on this Earth to do. Noah dove forward, crashing to his knees and pushing the thought of a bullet as far from his mind as he could. He fumbled to pull his brother out from under the truck so he could have a better look.

Robert winced. Noah pressed against his brother's chest. Rib. Intercostal space. Rib. Robert screamed in pain as Noah's fingers found the open wound. In the brief silence that followed Noah swore he heard the man with the gun. . . laughing.

Robert was bleeding from the shoulder. Noah pressed his hands down, causing his brother to groan. The blood warm and sticky against his palms.

There were sirens in the distance. A small feeling of relief fell on Noah's shoulders. Madsen had listened. Now, how to stay alive until she arrived? He steadied his breathing. Inhale. Exhale. Noah turned his attention from his brother and back to the man lording over them. Their eyes met, the glare of the headlights illuminating his entire face. The same face from the diabetic call. The same face of the EMT in the video. From the first call so long ago.

"Who are you?" Noah asked.

"Back up," the man said.

Noah remained still.

Lechmere walked forward. His movements were as fluid and calm as his voice. Each muscle acting with cold calculated purpose. He seemed almost inorganic. This was not the same man Noah had encountered on scene. This was—the man bent down, holding the gun angled toward the ground close enough to Noah's face that he could smell the pungent odor of burnt powder. The man spoke each syllable slowly, each word almost its own sentence. "You will see me again, Noah."

He jumped in Noah's truck and reversed out of the embankment. The engine ticked; the front bumper hung half-off as the man sped away.

Robert coughed. No blood came from his mouth. At least that was something.

"What the hell were you thinking?" Noah demanded.

Noah pulled his sweatshirt and undershirt off, tying the thinner of the two in a tight band over the hole in his brother's shoulder. Behind them, flashing lights lit the intersection and turned left.

Robert groaned and held his shoulder. Blood seeped through the makeshift bandage, nerves burning inside Noah's chest.

It was a cop, not the ambulance that approached them. He slowed to a stop, a second cruiser just behind him. Had it been two minutes earlier, Noah would have been overjoyed. Now all he wanted was the ambulance.

"I need an ambulance," Noah shouted. "He's been shot."

No sooner had the words left his mouth did Buckland's rig turn onto the road. It stopped in front of the lead cruiser. The technician jumped out, a confused look on her face. Noah rambled through a quick version of what had happened. The second cruiser sped ahead, tearing down Grey Road toward the house that the original call had been in regard to. Noah was sure there was a woman inside. And he was sure she was dead. She would look like the others: throat slit, abdomen mutilated. A wide array of carefully selected items arranged around her body, each one placed with precision and purpose.

"This isn't the Sara's Point call?" the tech asked. Her partner jumped out of the passenger seat and ran around.

"No. Call for another ambulance to deal with the original scene. He's been shot, and he needs attention now."

He couldn't wait more than a second.

"God damn it." Noah jumped up and sprinted for the ambulance. Tore open three compartments until he found the med bag. The technician started yelling, but he cut her off. "Then do your damn job. Get the stretcher out of the back. Let's go."

He tore open the bag and pressed gauze against the wound. He rolled Robert on his side in an effort to elevate his shoulder above his heart. The remaining police officer rattled off questions. Noah fumbled through the answers in a state of half-attention. The stretcher bumped as they pushed Robert into the back of the rig.

He spun around. "Look, I'm going to the hospital with him; either follow us or have Detective Madsen meet us there, and I'll tell you whatever you want to know."

They shut the rear doors and drove off toward Caligan General, the lake and the woods behind them. Somewhere in that house was a dead woman with her throat slit. Noah wondered, if only in the back of his mind, what little trinkets and clues the police would find next to the body.

TWENTY-ONE

With Robert in surgery, Noah hung around the waiting area of the emergency room, a place he at least felt somewhat comfortable. But, despite the feelings of familiarity with every cough or sneeze he heard, each page that crackled through the PA system above him, Noah was on edge. He wiped sweaty palms on his jeans for what felt like the hundredth time while his brain envisioned the man who had shot his brother.

The moronic first responder that arrived on scene without a blood pressure cuff or a stethoscope. The stoic man who nodded at Noah as they shared a quick glance outside a dead woman's house. A dead woman that this man had murdered. Sliced nearly in half and then proceeded to draw pictures with her blood.

"Stop," Noah said out loud.

A mother looked over at him, her hand protectively gripping her sick child's shoulder. She asked, "What?"

When he didn't answer, she hid herself behind a magazine, her eyes creeping over the top of the pages.

Noah looked at the clock: 10:17. His stomach grumbled. At the vending machine, he punched the combo for a bag of chips and tore them open the second he had them in his hands. Four people were in the waiting room with him, not including the mother/daughter combo. A heavyset man with a graying beard sat hunched over a basin, dry heaving like clockwork in a valiant attempt to garner attention. Another woman, taking up several seats by laying down rather than sitting. And two college-aged kids—guy and girl—who were there for…?

Through the glass doors, he could see a police cruiser pull up to the curb. The logo on the side read *Caligan PD.* Where was Sara's Point? What was taking them so long? Then he froze. Maybe the victim hadn't been dead. Maybe they had gotten into the house, and she was still alive or even just barely alive. Maybe by stopping the ambulance, he had inadvertently caused her more suffering.

"Stop," he said again.

Mombie glared while her spawn looked between her and the crazy man who talked to himself. But Noah's mind continued to race. The person in that house had been dead. Lechmere wouldn't have left her if she were still alive. He would want her dead. The same way that the Ripper had sliced open the women of Whitechapel.

"Maybe we should start calling him Jack." Noah laughed to himself.

"Jack," the little boy repeated and the look on Mother's face was priceless.

Where was Detective Madsen?

Noah pulled his phone out to dial her a third time, when he caught himself. Two voicemails later, and he was still sitting by himself. The wretched little witch. This was when he needed her, and she was off doing something else. Just like every other person he ever depended on. But if he had been the one who had been needed, he would have been right there. Professionally and personally.

"Shit," he said.

"Do you mind?" The mother finally summoned the courage to say something.

Noah could only stare in disbelief at this person who had dragged her child—who looked not the least bit ill—to the emergency room at almost ten-thirty at night.

"If it bothers you," he said. The calmness in his voice surprised him. "You can bring him to your pediatrician's office when they open in less than twelve hours."

Noah glared at the woman until she looked down and began thumbing through the same magazine for the twentieth time.

Resuming his pacing, Noah had a sudden, dreadful thought: what if they were arrested for obstruction of justice? Was that a felony? He had never been arrested before. That wasn't true. He had been picked up a couple of weeks ago. How could he have forgotten that? He was sure Madsen would sink her teeth into any reason to lock them away.

He cursed his brother. Promised that he would hit him square in the jaw when he saw him, and then instantly retracted the thought in exchange for a promise: *I'll forgive him if he makes it through surgery.*

Sick of waiting, Noah snuck through the doors leading from the waiting room to the ED proper. Behind the computer desk, Tanya tapped her fake nails against the keyboard. She looked up at him and smiled. "Nothing yet?"

"Not yet," he said. "Hey, is Amber on today?"

After dialing the detective, he had called Amber and sent her two text messages, but she had yet to respond. He chalked it up to working a different shift and quite possibly trying to catch up on sleep, but now that he was standing here, he figured it wouldn't hurt to ask. Unknowing had such a detrimental effect.

Tanya offered a half-smile before pulling up the schedule on her computer. "Actually, she took the overnight tonight. Should be in at eleven."

He nodded, knocked his knuckles on the counter, and said thanks.

She said nothing, only winked.

Behind him, the on-shift triage medic walked the man with the basin from the waiting room into an exam room. He gave one of the nurses a disinterested report before heading back out to screen the next patient.

In the medic's place, Noah saw himself. Because that's all he would be doing if he gave up the fly car and sat behind that desk. It was a change set to happen in two days. He thought of the resignation letter he had almost handed Paul and laughed out loud.

"What?" Tanya asked.

"Nothing, just thinking of the stupid things we do sometimes."

"We meaning, like me and you?"

"No, no, just people in general."

"Ah," she smiled.

Back in the waiting room, he decided to forgo pacing and simply took a seat with his elbows on his knees. The glass doors parted, and he heard his name called out in a shrill voice he'd hoped on more than one occasion that he would never have to hear again.

He watched Claudia awkwardly rush in, unable to move quickly in her designer heels. Little Mikey trailed behind her, yanked about by the death-grip she had on his wrist.

"Hey, Claud," he said.

"Hey, Claud," she exclaimed. "Is that what you're going to say to me?"

He held his palms up. It didn't matter what he said; it would all garner the same response.

"Where is he, Noah? Where is your God damn brother?"

Even through the layers of makeup, her face was flushed. Cheeks red. Brows arched perfectly. Her nails were pristinely done in a light teal while thin bracelets dangled on both wrists.

Noah exhaled. "He's in PACU right now."

Her face contorted. "In what?"

"Post-anesthesia-care-unit. He had to go into surgery to get the bullet." Saying the word bullet made him look at Robert's six-year-old son and wish he had chosen a more tactful response, if not an outright lie. But the damage had been done, so he owned his words, though he looked at the ground while he finished. "To fix his shoulder."

Claudia pulled at her son's arm and stalked to the registration desk, demanding information regarding her husband. Noah rolled his eyes and looked at the other woman and her child.

"Bet you wish it was still just me, huh?"

The child giggled. Kicked his legs and yelled out, "Jack!"

Noah chuckled, never ceasing to be amazed at the things that happened around him. He could have told Claudia anything she wanted to know; he wasn't about to keep secrets from her. Would it cause a divorce, though? The tension between the two was at the highest it ever had been, that much he knew. But would it end them?

He glanced over at Mikey, and the thought of Robert and Claudia separating left an awful taste in his mouth. He watched her continue to badger the woman behind the desk. Pestering. Questioning. Not believing any of the answers she was being given.

"Noah," someone called to him.

He turned to see Tanya standing in the open door to the triage area. She motioned him over and, under the glaring scrutiny of his sister-in-law, he abided.

She spoke quietly, "He's awake and asking for you."

"Thanks, T."

He started to leave when Claudia yelled after him. He rolled his eyes and took a sharp inhale. "Follow me."

Her heels clacked against the floor as they walked.

"How's school, Mikey?" Noah asked.

The boy started to answer, but Claudia cut him off. "He's doing fine. Can we hurry up?"

Noah paused, causing her to nearly walk into him. Their eyes met and despite his glare, she refused to back down. The desire to tell her off once and for all burned in him. *Do it. Tell her what a cunt she is and how much better off Robert and the kids would be with her gone.*

She could be in denial all she wanted, but the fact was that Robert chose to be gallivanting off with his brother rather than at home with her. Though she was probably fucking another member of the PTA while Robert was lecturing at Northern. But he could never prove it, so Noah kept his mouth shut, because why stir trouble?

A nurse wearing maroon scrubs led them into a recovery room. Robert lay in the only bed, groggy and fumbling with the remote. Claudia's shoulders dropped with visible relief, proving that she did care, even if only on some minute level.

Mikey stood at the foot of the bed, flicking the end of Robert's blanket. Claudia leaned over the rail, head pressed against her husband's forehead, and began to sob. Robert raised his uninjured arm and hugged her, the exertion causing him to groan.

"What the hell happened?" Claudia suddenly yelled.

Noah raised his hands, palms out, the same way he did when Jack had yelled for him to stop. In a flash, Claudia was gone, replaced by the man with the gun. Noah shook his head, shredding the vision away. When he did, he realized they were all staring at him.

"We got into a car accident. Road rage and all that shit—sorry." He looked at Mikey. "Stuff. And when Robert hopped out, the guy pulled a gun and shot him."

Claudia's face went pale. A second later, it turned bright red. She stalked toward Noah, finger pointed like a knife. "This type of shit only happens when you're around. Last time he almost got stabbed at one of those God damn drug houses you were called to, and this time he got shot. You won't be happy until he's dead. What is wrong with you?"

Noah remembered the night Robert nearly got stabbed. Only it hadn't happened the way she was insinuating. It was a routine difficulty breathing that ended up being a patient refusal. They were walking back to the SUV, arguing about some movie they had just seen, *Cloverfield*, and the minute details hidden in certain frames, when a junkie jumped out at them, knife in hand. Noah reached for his wallet when Robert shoved the guy. The addict swung, sliced Robert's arm, but twisted off balance. Robert threw a punch, connected with the guy's jaw and dropped him.

Claudia stomped closer, causing Mikey to climb onto the bed with his father. "What's next, Noah? Are you going to push him into traffic? Throw him into a fire?"

"Claud," Robert said, but she paid no attention. Warpaths generally have only one target.

"Claudia, I had nothing to do with it. The guy's going to be arrested." Though as he said it, a voice inside his head, speaking quite loudly, argued *no he's not.* There was a knock on the wall behind them. Detective Madsen stood in the doorway. She wore a long coat that fell to her knees, wet from rain.

"Who are you?" Claudia spat.

"Claudia," Noah tried to calm her.

Madsen eyed Robert's wife with an odd look. She was studying, Noah realized. Profiling. "Mr. McKeen," she said. "Do you have a minute?"

"Yeah," Noah said. Behind him, Claudia launched into a second tirade.

"You had quite the night," Madsen said, leading him into the hall.

"Yeah, well, you know."

"No, I don't know. But not to worry; eventually, I'm sure you'll tell me everything. However, in the meantime, I'm inclined to tell you that we found your truck."

A shimmer of relief hit him. "Good."

"Not so much: It was on fire."

Noah closed his eyes. *God damn it.*

"We have a team going through it to try and pull any forensic evidence that we can. However, I don't think we're going to find much of anything."

He leaned against the wall. A few yards away, a nurse stepped up to an Accu-Dose machine, pressed her finger on the scanner, and typed in the medication she needed. A drawer popped out, and she pulled pills from the correct container.

There was a sudden longing in his chest. He twitched when he heard the plastic pop of the drug being removed from its package. A chill when he heard it rattle inside of a small plastic cup.

"Noah," Madsen said.

He looked at her, surprised at the softness in her voice. She had never spoken like that around him. He rubbed his palms on his legs and launched into the story, telling her what had happened right from the point of leaving the station.

TWENTY-TWO

Detective Madsen stared at him, her expression a mixture of disbelief and subtle approval. Noah watched it fade, could see the stone cold mask reposition itself. Alyssa Madsen had appeared for a second, and then she had vanished. Replaced by the stoic, gargoyle detective.

"Okay," she said. "I'll level with you. This is the third murder scene that you have been at or had something to do with. And this time you were not even working. You had no reason whatsoever to be over on that side of the lake."

"Detective." Noah cleared his throat. "With all due respect, you heard my brother. This was going to happen regardless. And, if he is correct, then there are two more women that will be killed. Did you find anything in the house? Anything that confirms his idea?"

"If I showed you anything, would you recognize it?" Madsen asked.

Noah shook his head.

"I didn't think so. I don't think you had anything to do with this, but you have to think about how this looks from the outside. This town is scared. The newspapers are beginning to pick up the story. They haven't tied it to Jack the Ripper yet, which could either be a blessing or a curse; I'm not exactly sure. Now, tonight you engaged this man in a different way than ever before. Did he say anything to you? Make any kind of remark or ask you anything?"

You.

Will.

See.

Me.

Again.

Noah shook his head. "Nothing other than what I told the officers on scene. Just yelling to back up and get away."

She nodded but her gaze lingered. Noah felt her eyes and swallowed hard. She was waiting. Waiting to see if he would blurt out anything he was trying to keep in.

You.

Will.

See.

Me.

Again.

"Okay," Madsen said. "Bring yourself back. Did you have any contact with this man prior to the call on Oak Street? The first murder?"

"No." Noah shook his head. "But—"

"But what?"

"I saw him on a different scene." Noah recalled the idiot of an EMT he'd had to deal with. "A chest pain—no a diabetic—he was the first on scene. I'm telling you though, he was a different guy."

"What do you mean? There's possibly two people?"

"No, no." Noah hesitated, tried to find the right words to explain, because as he ran them through his head, they all sounded absurd. "It's like he's two different people. When we were at the diabetic, I thought he was just another volunteer. I also thought he was an idiot. I mean, he was dropping things, didn't know one medication from the next, couldn't get a set of vitals. I brushed it off. But tonight? He was—he was in control."

Madsen paused as a nurse walked by. Claudia's yelling had dropped to stern anger.

"It could be that he was nervous around you. Nervous you would recognize him."

Noah thought for a second. In his ears he heard the man's laugh. The out of place, *genuine* laugh.

"I don't think so," Noah said. "Why would he respond to the call then?"

Noah watched the detective's mouth twist as she tried to come up with something off the cuff, but she couldn't.

"Possible that you caught him before he could finish," she finally said. "That he was planning to kill the diabetic man, but you arrived too quickly."

"No," Noah said. "It took me a while to get to the scene. If he was going to kill him, he would have killed him. Besides, the canonical five were all women."

Madsen's phone rang. She turned away from Noah and answered it, giving him a second to breathe and collect his thoughts. Few words were said on her part before she ended the call and returned her phone to her pocket.

"Alright," she said, adjusting her coat. "You've had a rough night. Swing by the station in the morning, and we'll give you a copy of our report. That way you'll be able to contact your insurance company regarding your truck. In the meantime, if you think of anything—"

Noah pressed his lips together before finishing her sentence. "Call you."

She nodded. "And do yourself a favor, Noah, be careful."

Stepping back into Robert's room, he was greeted at once by Claudia's high-pitched accusations. "You're a liar. What really happened? Why is he spewing on about people dying?"

Noah stumbled. The question caught him off guard. Why had Robert said anything? And then Noah remembered. Morphine. The miracle drug that's secondary purpose was truth serum.

Claudia stormed toward him, pushing him against the wall. A nurse appeared in the doorway.

"Everything alright?" she asked.

Claudia glared at her, but the older woman refused to stand down. Jaded? Not likely. Experienced? Definitely. Tense seconds passed until the nurse spoke again.

"I don't want to call security, but I will if I have to. Do you want to talk to someone? I can get the doctor if you're concerned about something."

"We're fine." Noah offered her an apologetic nod.

"It wasn't a car accident." Claudia snapped as soon as the older woman had left. He could smell vodka on her breath. "What were you really doing?"

She smacked him on the side of the head, causing Mikey to squirm on the bed.

"Mommy, stop," he yelled.

"Claudia," Noah started.

"Shut up. Unless you're answering me, I don't want to fucking hear it."

She swung at him again. Open palm against the side of Noah's face. He ground his teeth together. Muscles in his face tight.

"Well," she shouted. "You going to answer me or what?"

There was a knock at the door. Two security guards sauntered in.

"Ma'am," the one whose badge read Miguel said. "I need you to calm down."

"And if I don't? What are you going to do?"

The portly man adjusted his belt. "We'll have to escort you out of the room. That's all. It's a patient's right to recover in peace."

"Oh, shut up," she snapped. "He's my husband. I can talk however I want."

"Ma'am, I'm only going to ask you one more time, okay?"

"Touch me," Claudia said. "And I'll have you deported."

Noah cringed. Both security guards came forward.

"Guys," Noah nodded to his nephew.

They acknowledged the boy but did their job nonetheless. Claudia slapped at them. Shouted as they grabbed her by the arms and led her from the room, leaving Noah to comfort Mikey.

"Noah," Robert said and waved him over. He licked at dry lips before trying to continue speaking. "There's another body."

"Yeah, I know," Noah said. "Two more. I told the detective. She'll take care of it, Rob."

"No," Robert rolled. He grunted and gripped Noah's shoulder as he struggled to sit up straight. His movements escalated his heart rate, causing the monitor above his bed to begin beeping. Noah quickly pulled the sensor off Robert's finger. One line went flat and the oxygen level changed from numbers to a dash. They would have a minute, if that, until the nurse or an aide realized there was no reading being transmitted to the central monitor at the nurse's station.

"Jack the Ripper killed two women on September 30. It would later be called the 'double event'. If our guy is really trying to mimic the real killer, then there's another one out there. Another one tonight."

Noah remembered Rob previously bringing up the double event, but he hadn't realized it would be tonight. "You're sure?"

Rob nodded vehemently. "It was the only thing that gave credibility to some of the letters. The following day they received the 'Saucy Jacky' postcard, and he referenced the two murders in it. The bodies had barely been discovered at that point."

"Maybe we got him after the first one, and now he's too worried to keep going."

"You know as well as I do that that's bullshit. If we did anything at all, we pissed him off, which is apt to make him all the more likely to do it. It's not even midnight yet. He still has all night to skulk around."

Noah pressed his palm to his forehead and closed his eyes.

"Noah," Robert insisted. "He's going to do this. If he gets away with it tonight, then all that leaves is number five on November 8—no 9. Damn it. It's the 9. The fifth and final victim was on November 9, just a few weeks after the From Hell letter.

"Okay," Noah said. "Just rest for a bit."

"Rest? We have to go."

Noah pushed his brother backward. His voice was stern, determined. He felt Mikey's grip squeeze tighter. "No. You need to rest. Your son wants you to feel better. And resting until the doc says you're good to go is what will do that."

Mikey bit the webbing of skin between his thumb and index finger. Robert deflated. Reluctantly, he scooted back in bed and patted the mattress next to him. "What do you say Uncle Noah lowers this rail and you hop back on up, buddy."

The kid crawled onto the stretcher and looked up at the television. Robert mouthed *thanks*.

"I'll be in touch," Noah said.

Neither Claudia nor the security guards were still in the corridor. Several lights had been dimmed over the nurse's station, meaning only third-shift people were on. Day-walkers would never dim the lights. They hated darkness, found no sanctuary in it.

Robert would be kept overnight for observation. Noah didn't need to speak to anyone to know that much. He was surprised however, that no one had noticed the monitor going off. With his hand on the doors to the ER waiting room, he hesitated. Rather than push them open and leave the hospital, he turned back and went through the rear doors leading from radiology into the emergency room.

He passed by the urgent care section where he had learned about Amber and Neil. Had she told him yet? Would she tell him? If she was going to end it and things were going to go back to normal, then she would have to. Hopefully sooner rather than later. Noah wanted his life back. He was so close, he could taste it.

Passing by exam rooms and the back hall, he couldn't find her. He stopped at Tanya's desk, leaned over, and playfully poked her in the shoulder while asking where Amber might have been hiding.

"Don't know," there was a slight annoyance in her voice. "She ain't here yet."

He looked at the clock. 11:47. "She's almost an hour late for her shift?"

"Mhm."

"Wait, why are you still here?"

"Double. Overnight was empty," she said.

"And Amber just didn't show up? Did she call?"

Tanya shook her head. "Are you guys seeing each other again?"

He held her gaze for several seconds before allowing his eyes to drift to the countertop.

"Never mind. Sorry I asked."

He waved her apology away and returned to the waiting room. Through the glass doors, he saw Claudia outside smoking a cigarette, yammering away on her cell phone. He wondered if she was relaying what had happened to Emma. Based on the girl's attitude from the other night, Noah doubted she would even pick up the phone had her mother called. Didn't matter. She would see her father soon.

You.

Will.

See.

Me.

Again.

The words rushed into his head like a tidal wave, carrying with them the vision of Jack. Only, he didn't look like he did on the side of the road. Blood dripped from his fingertips. There was stubble on his cheeks and chin.

Short hair with dark brown eyes and a quiet serenity on his face. It was scary what stoicism could hide.

A chill shook him to the core, crashing Noah back into reality. He blinked and felt his legs go weak. Every noise around him had become amplified. The creak of chairs as people rocked back and forth. Vomit hitting the inside of a plastic basin. A child crying into his mother's side.

He slowly spun around, looking at all the hurt and sickly faces, but he truly saw none of them. The only vision in his head was Amber, dead on the floor and gutted like an animal, her throat lined with a permanent necklace deep enough to see her spine.

You.

Will.

See.

Me.

Again.

He called Claudia's name as he rushed into the parking lot. "He's asking for you."

"Of course he is," she spat back. "I'm his wife."

She pushed past him and toward the entrance when Noah yelled after her. "Mikey left his Gameboy in your car and asked me to get it."

"Mike didn't bring his Gameboy," she said.

He held his palms up. Claudia grunted and stalked toward her SUV. The horn beeped and the lights flashed as she unlocked it. With the door open, Noah shoved her, snagged her keys, and jumped in. He jammed the key into the steering column, missing the ignition completely.

"Fuck." He retried while Claudia slapped her palms against the window.

"What the hell are you doing?"

Noah slammed the SUV in reverse. He pulled out of the emergency room parking lot, leaving his sister-in-law waving maniacally at the security guards. The speedometer arched around the half-dial as he blew through a red light. Instinct caused him to reach for his lights and sirens but neither were there. He was alone.

Amber's car was parked outside her condo. An end unit, closest to the cul-de-sac. *Okay, no Buick yet,* he thought as he jumped out. And then he remembered: the Buick was in a ditch, undoubtedly surrounded by police tape and forensic people.

Noah patted his pockets for his keys and felt the second hit to his gut: his pockets were empty. He grabbed the handle and banged on the door but to his surprise it popped open. Jack was there. He knew it. Amber never kept her doors unlocked.

The door opened to a small foyer and a stairway. Noah hit the lights, but only the bottom bulb flicked on, leaving the top of the stairs masked in shadow.

"Amber?" he called.

Nothing.

He had his foot on the bottom step when he heard his name. "Noah?"

She leaned out of the hall at the top of the stairs. Her silhouette just a dark line. He took another step up and stopped. Tension held him there, as if their bodies were polar ends to a magnet.

"What are you doing here?" she asked.

"Rob was shot."

"Oh my God. Is he alright?"

"Yeah," he took a few more steps. "Yeah, he's alright. Amber, why aren't you at work?"

She said nothing. She disappeared from the top of the stairs. A second later there was movement and neither Amber nor Neil stepped onto the landing. Noah looked up and met eyes with the man who had shot his brother. The man masquerading as Jack the Ripper. Jack held his arm out into the hallway at the top of the stairs, and though Noah couldn't see it, he knew there was a gun being pointed. And that meant Amber was on the other end of it.

"I told you, you would see me again," Jack said.

Noah froze on the stairs. He fought the urge to rush forward and swing. Tackle this man to the ground and drive his fist into his jaw until it was broken and unhinged. He squeezed the railing until his knuckles turned white and the wood pressed the pads below each finger into tiny burning folds.

He imagined the gunshot. Heard the sound in his ears and imagined Amber dropping to the floor, her carpet and walls sprayed red. Noah stepped forward. Jack rocked his arm that held the gun. Was he smiling?

"Uh-uh-uh," he taunted. "A few things first: give me your phone."

"What?"

Jack spoke slowly. "Throw me your phone."

Noah pulled his mobile from his pocket and tossed it the remaining five steps.

"Thank you," Jack said. "Now, if you don't mind, stay still until I get back."

Jack disappeared leaving Noah gawking at darkness. A shuffle. The sound of a thud. Tape being pulled. Amber whimpered and the sound propelled Noah to jump three stairs, only to be met by an angry man lording over him.

"I said stay!"

Noah felt Jack's hand against his chest. The shove came quick, no time to react. Noah lost his balance, flailed his arms, but couldn't catch the railing. Step after step he tumbled backward. His knee. His head. His shoulder colliding with the edges of the step. Impacting his body like blows in a bar fight. The bottom of the stairs crashed into him. Pain pulsed through his entire body.

Jack was on him, the gun barrel pressed against his cheek.

"Do as I say," he hissed. "Or I will bury you together."

Noah's eyes burned. He squeezed his fists together. One clean swing. But Jack had the upper hand. The gun. The position. Standing over Noah's body in its contorted crash landing. As fast as the man appeared, Jack was gone. Back up the stairs and out of sight.

Amber's muffled voice was silenced by the smack of skin-on-skin. Noah pulled himself to his feet. Dizzy, fighting to find a steady calm. She screamed. Gagged by something. Again, the painful shriek filled the hall. Falling into a whimper before reducing to nothing but sobs.

Noah climbed, easing his weight onto the first step in order to make sure it didn't creak. Just nice and slow.

Jack reappeared on the top step, though this time the gun was aimed at the floor; he flicked his wrist, beckoning Noah to follow.

Noah reached the top of the stairs. Looked left into a dark empty kitchen and then right into an occupied living room. The small room was lit by a single light on an end table. The slider door was closed with the curtain pulled, blocking the view of the balcony. Amber was in the center, duct tapped to a wooden chair. Her mouth silenced by shimmering silver. Ropes bound her wrists and ankles. Tears streaked her face. Coupled with...lines of blood.

Amber's cheeks had been sliced in several places. Gashes in her flawless skin.

Noah felt his muscles tense. He looked at Jack, his voice flat with the levelheaded view years as a paramedic had given him. "There is no happy ending to this, is there?"

Jack, still holding the gun on Amber, said, "No. I'm afraid there isn't."

"Then what do you want?"

Noah felt like someone was standing on him. Unbearable weight on his chest and shoulders.

"I want to see you work," Jack said. His smile flashed. Brief as it was, it had stretched ear-to-ear. The man circled behind Amber, pausing between her and the television. He stood for a moment before resting his hands on her shoulders. She recoiled at his touch. He gripped harder.

Noah took a step forward and was suddenly overpowered with the smell of gasoline. He put his hand to his nose as he sniffed the fumes that hung in the air. What was the end game? One shot fired and the entire place would go.

Another step forward and Noah saw the gas can next to the couch. Sporadic circles of liquid darkened the carpet. With a smile, Jack lifted his hand from Amber's shoulder and pressed the gun against the side of her head. She tried to lean away. In his other hand came a flash. The blade of a knife. One that wasn't completely clean.

Jack ran the sharp end of the blade against the skin that connected the bottom of Amber's ear to her head. She squirmed against the touch. Wincing. Eyes squeezed shut caused fresh tears to run in rivulets down her cheeks.

Noah stepped forward, fists clenched, but Jack just shook his head. "It would be heroic, but pointless. You really don't remember me, do you?"

Noah wanted to scream in frustration. "From the other call? Yeah, I remember you; you couldn't even take a blood pressure."

Jack's nose twitched.

"No, not from that." He cocked his head to the side. A twitch. He stepped away from Amber and toward the fireplace. "Think, Noah. Before that. Long before that."

Noah tried to think, but every thought was consumed by his and Amber's impending deaths. Of guns and gasoline. His mouth open, Noah fumbled.

"Think!" Jack yelled. A momentary break in his composure. He returned to point the gun at Amber. "If you really don't remember, this entire thing is for nothing, and well, she really doesn't need to live then."

"It means something. It means something." Noah waved his hand. "I get it. I get what you're doing. We idolize our heroes and—"

"Stop." Jack turned his back, resting a hand on the mantle above the fireplace.

Noah took a quick step forward.

"I can see you in the reflection." Jack pointed the gun at the pane of glass covering the propane insert. Noah cursed himself before taking a breath and standing still. He looked to Amber, met her gaze and nodded. Anything he could offer to reassure her. Those cuts in her face. . . The blood.

"Do you remember the clinical portion of your paramedic program, Noah?" Jack asked. "When we'd run through different stations, respond to mock scenarios with volunteer patients? You always finished first. Not like a cocky first either, but a confident body of reassurance. You were there when I botched a monitor reading, forgot to run a course of epinephrine."

Jack's voice trailed off, but the memory pushed itself to the front of Noah's head. Resurfacing after it had been buried under years and years of calls, of hookups, of Amber, and of the final crash as he went over the edge.

"You said no worries, man," Jack continued.

But Noah finished. "It's only a mistake if you don't learn anything from it."

Jack turned from the fireplace and slumped slowly to the floor, almost as if he had been beaten. "You actually helped a handful of us. In the end, there were only two who didn't pass the practical or the written. Dave moved to upstate New York, some place remote."

"And you stayed here…" Noah concluded. His mind raced. Why couldn't he place who this man was? Who he had been in their program?

Noah squinted. Tried to think. Everything had come naturally. Larger than life in the flesh. Had he really not paid close enough attention to those around him? Or was it the byproduct of the chemically abusive life he had been living since the accident?

He scanned the room. Tried to find his phone. He knew Amber didn't have a landline, but if Jack had left his cell somewhere, then he could snag it.

"Yes, I stayed here. I had other things to do, couldn't exactly leave." He spoke with unnerving nonchalance

"So, is this some sort of payback?" Noah asked. "Did I do something that I don't remember doing? Because if I did, then I'm sorry. Whatever it was, it's not worth killing more innocent people over."

Amber tugged against the ropes and tape. Every time she moved, Noah could hear her restraints rub against the chair. Jack stood, stretched his arms forward.

"You gave up, Noah," he said solemnly. "You were the best, and yet you let yourself be beaten. So, I decided to help you. I knew you were better than your accident. Better than her!"

Jack moved quicker than light. The knife was again against the bottom of Amber's ear, only this time it touched her skin when he yanked it backwards. Amber screamed against the gag as the bottom third of her ear separated from the side of her head. Blood oozed in a thick stream.

Noah couldn't take it. He rushed forward, but Jack met his steps with the gun pressed against the back of Amber's head. It clicked. Safety off.

"I will kill her," Jack said. "If you take another step. She doesn't have to die, but whether or not she does is up to you. This, this is my repayment, Noah. For your knowledge; for the help that you gave me. I want nothing more than to return the favor."

"What are you talking about?" Noah exclaimed. "You're just murdering people based on the killings of someone from over a hundred years ago!"

Jack's face flushed. When he spoke, drops of spit spewed from his lips. "I am helping you! I'm offering you the opportunity to save people. To do what you do best, rather than wallow around in the depths of your own self-pity."

Jack shook his shoulders. Regained composure. "Here's the deal, Noah: if you catch me, then all ends well. You'll stop a killer. You'll remember what it's like to help society. And hopefully, hopefully, you'll go back to the person that Amber and I know you can be. But, if you don't? Then, well, I get to pay homage to the greatest enigma of all time and slip away into oblivion."

Noah met Amber's tear-soaked eyes. Black mascara streaked her cheeks as Jack stroked her hair with the back of his hand. Noah felt his stomach turn. He took the chance, stepped forward, but Jack anticipated and raised the gun. A fatal game of stop and go.

"Where do we go from here?" Noah asked.

"I'll give you a choice: save her life or catch me." He shrugged.

"You're full of shit," Noah said. "If I run after you, then you'll shoot me. So she dies, and you still walk away."

Jack smiled. "See? This is the Noah we know. Always thinking. Always anticipating. I will be honest, I was not planning on coming here tonight. I had another individual, another lovely lady, in mind for the second part of this evening, so I am without a few things that would mark the occasion for number four. Nevertheless, here we are."

Jack raised his hand, unloaded the clip from the gun, and laid it on the television stand. He pulled a flip-top lighter from his pocket and crossed the room in three easy steps, winking as he stood in front of the sliding glass door.

Noah jolted forward, just as he heard the scrape of the flint and stone. The room exploded in a flash of white and red, knocking him backward and driving the back of his head into the corner of the wall at the top of the stairs.

TWENTY-THREE

Amber was crying the first time Noah met her. As bad as that was, it would have been worse if she hadn't had tears in her eyes. If she had just stood there, outside the exam room of a deceased baby, stoic, expressionless.

Sudden Infant Death Syndrome, or SIDS, was what was written on the death certificate, but only Amber and two others knew what had really happened. The child's mother, exhausted from the tiring ordeal of being a new parent, had fallen asleep with her daughter in the crook of her arm. . . and rolled over.

There was no maternity unit at Caligan General, nor did they specialize in any form of pediatrics, aside from bumps and bruises, dinosaur bandages, and popsicles. Children presented to them, once stabilized, were transferred to the children's hospital in the city.

The June SIDS case (as it came to be known) hadn't been Noah's call. He had been dispatched to a palpitations in Buckland, leaving the infant to a backup medic. It turned out that the family couldn't wait, and after hanging up with 9-1-1—against the dispatcher's advice—they threw themselves into their car and drove as fast as they could until they skidded to a stop outside the emergency room doors.

Noah, consumed by his own call, transported to Caligan, unaware of what was unfolding in their halls. When he arrived at the hospital, his patient stabilized, Amber was walking out of the room, her hand over her mouth, her eyes watering.

There was a twisted beauty in her sadness. In that moment of vulnerability, she looked more like an actual person than any other human being he had ever met. He wanted nothing more than to walk over and put his arms around her. Pull her close, and let her cry into his shoulder.

He put his laptop down near Tanya's desk and watched as Amber went back into the exam room for several minutes. Tanya looked up at him, shaking her head. "First day on her own."

"What happened?"

"Pedi code."

His eyes opened as if to ask what kind of sick joke it was, but there were no jokes, not in real life anyway.

A chaplain walked through the back doors of the emergency room. She was an older woman with gray hair that framed her face in a triangle. She held her hands folded in front of her, rosary beads wrapped around them. Noah watched as she entered the exam room. He heard the sobs. Aside from the sounds of loss, the department seemed eerily quiet. A draft blew past him. Amber stared from the hall outside the room, vacancy in her eyes.

Noah's pager beeped. Dispatch contacting him for stroke-like symptoms in Sara's Point. He closed his computer and headed for the ambulance doors but stopped as he passed Amber. Behind her, he could hear the soft voice of the chaplain accompanied by the mother's sobs.

"Hey." With the tips of his fingers he touched her shoulder. She looked at him, raised her eyebrows and nodded, her eyes completely blank. It hadn't registered that she had never seen him before. Noah knew there was a chance she didn't comprehend the words he was saying. Her nods merely quiet acknowledgements that he was speaking.

"It get's easier," he said.

The mother drowned herself in the bathtub a week later. Amber asked Noah to take her to the service, making for the darkest first date he had ever been on.

***

Noah stirred, groggy. His head heavy. A mass atop his shoulders that swayed and teetered, balance near impossible. Pain pulsed through the back of his skull. He smelled fire. Ash. Gasoline. Then something putrid: hair, skin. All around him the world was burning. Smoke detectors wailed as the sound of fire roared and crackled in his ears. He rolled, fell to the landing at the top of the stairs and his eyes shot open while everything rushed back: Jack. Amber. The gasoline and the lighter.

On his feet, ignoring the pain that gripped his head like a pair of shadowed hands, he raised his arm and ran forward. The heat pushed at him, like a charging army fighting back. Everything was a twisted blend of yellow, orange, and red.

"Amber!" he shouted.

He could hear her. Muffled and sobbing. Trying to scream against the tape. He called her name a second time and sobs turned to wails. Pain laced her howls. Heat burned his arm as he tried to shield his face. Stinging. Burning. Incinerating the hairs. All of it adding to the morbid stench that filled the room. He planted his foot, pushed off, and jumped.

Flames licked at him as he jumped, falling into Amber and the chair she was tied to and knocking them both backward from the middle of the room. The curtain rod above the slider door gave, fell from the wall and crashed down onto the television. Amber bawled. Flames reflected in her tears like sparking red gems. The ends of her hair were singed. Noah could smell the burning. He yanked at the tape. Ripped it from her face. She erupted with sobs and saliva-filled words. Noah tried to hush her, tell her everything was fine as the fire oppressed them, curling like rounded arcs on the ceiling.

The ropes stung his hands as he pulled at them. Amber kicked at the ties on her legs, inadvertently hitting his hands. Sweat dripped from his forehead. His fingers fumbled with the knots until they finally gave. Hand-over-hand he pulled, yanked, forcing the ropes to come free. He tossed them aside; more fuel for the fire.

Amber tried to stand but her legs gave out. She fell backward, toppling over the chair and dropping her arm into the flames. She whipped it back but it was too late. Her skin sizzled and bubbled.

Noah helped her up as something above them cracked, the heat stressing the fire-weakened walls and beams. Smoke bellowed at them as the couch erupted in flames. Thick, black rolls pushing toward the slider. His lungs burned as he tried to breathe. The sting forced him back to the floor. They couldn't crawl. There was nowhere to crawl. Nowhere to jump. To run. Flames circled them, and if the floor gave, it would drop them both to Hell.

Amber hacked up blood and spit. Her skin was fire against his touch. He pulled her forward, toward the shattered slider door, when he felt her collapse, his arm suddenly tugging at dead weight.

"Amber!" Noah yanked at her arm.

Her skin moved more than it should. He recoiled, shook her clothes as the fire kissed her feet, the hem of her jeans dotted with embers.

The smell was foul. A mix of disgusting chemicals and burning fabric. Singed skin and hair. The feeling of a thousand nails dragging themselves down the inside of his esophagus with every breath. He squinted, smacked at his eyes to try and wipe the blurriness away. All he could see was smoke and fire.

Desperate, seeing no other option, Noah jumped to his feet, grabbed both of her arms and dragged her upward, threw her over his shoulder, and stumbled through the flames into the shattered opening of the slider door. His foot caught the edge causing him to trip. A jagged piece of glass ripped into his arm. Amber's weight shifted, throwing his balance too far to the left. He teetered and fell, dumping her into the patio chair and crashing down next to her.

Noah rolled. Someone shouted, and he could see flashing lights below him. Firefighters. He could hear the hiss of water on flames. Sirens wailed in the distance. He shook Amber, but she didn't stir. The skin on her arms and neck were pink and bubbled. The straps of her tank top burned into her shoulders.

"Get up!" he yelled. "Amber, get up."

He pressed his head to her chest but felt no rise. Flames snapped through the open slider. Smoke curled out into the night air. A firefighter yelled. A bucket was being raised. Noah rolled Amber to her back, her face smudged with ash and burns. He put his mouth on hers, tilted her chin and blew. She gave no response, no inhale, no rise in her chest. He put his hands together over her ribs and pressed.

Pain hit him with each compression. His arm. His knee. The back of his head. A barrage of fists and knives into his body. Pushing the feeling down, he kept going. And then there was someone else on the balcony, followed quickly by a third person.

"Is there anyone else inside?"

The first man pulled at Amber, but Noah kept pressing on her chest. He felt the crack and crunch under his palm as one of her ribs snapped. Someone's hands were under his arms. He was yanked back. Amber being pulled away from him. The edges of his vision were black. All he saw was her not breathing.

"Come on, come on," the firefighter was yelling at him as two others lifted Amber into the bucket. One immediately resumed CPR.

Noah was guided over the side of the balcony and onto a ladder. He fought to look back. Was she breathing? She had to be. She had only been out for a few minutes. It was just the smoke. Once they got oxygen on her, she would be fine. Halfway down the ladder, the firefighter a step below him to guide his descent, Noah heard the sound of wood cracking, splintering. The ladder wobbled, steadied until the balcony gave, ripping away from the side of the building.

The ladder went, Noah and the firefighter with it. Wood beams and posts crumpled and fell around them. An immense weight collapsed onto him. A sudden, sharp pain in his chest.

His entire body was agony. He gagged, wretched as he lay face down on the pavement. People shouted around him but his arms and legs were pinned. He tried to turn, the pain so violent his vision blacked. Opening his eyes revealed a similar darkness. The heat was gone. But so was Amber. He couldn't feel her. He tried to reach out. She had to be here somewhere with him. She had to be with him.

He thought of every fight. Every time he had called her a bitch or the sole time he had used the other word. Every time she had yelled or swung to slap him.

The weight was suddenly off his body. An exponential relief. Two people were on him, dragging him away from the building. He was dizzy, exhausted, and nauseous, but he still clawed at the ground, trying to drag himself back to the rubble, back to where she was. A mask was on his face. Oxygen flowed into his mouth and nose. The world was slipping. The glow of fire and the shouting of those trying to put it out. Amber's face. The sadness in her eyes from that first night. Noah felt himself let go, slipping in and out of consciousness.

In the chaos he heard the crackle of a radio. "Transporting to St. Vincent's. CPR-in-progress."

TWENTY-FOUR

The doctors and nurses had left the room in order to give Noah a few minutes alone. It smelled like smoke and ash. Everything smelled like smoke and ash. Burn marks scarred his hands in blobs of pink and red. The skin of his neck and face had been coated with a topical medication, but he knew how red the spots were. It hurt to breathe—pins and needles pricking the inside of his lungs. His head felt almost too heavy for his neck.

Beige hospital blankets covered Amber's body to just above her shoulders. Pink blisters had formed on her cheeks and her hair was singed to nearly half its length. He stood there, leaning against the counter in the room, and stared.

He saw nothing but a blur of cream color blanket. She was under there, he told himself, skipping the denial stage. Or maybe he had known in the condo, and his efforts at CPR were his denial. It didn't matter either way. It was done now.

You know you're going to be the death of me. She had said it after an aggressive round of make-up sex while lying on her back, sweaty skin sticking to the kitchen table. Her bare legs hanging off the edge, toes a few inches from the ground. When he grabbed her hand to pull her up, her skin made a wet *ssssnnnnnn* sound as it separated from the wood.

His eyes drifted from the hospital bed and focused on an arbitrary spot on the floor, his head leaning slightly to one side. Everything felt empty and cold. Muffled emergency room noises so distant, he couldn't be sure if he was really hearing them.

He could feel her though, in his head. The touch of her fingertips or the softness of her hair as she put her head on his chest. He could hear her laugh and see her smile, and then it was gone. Everything. Because the part of his brain that had been trained to analyze and focus on situations could not ignore the fact that she was gone. That none of the other stuff: the memories, the feelings, the emotions, none of it mattered because she was no longer there, and now he must move on to the next person who needed his help. Except there wouldn't be a next person for him. Ever.

His legs gave and Noah slid down against the cabinets, drawing his knees to his chest. The movement caused pain in his two broken ribs and sprained wrist, but he welcomed it. Just to feel it more, he pushed his wrist against the top of his knee until the sharp stabbing caused his fingers to go numb.

There was a soft pop in his ear. Someone's knees. He turned to see Robert crouched next to him, a bandage and sling on his arm. Together with a nurse, his older brother hoisted Noah from the floor and guided him back to his own room. Detective Madsen walked in shortly after. Noah didn't look at her, simply kept staring at a spot on the wall. A smudge missed by environmental services.

"I'm sorry," she said. Her voice was surprisingly soft.

Noah's throat felt tight. If he spoke, he knew the words would be scratchy. How much smoke had he inhaled? Apparently not enough to kill him. Though maybe enough to have some lasting effects? Could he be that lucky? The nurse reattached a pulse oximeter to his finger.

"Just because of the amount of smoke you inhaled," she said, as if she'd read his mind. She kept her head down as she scooted past Robert and the detective.

Noah spoke without taking his eyes off the smudge on the wall, without blinking. "How's your shoulder?"

It took a second, a confused look before Robert realized what Noah was referring to. "Um, it's good. A little sore, but how are you? Your ribs and everything?"

"What about them?"

His brother shot a quick glance at the detective. "Do they hurt at all?"

"Why would they hurt?"

"Noah," Robert stepped forward. Spoke with hesitancy. "You had a balcony fall on you. You could have been crushed to death."

If there was a look of regret for mentioning death on Robert's face, Noah didn't see it. He just sat there, eyes burning their unwavering gaze into the wall.

Finally, breaking his trance, Noah rubbed his eyes causing the lights in the ceiling to flicker. To flash orange like curled flames on the ceiling of Amber's condo.

"Do you guys smell smoke?" he asked.

Robert exhaled. "No, Noah. No, we don't."

"Right." He spun from the stretcher. A woozy feeling flooded through him as his feet hit the ground. "Alright, I'm good."

"Good?" Robert asked, the concern on his face evident.

"Good to go."

"Noah."

Detective Madsen raised a hand. "Why don't I grab the doctor?"

Robert nodded, and she retreated into the hall. Noah looked at him, not missing a beat. "Can I borrow one of your cars?"

"Noah, are you okay? I don't think you're really processing what just happened."

Noah's head twitched. What he could not process was how his brother, who had not been there in Hell, thought he knew best. How he felt like he had any ground to stand on. Noah looked Robert straight in the eye, his face stern and his voice calm.

"Amber's dead. I broke two ribs, nearly shattered my wrist, and wound up with this lovely gouge in my arm. Yeah, Rob, I get it. Doc." His attention shifted as Detective Madsen and an older Middle-Eastern man walked in.

The doctor took off his stethoscope and rinsed his hands in the sink. "Noah," his voice was deep and heavily accented when he spoke. "How is your chest?"

"Feels like I broke two ribs," he said.

The doctor motioned for the bed, and with Noah sitting, he pressed his hands against each side of his torso. "Any pain?"

"A little."

He retrieved his stethoscope and listened while Noah breathed.

"You were lucky, Noah. Very, very lucky. How you're not in more pain, I don't know."

"How much medication has he gotten, Doctor?" Robert asked.

Noah looked at him with an unsettling smile. "None."

The doctor shook his head in confirmation. "Refused all pain medication. Now, are you doing alright? Other than the chest?"

Noah kept the smile, a curved set of lips under hollow eyes.

"I want you to meet with the hospital's grief counselor," the doctor said. "This was an unbelievably traumatic experience. You most likely won't exhibit, or even feel, any sense of loss or grief for several days or even weeks. Still, I would like to keep you overnight for observation, make sure your breathing is maintained, and have you talk to the counselor in the morning. Lovely woman, Eliza, been doing this for a long time. She can help you with everything."

Noah eyed his brother and the detective. "Thanks, Doc, but I'm good. I'm ready to go."

A hint of concern flashed in Robert's eyes. The doctor shared the sentiment. "I really must insist."

Noah hopped off the stretcher, no hint of pain. Of external pain. "I really just want to go home. I'm exhausted and could use a drink, to be honest."

"I think it would be better if you stayed, Noah." Robert said.

Claustrophobia. The feeling of people around him. Three of them. Their bodies suddenly flashed orange. Noah's chest tightened. The alarm on the monitor beeped. His pulse was climbing. His heart beginning to pound. If he didn't stop it, breathe and remain calm, they would make him stay.

As calmly as he could, Noah removed the sensor from his finger in order to silence the beeping.

"Guys," he said after a deep breath. "I'm going home. I'm not suicidal. I'm not homicidal. I'm sad. But you can't hold me because I'm sad. I just," he looked at the ground. "I just want to go home and rest."

"How about this?" the doctor said, washing his hands in preparation to leave the exam room. "I give you something, a small something, to help you sleep while we draw a repeat set of lab work to verify that everything is alright internally. If you wake up in the morning and want to speak with Eliza, we'll fetch her down here. If you decide you want to leave, at least you had time to think about it."

Noah slumped back on the stretcher, wincing as the impact shot pain across the right side of his chest. He had no energy to argue. He wanted nothing more than to sleep.

"Fine," he said. "I'll stay overnight."

"Good," Robert said and smiled. "Good. Thank you, Doctor."

The man nodded and stepped out of the room.

"Detective," Noah said. "If you don't mind, I'd like to talk to my brother."

There was animosity in his voice, and he knew she could hear it. She dragged her teeth over her bottom lip and nodded. "When you're feeling up to it, maybe tomorrow, you can come down and talk to me about what happened."

"No. This would be the third time that I sit with you after the fact. In the past twenty-four hours alone, my brother has been shot and the only other person close to me is dead."

"Which is all the more reason for you—"

"Detective, I handed you this psychopath, and you fucked it up. Now four women are dead with—Rob, how many more to go?"

Gaze fixed at the ground, his brother said, "Assuming Amber is part of the count?" Robert held up a single finger.

"One," Noah said. "One person left, and then this man walks away. So no, I won't be sitting with you talking about shit that you already know. And if you feel like bringing me in, then I will gladly hand you my lawyer's business card. Good enough?"

Madsen stalked from the room, her heels clacking on the floor.

***

The dreams came as he knew they would. Despite, after pressure from both the nurse and the physician, relenting and allowing them to push a small dose of Ambien into his veins in an effort to allow him to sleep.

Noah was in the cathedral again. Every person dressed in black with the exception of him. The outcast. Next to him the southern woman turned. "You have to go up now."

Noah gripped the edge of the pew, squeezed until his knuckles turned white. Back and forth he shook his head, desperate to leave the hallucination, but he felt the woman's frail hand on his knee. When he looked at her, she was crying, her face ashen.

"You have to go up now," she repeated.

He wanted to scream in her face. Shout gibberish. Anything to silence her voice.

But it wasn't just her. The congregation had turned their attention to him. Sets of eyes from both young and old, staring through him like his skin and body were a transparent shell. Housing something else. He squeezed his eyes shut, gripped the bench harder and felt his wrist begin to ache. When he opened his eyes again, he was no longer next to the southern woman but on the edge of the pew, one foot in the aisle. Standing there, with his little hand stretched out, was the young boy from before. Only this time, there was no smoke that masked his face, making it painfully clear who he was. Noah broke, dropped to his knees, and took the boy's face in his hands.

"Adrian, I'm so sorry." He repeated his apology over and over and over until his voice scratched and his words were silent. The boy looked so old. Noah had last seen his picture on the year anniversary of the accident. How much he had aged in such a short time.

"You have to go up now," the boy said.

Noah mouthed the words *I can't*, but Adrian remained there, hand out, waiting.

"Adrian." His chest ached with the feeling of breathing smoke.

"I'll go with you." The boy took Noah's hand.

Noah stood, his feet and shins dragging against the movement. As they approached the base of the altar, Noah began to smell the faint scent of smoke. Adrian let go, the sudden weightlessness in his hand making Noah panic.

"You have to sing for her."

Atop the altar was the same casket from before, only this time it was not empty. Noah could see the curve of a woman's head, the strands of hair falling to either side, her hands held atop each other over her waist.

The boards creaked as Noah climbed. In each nostril, the smoke was overbearing. Charred wood. The third step bucked slightly, and the skin on his forearms began to feel warm. He looked but saw no source of heat. No fire.

He could see her face now, her untouched beauty, and he tried to think back to the first time they had met, the beautiful sadness in her eyes.

Noah willed her to move, but he knew she wasn't really there. That Amber was gone and only her body lay in the casket. He willed it regardless.

The cathedral was silent. Behind him, the congregation stared. He could feel their collective gazes on his back, and he wondered who they were underneath the tilted hats and thin veils. Brides and grooms of other-worldly things.

"You have to sing to me," Amber said.

The sound of her voice caused his heart to pound. His hands to shake. Her body remained motionless. A fixture.

He heard shuffling behind him. In the place next to Adrian, there stood a beautiful woman in a dark blue dress. Noah's heart stopped as his vision focused, thinking for a second that it could be what? Amber?—but it was Michelle, the boy's mother, uninjured and safe with her son.

From the corner of his eye, Noah saw another woman walking toward the altar in a faded white dress, hair the color of deep red, eyes that sparkled blue. And without a second guess, he was sure. Amber looked up at him and waved him down from where he knelt.

With solemn steps he descended, humming the tune he had started to sing, finding strength in the melody. He stared in Amber's eyes. Around them, the others circled, their focus on Noah. The door to the cathedral creaked open, allowing rays of light to shine in, illuminating the top of the aisle.

Noah continued to hum, and with Amber's hand tightly in his own, he lead them all forward like the children of Hamelin.

TWENTY-FIVE

After deciding not to meet with the hospital's grief counselor, Noah met his brother outside St. Vincent's emergency room. Robert was leaning against the driver door of his SUV, scrolling through feeds on his phone. Noah wrinkled his nose at the smell of city air. Grime and trash mixed with old grease and snuffed cigarettes. Robert slid his phone into his pocket and walked around to open the passenger door.

"I'm not crippled," Noah said. Though he supposed the sling around his neck and the tight band of padding around his chest argued otherwise.

"Just get in," Robert said.

They drove for a few minutes in silence. Noah flipped through radio channels but found nothing appealing. He was coming down. A high that he barely noticed because the dose was so small, it treated his pain and nothing more.

Thoughts semi-collected, Noah tried to picture Jack's face. Not the man who stood in Amber's living room, but the decade younger paramedic student that Noah supposedly had coached. The man's face appeared like it would in a dream. A blur. Distinctive not by looks, but by foggy recollection in a person's head.

"I talked with Madsen," Robert said. "Explained how everything happened, at least what you told me. I apologized for you snapping at her yesterday and told her we'd come down and see her as soon as we could. We're going to get this guy, Noah."

Noah clicked his tongue, glared at his brother for a second and then shrugged, trying to figure out what point a dirty look would make.

"Well, I hate to make a liar out of you, Rob, but I won't be going to talk to her. I meant everything I said yesterday. She can do her job and figure it out on her own." And in his head, Noah thought, *if Madsen can beat me to the fucker, then God help both of them.*

His brother slowed to a red light, a police cruiser behind them. "Noah, we can't just abandon this. He's almost done. If he kills one more woman then he's gone forever; you said so yourself. We have to find him."

"We," Noah snapped, "don't have to do anything. If you want to help Madsen, then do it. I'm not going to stop you. But, you are going to drive me to the pharmacy, so I can fill this script, and then drop me off at home, where I will be relaxing while my two broken ribs heal. Okay?"

Robert pulled onto the interstate, and Noah watched the light posts flick by, struggling to keep his eyes open as thoughts of retribution flooded him.

***

Noah's apartment was cold. The heat was still off. His refusal to turn it on a silent ode to summer. Without turning on a light, he walked through and sat on the edge of his bed, phone in hand. The screen glowed and died. On. Off. Awake. Standby.

A twinge hit his back. Muscles twitched on their own accord and he could see, softly glowing in the darkness of his room, a faint hand resting on his shoulder. His breathing became shallow and panicked. Short gasps.

The temperature dropped, and he could feel himself shiver.

Noah.

Amber's voice was in his head. He searched the room, dropping to the floor as his eyes began to water. A cold touch graced the back of his neck. Every inch of his skin grew goose bumps.

Noah.

The touch was gone, but her voice echoed. It came from everywhere. Surrounded him. Penetrated his ears from every dark corner.

And as soon as he blinked, it vanished. An absolute emptiness surrounded him.

***

Passing the crucifix in his hallway, Noah raised a hand without looking and touched the bottom of it. He sat on the edge of his bed, sheets half off. They smelled like her. Who had he been kidding? Find and kill someone based on revenge? Noah laid back and spread his arms out, willing the blackout-curtained darkness to envelop him. Minutes passed, and when the faux night didn't suffocate him, he pushed himself back to his feet in order to retrieve something that definitely would.

Noah twisted the top off the orange pill bottle and shook three into his palm, shuffling them back and forth like dice. He stared at the label, the ER doctor's name looking back at him. He exhaled, swallowed them down with a glass of water and returned to his room, asleep before his feet were off the floor.

***

Noah woke in a start. Jolted upright. Something in the room shook him from oblivion. How long had he been out? His eyes fought to adjust, the room spinning around him like a slow oscillating globe. Light crept in from under the curtains, which meant it was still daylight. . . Or he had slept through the entire night. He tried to stand, his legs weak, wavering.

The temperature had dropped, and he fought the urge to shake. Breath escaped him. Sucked from his lungs like life was freezing him in place. Leaving him to suffer in a state of permanence.

Noah.

He crawled back into bed, pulled the pillow over his ears and pressed until he drifted off a second time. High and willfully ignorant.

TWENTY-SIX

Two pills rattled from the bottle, circling inside his palm like little tokens. That left six still inside. Damn. Despite slowing down on how many and how often, they had only lasted a week.

Had it really been that long? Caligan General had called and fired him. Three no-call, no-shows in his first week? Unheard of. He had laughed when he heard it on his voicemail. If they only knew.

Noah finished a granola bar and flipped over to a different sitcom. Nothing held his attention. When the clock reset and he was pushing sober, coming up on that lovely timestamp that marked when he should take another round, he began fidgeting, unable to make up his mind on what to watch, to listen to, to eat. When he was high, well, he frankly just didn't give a shit. Anything would do.

His mind returned to the six pills in the bottle on his kitchen counter. No doctor's offices were open over the weekend, so that option was out. Never mind that his primary care physician wasn't exactly up for prescribing him narcotics, although now with the two broken ribs, that may prove a different story. Regardless, her office would be closed until Monday, and the likelihood of getting an appointment more than a week-and-a-half out was borderline lottery level.

He would have to ration. There was no way around it. It was almost eight o'clock on Friday night, which meant he would wake up around two and need to take more. He would have to try with just one to get him back to sleep. Yeah, one he could do if it were the middle of the night. Okay, so that left five. He would take two Saturday morning, which left three, and then two Saturday afternoon, which left one.

"That's not going to work," he said to no one.

He tried recalculating: take none overnight (he jittered his leg nervously at the thought) take two Saturday morning which left four, two at night which left two, but that would only leave two for Sunday.

He screamed out, threw the remote against the wall, shattering the plastic backing and sending AAA batteries spewing into different corners of the room. Staring at the hole in the plaster, Noah gripped at his hair and started laughing.

"Fuck it," he said as he got up and swallowed another pill. "That leaves five." He laughed at himself and went down the hall to his bedroom.

***

Noah woke to a rattle. Little pills in a little vial. His room was dark. To his disappointment, there were no medications on his nightstand. He knew he had heard the noise. Was sure it hadn't been a dream. Groggy, eyelids heavy and half-open, he swung his feet off the side of his bed. His bare soles hit the floor like anchors in water.

"Whoop," he leaned back, his movements amplified, and tried not to fall forward onto the floor.

He heard the sound again. *Rattle, rattle, rattle.* Like a child's toy. A plaything filled with rice or whatever it was they were filled with.

"Fuck off," he yelled into the darkness.

And laughter responded.

Noah's back went rigid; his skin tingled.

He reached for his phone, but his hand hit wood. His cell was gone, and so was the lamp that normally occupied the space adjacent to it.

He swallowed hard and slid from the edge of the bed to the floor. The world spun, its axis tilted in his vision. How many pills had he taken? He remembered being in the living room, storming to the counter, but had it been one or two. . . Or did he choke down three?

Again, the rattling sound echoed down the hall. A taunt. Come child, there's candy in my hand.

Noah grabbed a shirt from the floor and tugged it over his head, twisting his arms to get them from the neck to the sides. His fingers gripped the hems of the fabric, dragging it down his body and across his burned arms as he did so.

There was no pain.

That was the beautiful part about the candy: it replaced all the ugly with a calming sweetness. His hand on the wall to guide him, Noah crept down the hall. Each step required maximum effort as he fought to remain on his feet. Bobbing sensations, like buoys on waves, filled his head. A seafaring journey.

He stopped and peered into the kitchen. No one was there. The only light came from the oven clock and its green glow. Were the pills on his counter? He squinted, tried to focus, but the slab of black plastic teetered on its side, everything held to its surface by some remarkable force.

"Where?" He looked to the living room but there was nothing.

As he stepped forward, the door to his apartment clicked shut. Noah frantically dragged his hand across the wall until his palm collided with the light switch. Brightness shot down from the ceiling lights, momentarily blinding him. He raised a hand in front of his eyes and squinted, waiting for the world to refocus into something discernible.

When it finally did, the blurred edges of his vision sharpening, he saw the physical items in his kitchen and living room return to form. On the counter, just as he remembered, was the little orange bottle of pills. Relief washed over him. The calming effects of the medication returning.

He walked over and popped the top only to find that the bottle was empty.

"What?"

That couldn't be. There couldn't be none left; there were five when he went to bed. Or were there four? Why couldn't he remember how many he had taken? Had he finished the bottle?

Noah lifted his gaze from the bottle and stared until his vision lost focus. He rushed to the door and yanked on the handle. To his surprise it was unlocked. He froze with one hand on the knob, the empty bottle of pills gripped in the other. Had there actually been someone in the apartment? Did someone come in and take his medication?

He shut the door and slid the deadbolt across as he always did. There was no way he had left it unlocked. He couldn't even recall the last time he had been out of the apartment, which meant if someone came in, they would have needed a key. Only two people aside from himself had keys: Robert and Amber.

Noah looked at the ceiling, a feeling of stupidity hitting him square in the face. He whipped the bottle into the kitchen. It clattered against the stove and rolled in front of the dishwasher.

"That son-of-a-bitch."

TWENTY-SEVEN

Three voicemails. Eight text messages. Noah, after tossing and turning through the rest of the night, ignored the notifications and dialed his brother's number.

"Noah," Robert said. "Jesus Christ, it's about time. What the hell happened to you? Where are you?"

"Where do you think I am?" Noah snapped. Nasty.

Robert's voice immediately hardened. A brother's love for a brother's love. "I don't know; that's why I'm asking you."

"You know damn well where I am, Rob. I'm at my apartment. Haven't moved since you were here last night."

"What are you talking about? Noah, how much medication have you taken today?"

"None!" he shouted.

His brother became silent on the other end. Noah pulled the phone from his face and laughed. He ran a hand through his hair and it clumped together with grease.

"How could I have taken any? You stole all the ones I had left."

JACK BE QUICK · 215

Noah heard muffled voices, and then his brother came back on the line. "Noah, I'm coming over, so get dressed if you're not wearing anything."

"Rob, you come here, and I will slam the fucking door in your face." He threw the phone down.

Following a shower, Noah wanted air. His head ached and his stomach was doing somersaults, but he hadn't given in. Hadn't thrown up yet. He refused to withdraw again. His muscles would burn, acid turning inside his stomach, but that's where it would stay.

Noah walked down the steps of his building and to the end of the parking area where the mailboxes were collected in large square banks, like safety deposit boxes in a vault. He turned the key and could barely fit his fingers around the stack that had built up in the rectangular cubby.

"Jesus," he said as he shut the door.

He thumbed through the bundle, mostly junk mail, rubber banded to a few bills and back issues of magazines. In the kitchen, he tossed what he'd sifted through on the table and continued flipping through the rest.

Bill, credit card offer, loan offer, refinance offer, magazine.

Noah suddenly froze, his thumb and forefinger pinching the corner of a postcard. The image on the front was of the Palace of Westminster. A red fingerprint smeared across the clear blue sky, just above Big Ben.

He dropped the rest of the correspondence to the floor. A sudden weight pressed against his broken ribs as he tried to breathe.

He flipped the card over. It had been postmarked on October 1. A week ago. There was no return address. Only Noah's apartment complex and number, scribbled in handwriting that bled some line between print and cursive.

You've made your return, Noah. I am truly sorry that it took her life to mark the occasion. I had not planned on that. But you had to press me, prematurely arrive at number three. Tsk. Tsk. Made the double event that much more exciting though! I still owe you something. A memento before I go. Till then, all the best, Jack.

Noah stood frozen, rereading over and over until he had it memorized. With the words burned into his brain, he bunched his hand into a fist, crumpling the card inside. He stalked to his room, seething, and ripped his phone from the outlet, charger and all.

"Damien," he said when the call connected. "Yeah— hey, it's Noah. Yeah, I know, too long."

The phone pressed against his ear, he continued to nod until there was a break. "I know, right? Look, I need something. I hate to do this, but you're always saying you owe me.

I need a gun."

***

Damien would follow through on the gun—that Noah was sure of. It had been ages since he had last gone shooting. On any other day, the idea of getting a firearm from Damien would make him laugh. And yet, here he was: standing in his kitchen drinking a glass of water, imagining putting a bullet into Jack's head. Except that wasn't good enough. That wouldn't do it.

Noah would shoot him in the knee. Watch as shards of his patella spewed into the air like jagged confetti. He nodded as he stared into the abyss of his living room, unblinking. And while Jack was crawling, hand over hand, dragging his limp leg, Noah would shoot him again. He would put a bullet into his thigh and watch as blood pooled around him, seeping from his wounds until there was nothing left in his veins for his heart to beat. *Thump. Thump. Death.*

Having the gun wouldn't be enough. He still needed to find Jack. To at least know the man's real name so he could stop referring to him *as* Jack. Noah had shifted through the few boxes in his closet, looking for a roster or a class picture or something from the program he had gone through, but there was nothing left. Everything trashed in an angry fit after Amber left. And, unfortunately, Facebook had just been in its infancy, Noah not a babysitter.

No, he would have to draw him out. Play into Jack's wheelhouse, and Robert had the knowhow.

Noah refilled his glass and stared at his phone. His brother had called a second time. Another fifteen minutes and there would be a knock on his door. While Noah needed information, he wasn't sure he could tolerate talking with his brother. But, he wasn't up to looking up all of this shit on the Internet. His head hurt at the thought.

Robert it was.

"Well," his brother said when the call connected. "Are you sober yet?"

"We're not going to go there. I need something, though."

"Yeah? And what's that?"

"I need a car."

"Um, I can't exactly give you my car. What do you need? I can go to the store and get it for you, or if you want to just get out, we can go do something. After the weekend, we'll get your insurance information straightened out, and we'll get you another truck."

"That's great," Noah said. A sigh of relief on the other end of the line until he added. "But until then, I need to borrow a car."

On the other end of the line, a door closed and Robert released an exasperated exhale. When he spoke, his words were quieter, hushed. "I'm not giving you my car, Noah. If I do, I swear Claudia will divorce me. She's already losing her mind over some stupid argument with Emma."

He squeezed the glass of water so hard it shattered in his hand, slicing his palm and causing blood to run from the gash in his flesh and drip onto the kitchen floor.

"What was that?" Robert asked.

"I dropped a glass."

"Right," Robert said. "Have you eaten today?"

"What?"

"Have you—hold on." Robert called to someone, not bothering to take the phone away from his mouth.

Noah grabbed a rag from the bathroom, pressed it to his palm and applied pressure while he searched through his bag of stolen medical supplies and found a pack of butterfly strips.

"Let's grab dinner," Robert said. "I'll pick you up, and we'll go to Carroll's Grill."

"I'll meet you," Noah relented.

"How? You don't have a car, remember?"

"I know, I asked to borrow yours, but there's a taxi; there's Uber."

Robert exhaled loudly into the phone. "If you want to be a petulant child, fine. I'll see you at seven."

With the conversation over, Noah applied the last of the butterfly strips and looked at the slice across his palm. The edges of the skin pursed like thin, bloodied lips. Noah chuckled and kissed his palm, the tangy taste of blood on his mouth.

TWENTY-EIGHT

It was the first time Noah had used Uber, and it was the first time Noah had been uncomfortable while using Uber. He followed the little GPS arrow that represented his driver—Amelio, an older man who was most likely retired and driving either out of boredom or because he hated his wife—as it banked around this corner and down this road until it finally pulled into a spot in the main parking lot of his apartment complex.

They drove to the destination Noah had plugged into his phone. Down Carriage Street, three blocks away from the hospital. A street where houses were far enough apart for there to be a strip of grass between them but too close to fit a lawn mower.

"Up here," Noah said. "Keep the engine running."

"It doesn't—I'm not a taxi."

Noah leaned inside the car, his hand on the open door. "Just hang around, I'll be right back."

Noah half jogged, half jumped up the two steps and knocked on the front door. His body was betraying him. His chest reverberating pain with each bounce or sudden movement.

"My man," Damien said as he opened the door.

Noah was pulled into a rough embrace, suffering through several meaty slaps to his back, each one forcing him to recoil and wince.

"Sorry homes, you good?"

"Yeah," Noah waved the concern away. "Busted a couple ribs, but I'm good."

"Ah, tough out there saving lives, huh?"

"I really don't save lives all that often," Noah said.

"You saved mine. Come on."

The house was cluttered with old magazines and ash-trays, though the smell of cigarettes was oddly absent. Noah followed Damien up a set of steep stairs. On the second floor, the boards creaked under their weight. They passed an open room with boxes piled high and the floor covered with even more magazines.

Trailing behind, Noah said, "You know, you have to stop saying that I saved— Hell, Damien, you read all these?"

Damien turned back. Reached in front of him and pulled the door closed. "Collector's items. And, yeah, you did. I'd be dead if it weren't for you."

"Lilly had already done the Heimlich; you were fine."

"No, I still couldn't breathe. I still couldn't swallow. You saved my life, Noah. Get that."

Lips tight, he gave the man a shrug. In a room at the end of the hall, Damien knelt at the foot of a bed. On top of the blankets, an orange and white cat uncurled and stretched. It eyed them for a second, mouth opening and closing, before deciding they weren't a threat or all that interesting. It walked to the head of the bed, kneaded one of the pillows, and curled back to sleep.

Damien pulled a gun from the trunk, shutting it as he stood. Noah guessed it was a nine millimeter, but for all he knew, it could have been a .22 or a .357. Some of the guys on the force used to take him shooting a few years back, but he had never really been sold on blowing holes in things. Just wasn't for him. He knew how to turn the safety on and off, and which end to point when you go to pull the trigger.

"This going to get you—"

Damien held his hand up. "I don't want to know what you do with it. You get caught doing whatever it is you're going to do, well, I'm not going back to jail. I'll tell them you stole it, plain and simple. Get me?"

"Got you," Noah said and felt the weight of the gun in his unbandaged hand.

***

The hostess at Carroll's Grill sat Noah at a round table for two on the left side of the main dining area. The restaurant was busy. A low rumble of conversations rolled at him as Noah studied a menu. The seat opposite him moved, causing Noah to lower the menu, mouth open, comment lingering on his tongue that was forgotten the second he looked past the top of the pages. Noah dropped the menu as Jack sat down and pulled the seat in.

Jack unbuttoned his grey suit jacket, the color nearly black. A white button up underneath with a tie patterned with shades of grey. His face was clean-shaven. Eyes heavy like a judge about to pass down a ruling he knew was wrong. A win by technicality.

"Can I get you guys something to drink to start off?" The waitress was middle-aged with straight, dyed-blonde hair and the hint of a tattoo on her left wrist.

She stood a foot away from Noah, yet she may as well have been on the other side of the restaurant. Noah ignored her. Clenched his fists so tight they trembled. Sweat beaded on his forehead while his stomach turned in circles.

He saw blood. Bodies. Sliced stomachs and bleeding women. Amber. The first call on Oak Street. When he walked right by this man. When he walked right by and *nodded at him.*

"Sir?" The waitress' voice was distant. Muffled.

Jack leaned forward. Noah skidded back in his chair, slamming into the person behind him. Someone shouted. The person he hit? Everywhere, people stared, their eyes boring into him. He took a breath, swallowed, and remembered where he was. The waitress hovered above him, a mortified expression frozen on her face.

"I'm sorry," Jack said. He reached out and gently gripped the woman's wrist. The contact—his skin against hers—it all made Noah sick. Was he feeling her pulse? Imagining taking the life from her? Jack's lips were moving. He was giving her some line, something. "Post traumatic stress. He was overseas twice: Afghanistan and then Iraq."

Noah looked at the table next to him. A woman shook her head. Across from her a bearded man looked down at his plate of food, refusing to meet Noah's eyes.

"See," Jack spoke to the waitress. His fake concern had vanished, replaced by a subtle grin. "Already coming back from the edge. Just bring him a beer, if you don't mind. Whatever is on draught is fine. And I'm sorry, again…" He let the last syllable linger, waiting for her to give him what he wanted.

"Ashley," the waitress said.

"Ashley." This time his smile was real. "I'll have a glass of Macallan, if you would. Straight please." With her gone, Jack opened his menu and thumbed through the pages in silence.

His dispassionate movements ripped at Noah. Clawed at him like a predator whose reach was just. . . too . . . short.

You snapped Amber's ribs, felt them break under your palms, as she died because of him. Noah gripped the sides of his chair to steady his hands. They were betraying him. He took a sharp inhale and realized it wasn't just his hands that were shaking. He felt the cold metal of Damien's gun against the skin of his lower back. This was it. The fight or flight, do or die moment. Mind de-

termined, he leaned slightly to one side only to freeze as
Jack made a *tsk, tsk* sound.

The man's eyes never left the menu. "Now, let's have
a drink before we get into all of that."

Noah's mouth dropped. The nerve. The unbelievable—

Then it dawned on him.

Through gritted teeth, he demanded to know where
his brother was.

"Robert?" Jack asked. "He's dealing with something
at the moment."

"With what?" Noah demanded, just a little too loud.

Jack lifted his hand as if to shush him. The man
mouthed an apology. The woman at the next table continued to stare.

The waitress reappeared, a drink in each hand. She
took Jack's order. Her unease evident when it came Noah's turn. His lips twitched.

"Burger," he could barely say.

"Fries or salad?"

"I don't care," he snapped.

Jack narrowed his eyes, and Noah felt the man's look
of disapproval like a physical blow. "Fries."

She left as quickly as she could, and Jack raised his
glass. "To closure. And, more importantly, our heroes."

Noah refused to lift his hands from his seat, but Jack
remained steadfast, glass in the air unwavering. He could
wait all night, Noah realized. Which meant that despite
Noah being armed, despite the multitude of witnesses
surrounding them, there was a play that Noah couldn't
see. Something Jack was hiding deep up his sleeve.

He raised his beer. They touched with a soft clank.

"Talk." Noah's voice was low.

"Rush, rush, it's been the basis of your entire career.
Take a breath. Relax. After all." Jack swirled his glass.
The copper liquid curled around the inside. "This is
twelve-year-old scotch, Noah, not cinnamon flavored
whiskey. You sip twelve-year-old scotch."

The restaurant hummed with chatter and utensils hitting dishware. People laughed in short bursts. Noah dragged his thumb over the label of his beer, digging into the corner.

Just shoot him.

But he couldn't.

"What do you want?" Noah asked.

"I'm simply here to check on you."

"Excuse me?"

Jack took a sip. "This was your redemption, Noah. Not your undoing. You made the choice I knew you would make. Unfortunately, the outcome wasn't favorable, but from ash comes rebirth. Know that with Amber's untimely passing, another life was saved. The original that I had intended for number four, well, she will see the sun rise tomorrow. And that, that is thanks to you, my friend."

Noah spoke through gritted teeth. "I am not your friend."

Jack lowered his head. Pouted at the glass of scotch in his hand. "You need to be done with the pills, Noah. You can't go back to that."

"You," Noah said. "You took them. You took them from my apartment. Off my *fucking* counter."

Jack nodded. Gave a meager shrug, as if his hand had been slapped while reaching into the till; but it didn't matter, because he'd already stuffed the hundreds into his pocket.

"You were being reckless, and I was concerned. One overdose is hard enough on the body—the odds that you would survive a second aren't in your favor."

Noah's heart pound against his broken ribs. This man had been in his home. He had been in his kitchen while Noah lay asleep in the adjacent room. Lowering his arms to his lap, suddenly conscious of the burns receding into scars like glaciers retreating mountainous landscapes.

Noah forced a laugh, because he didn't know what else to do. "I don't see why it'd matter. I'd just be another body on your count. Bring you that much closer."

"It would do nothing of the sort." Jack's tone had shifted. Had Noah insulted him? "Dear Jack never killed a man, only whores. And, apparently I must reiterate again, this was for you, Noah. I did this to help you."

Noah's leg began to bounce on its own accord. Amber was dead. The man who killed her had been in his apartment. He saw flashes of the other three women. He couldn't even remember their names. Digging his teeth into his bottom lip, he stifled a scream.

Just shoot him!

Noah reached behind his back, but before his fingers touched the cool metal, Jack was halfway across the table, finger pointed at Noah's chest.

"I am telling you that you don't want to do that. Not yet."

"I think I do," Noah said.

"Emma," Jack whispered.

Noah froze, the hem of his shirt raised, exposing his lower back and the butt of the gun.

After a few seconds Jack raised his eyebrows, titled his head to the side. "Would you pull your shirt down, please?"

Noah did so. Slowly. He struggled to get the words out. "What about Emma?"

Jack raised his hand slightly. "In a minute."

"Now." Noah glared.

"You're so quick to move this along, but I bet that when I'm gone, you might actually begin to miss me. I've given your life purpose again, Noah. Or would you rather be high and smelling like you haven't bathed in days? You're better than that."

Noah leaned forward, closed his fingers around his beer. When he spoke his words were low and overly annunciated. "The only thing I'll miss is knowing that you're going to die."

Jack laughed and ran his fingertip along the top of his glass. "Yes, well, I'm afraid that won't be happening. Two more things, and then I'm gone. Vanished. Like a magic trick. That was the greatest thing about Jack, you know: that he was never caught. He's an enigma. Over a hundred years, and he's still barely more than an apparition. And yet everyone knows about him. I will bet that if you ask a random person, any random person, they will know of Jack the Ripper. But, if you ask that same person how many presidents this country has had, they'll look like a child trying to count to four."

"You're not like him," Noah said. "You've been caught. You're sitting in front of me right now. I have you. I know who you are. The police can trace you back to our program."

Jack put down his glass, the faintest thud softened by the tablecloth. Noah felt the man's eyes on him, heavy. A thousand dying eyes throughout his career, and Noah had never felt a pair like Jack's.

"No," Jack said. "What you have is a fake name and a set of letters that I may not have even written. And sure, you can pull up our old roster; take a look with your finger down a row of pictures until you see me smiling back at you. But maybe that person died a few years ago. Maybe I forged a new birth certificate and ID. Made up an entirely new person, just for you. I promise you: I will never be caught. We all have a calling, a purpose in life. This is mine. Honoring the greatest ghost to ever walk among us."

He laughed.

The sound made Noah's skin crawl. He had to make it stop. Silence it.

"What did you do to Emma?" The words came like regurgitated molasses. Black slime that dripped in slow streams from the corners of his mouth.

Jack smiled. "Nothing yet. She's my insurance."

"Okay," the waitress announced. "A burger and chicken parmesan. Here you guys go. Another beer?"

Noah found himself nodding, even though he couldn't take his eyes from Jack.

"I'll end you. If you do anything to her, I swear I will end you."

Jack's lips twisted in distaste. "*I'll end you.* Original."

The smirk on Noah's face came naturally. "This coming from you?"

"Yes, well, when you're right, you're right. But that doesn't negate the fact that Jack is the most enigmatic serial killer in our world's history. He is a legend, and you would do best to remember that."

The waitress returned and placed the beer on the table. She hurried away without asking if anything tasted all right.

"I said it before, and I'll say it again: We know who you are."

Exasperated, Jack threw his napkin down. "Fine, because this is getting nowhere."

He reached into the inside pocket of his jacket. He smacked a folded paper, the size of an index card against his palm.

"Let's say that you do, in fact, know who I am. That the junkie paramedic and his historian brother figured out what the police couldn't. What the Whitechapel vigilance committee couldn't. What half the world still can't."

He flicked the paper across the table. It landed propped against the side of Noah's plate, and he realized it wasn't a piece of paper, but a photograph. Jack nodded but Noah was already reaching, his throat already tightening. His short, shallow breaths twisted into panic as he unfolded the picture and found himself looking at his niece, lying on a bed in her pajamas, propped on her elbows with her head buried in a laptop.

"It's taken from inside her closet," Jack smirked.

Noah sprang up, his chair flipping back against the ground. A woman shouted. Several men cursed before a hush fell over the entire dining area. Jack remained sitting, his smirk gone, replaced by a stoic, grim expression.

After a few seconds, the waitress and another individual began approaching. They had been waiting for this. Several of the busboys stood ready on the outskirts, like security in the emergency room.

With what appeared to be a manager at her side, the waitress cleared her throat and looked at both of them. Jack shrugged, finished his whiskey, and stood.

"Don't worry," he said as he handed the waitress two one-hundred dollar bills. "The scene's over. Give us one second, and I'm on my way out, I promise."

She looked at her counterpart, blinking rapidly, unsure of what to do. He nodded slightly, and they both backed away. Jack re-buttoned his suit and stepped around the table. Noah jumped back, but Jack only pointed to the picture.

"Noah," he leaned forward, three fingers touching the tabletop, and spoke just above a whisper. "Listen to me: I need one more to reach five. That place is reserved for someone other than her. Don't change that. You can tell Madsen you have nothing more to offer and be on your way. Go back to work. Back to what you do best. If you do that, she will be fine, and this will be our little secret."

Noah stared at him, his fingers shaking. "I'll shoot you. If you try to leave, I'll kill you."

"You could. But then you'd be taking the risk that I already kidnapped her and she's not lying on a bed, but strapped to one in someplace that you'll never, ever find. Now, do you understand what I've said, or are you going to allow someone else you love to burn?"

Noah felt his jaw tremble. His knuckles had gone white. Reluctant, he had no choice but to reply. "I won't do anything,"

"Good." Jack knocked his knuckles on the table and leaned farther in, his face inches from Noah's. "Because if you do, I will carve out her eyes and feed them to you."

TWENTY-NINE

Robert arrived at the restaurant a half hour after Jack had slid out the front door, a wave of smug arrogance trailing behind him. Noah was sitting on the round cement base of a light post, drinking a beer he had simply walked out with.

"What's this?" Robert pointed to the bottle. "Open liquor laws now?"

Noah stared at his brother, but all he could see was his niece's face on the photograph. His stomach ached. Pain worse than his knee, than his ribs. It ate at him. He could feel the teeth gnawing at his insides, shredding. How could he not say anything? He felt the picture in the front pocket of his pants. Its corner poked into the top of his thigh.

"Okay. . . Anyway, sorry I'm late. Emma's car wouldn't start."

Noah's eyes shot open. "Is she alright?"

Robert looked down, his eyebrows raised. "Yes? She didn't stall on the interstate or anything. She was leaving her dorm to come down and see us, and it wouldn't start. Not a big deal. To be honest, I needed the drive. Needed to get out of here for a while and to a place I at least felt a little comfortable."

"But she was okay?"

"Yes. Jesus, Noah. She forgot to put gas in it."

"Someone could have stolen it," Noah said.

"Really? You think someone would actually syphon gas from someone else's tank?"

"Been on the news before."

"Yes, because that means it actually happened. We don't pay five dollars a gallon anymore. I really wouldn't see the point."

"It's not you who has to."

Noah leaned backward, rocking slightly. His back touched the lamppost and he rested, exhaling into the night air. In his head, he tried to weigh the legitimacy of the photo. It could have been forged. You could do anything with Photoshop, and he was sure Emma had a Facebook or Instagram where pictures of her were plastered about.

It was taken from inside her closet, Noah. Amber's voice echoed through his head.

With bitter distaste on his tongue, Noah opened his mouth, ready to say fuck it and just tell Robert what had happened, when his brother spoke first.

"So," Robert nodded toward the door of Carroll's. "Shall we?"

"Hmm? No. I'm not hungry, really."

"Yeah, I figured."

The couple that had been sitting behind Noah came out of the door and began walking away from the restaurant. They hesitated when they saw him, their eyes meeting his for just a second before they hurried to their car.

"That was odd," Robert said.

Noah only nodded. Exhaustion filled him like a coursing poison. His mind was a muddied mess of nonsense. All he wanted was sleep, a sudden desire for nothing but oblivion.

"Can you just give me a ride home?" he asked. "Guess I wasn't ready to get out yet."

His brother nodded, "Yeah. Come on."

***

He didn't try to sleep. He didn't watch Netflix or even pace back and forth throughout his apartment. Noah sat at his kitchen table, the photograph of Emma in front of him, the crumpled postcard next to it. He stared at the front door, the deadbolt undone, willing Jack to visit. Tucked beside the stack of mail was Damien's gun, loaded with the safety off.

If the door opened, he would put a bullet in the man that walked through. He was stone sober and sure of nothing else. Jack's blood would decorate his kitchen walls.

Noah felt wary, unsure of everything around him. There was the distinct possibility that Jack was telling the truth. Emma could be safely running around Northern University, unaware that someone was following her. A romantic walk that she didn't realize she was on. He would finish his work, murder the last woman when it was time, and disappear. In his wake he would leave Emma and her father none the wiser.

But November 9 was a long way away. And according to what Robert had said before, and the articles he'd read online since returning from Carroll's, there was still one more care package to be postmarked. The From Hell letter. That letter would come in a little over a week. If it came at all.

It will come, Amber's voice assured him. *He's followed the pattern this far. Why would he stop now?*

"Because we're on to him," Noah said. "We know who he is."

But you don't. He was right, Noah, all you have is a fake name.

Noah rose from the table, his hands clasping the back of his head, and paced into the living room. Pausing, he stared at the darkness through the balcony door. "So what do we do?"

You, and only you, find him and do what you know you need to: kill him.

"If he's telling the truth, like you just said he was, and I go after him, then he'll kill Emma. That's what he said he would do."

Noah saw flashes of Emma's face. Carved to pieces in her apartment like Mary Kelly. Unable to hold it in, Noah began shouting.

"That's what he said he would do, and I can't do this again, Amber, I can't fucking do it. He's watching me. And if one more person dies because of something I did, then I'm done, I might as well—"

Noah dropped his hands to his side, his eyes wide. He looked at the gun on the table and sucked in his lips. A plan had formed in the hollow recess of his brain.

THIRTY

Come morning, Noah showered and ate the scraps that remained in his cupboard. Toast without butter. He left his apartment and checked his mailbox. A dog barked, causing him to jump. The old woman with the mini-mutt that lived in the next building. He gave her a weary smile and half-waved. The morning sun shone through bare autumn trees.

Noah headed away from the mailboxes, empty-handed, purposely leaving the few envelopes that had gathered in the box. Rather than head back to his apartment, he walked down the sidewalk toward the rental office.

Behind the counter was a woman with curly brown hair. Her desk wrapped back on each side, the top composed of green speckled marble. Pictures of the complex hung on the walls. Each one an ode to the various stages of development.

The woman smiled.

"Good morning," she beamed. He saw the twenty-four-ounce Starbucks next to her keyboard and was slightly jealous. "How can I help you?"

"I, uh," he pointed to the door in an attempt to feign helplessness. "Went to grab my mail and locked myself out without my phone. You guys have a business center or a phone I can use?"

"What's your apartment number? I'll call maintenance to head up and unlock you."

"Oh, no, that's okay. I don't really want to bother anyone. My brother has a spare key, and we were going out to breakfast in a little bit anyway. I just want to call and tell him to come earlier."

She gave him a perplexed look. "Are you sure? Someone can be up in just a few minutes."

"No, no, really it's okay."

The woman hesitated. Noah tried not to fidget, to just remain still. She finally pointed to a corridor on the left side of the office. "There's a copy room down there on the right. Dial 9 to get out."

He nodded. "Thanks. I appreciate it. Sorry to trouble you."

"Really," she chuckled, "it's no trouble."

Once in the hall, he dropped his shoulders and walked with purpose. At the end of the corridor was a radiator and floor-to-ceiling windows. He looked behind him to make sure the woman hadn't followed and jogged down to the end, peering outside the glass. Confident no one was looking, he ducked into the copy room and shut the door. He pulled his phone from his pocket, pulled up Detective Madsen's number and punched it into the office phone.

"Alyssa Madsen."

"Detective," Noah said hushed and quick. He slid his phone into his pocket and looked out through the narrow window in the office door. "It's Noah McKeen."

"I'm aware. What can I do for you, Mr. McKeen?"

He rolled his eyes. "I think you can call me Noah at this point—wait, how'd you know it was me? I didn't call you from my number."

There was a hesitation on the line before she answered. "Your voice."

"Oh, that's—anyway, I need to see you. I have something that I think you'll want."

"I'm headed into the station in an hour. I'll meet you there."

"Eh, I can't."

"Do you need a ride?"

"Yes," he made a fist. "Well, no. It's complicated. Look, I know this is going to sound insane, and I can explain it better in person, but I need to get to you without anyone knowing I'm getting to you."

Detective Madsen didn't answer for almost a minute. Noah looked down at the phone to make sure that the call time had not stopped, when she finally spoke. "Noah, I don't care if you are—believe me, I would understand—but are you on any medication at the moment? Have you been drinking?"

His grip tightened on the receiver. He wanted to smash it into the corner of the office table, shattering the plastic into bits and pieces.

"No," he said as calmly as he could. "I'm not on anything. I'm being followed. It's why I didn't call you from my cell. I think Jack has it tapped or is listening, if that's even possible."

It was evident in her voice that she did not believe him and worse, he felt she was losing all interest in the conversation. "I'll show you. Please, you have to trust me."

She exhaled sharply. "Fine, what do you suggest we do?"

"You said an hour right?"

"Mhm."

"Good, that's enough time for me to get an Uber and you to get an unmarked officer over here. And not one of the ones in a crown vic or anything, a real unmarked car."

He heard her laugh for a split second. "You want me to have an officer follow you to make sure no one is following you?"

"I do."

"Noah, I think maybe you need some sleep."

"I have his fingerprint," he blurted.

The line went silent. There was a knock on the door of the office and the woman from the front desk began to push the door open. Noah spoke fast, the syllables blending together in one long word. "An hour I'm leaving in an Uber have someone here or no deal, I have to go."

The woman stood in the doorway, hands on her hips. "I think I'm going to need to see some ID."

Noah shrugged and reached into his back pocket to grab his wallet. His wrist touched the butt of Damien's gun. The feeling of the cool metal against his skin gave him a chill, but he knew it wouldn't be cold for long.

**

The officer wasn't as inconspicuous as Noah would have hoped. He—or she, there was no way Noah could tell—pulled a Ford Explorer into a visitor spot in front of building three. Noah's apartment was in the fourth building, the back corner of the complex. There was only one main drive, and the cop was positioned to see anyone who came in or out.

The Uber driver pulled up, a dark gray sedan, and Noah slid into the back seat, craning his neck to see through each window. Satisfied that no one was watching him, he slumped back, slightly at ease.

The guy muttered something and pulled out of the spot near Noah's building. He tried casual conversation, but Noah barely responded, save for one-word answers and a few nods. Eventually, the guy gave up and turned the radio on.

Noah felt a little guilty for his behavior toward the driver, but he couldn't think about it. Halfway to the station he leaned forward. "Could I use your phone?"

"What?" The guy looked back at him.

"The speaker on mine is busted; I just have to make a call real quick. Please?"

The guy shook his head. "Sorry."

"Please, it'll only take a second." Noah pulled a twenty from his pocket and handed it forward between two fingers. "Here."

Hesitantly, the guy took it and gave him his phone. Noah snatched it and dialed.

"Alyssa Madsen," she said when she answered.

"Did your guy see anyone?"

"Excuse me?"

Noah laughed, noted that the driver was glancing up at him in the mirror every few seconds. "It's Noah. Guess you're not as good with voices as you thought."

"Mr. McKeen," she sounded angry, "I'll be at the station shortly."

"That's fine, but you didn't answer my question: did your guy see anyone?"

"Hold on."

He heard the static of a radio in the background and angled the phone slightly away from his mouth.

"Only another second," he said to the driver.

The man nodded. What else could he do already having taken Noah's money?

"No," Madsen said on the phone. "My *woman* didn't see anything."

If Noah had rolled his eyes any harder they would have fallen out. As if he were one to be sexist.

"See you soon," he said and hung up before she could reply.

THIRTY-ONE

Noah was led by a uniformed officer down the same stairs he'd been led every other time he frequented Sara's Point police station. They offered him coffee that he declined, remembering the vile taste of the sludge they drank. Bottom of the barrel gas station grime was better than that shit. Maybe it was ninety-nine percent caffeine, though he doubted it. If it had been, he would have devoured it. Maybe caffeine had been where his addictive behavior started.

The door opened and Detective Madsen walked in. Noah jumped up before she could make it to the opposite side of the table.

"Let's talk in your office," he said.

She pointed to the table, "Right here is fine."

He bit his lip and shook his head. "No. In here, I feel like I'm being interrogated, and I am not a criminal."

"If you don't give me the fingerprint you claimed to have, then I'll arrest you and make you one."

Noah lowered his eyes, nodded slowly. Rather than sit, he stepped toward Detective Madsen. He sensed her body shift slightly. Her hip—he assumed the hip that her gun was on—angled a little away from him.

"Arrest me," he said, his voice barely above a whisper. "Do you honestly think I have anything left to lose?"

They held each other's gaze. Noah had nowhere else to be; it was up to her.

With a quick breath, she relented. "Follow me."

She led him down a short hall to a room in the back of the station. Her office was small with no windows. A bookcase was pushed against one wall, a desk and two extra chairs in the center. She hung her blazer on the stand-up coat rack, took a seat behind her desk, and motioned for him to sit.

"Now," she said bluntly. "The fingerprint."

"You have to listen to the whole story," Noah said. "And you have to agree to something first."

"Mr. McKeen, I am losing my patience. I played your game and sent an unmarked car to follow you and nothing happened, as I said it wouldn't. Now, deliver on your side or get out. And the next cruiser that comes for you will come with cuffs."

Noah looked at the ceiling, gave a *whooo* sound and slapped his fingers on the edge of Madsen's desk.

"You obviously didn't listen to me. I don't care." He raised his fists. "Arrest me."

Madsen got up and pulled a set of cuffs from her back pocket.

Noah's jaw dropped. His heartbeat quickened. "I'm sorry, I'm joking. I'm joking."

He held his hands up in surrender and waited for Madsen to sit back down. She left the handcuffs on the corner of her desk.

Noah reached into his pocket, his fingers touching the edge of a photograph. He pulled out the picture of Emma and placed it on Madsen's desk. She snatched it up and stared before lowering it, her lips pursed in confusion. "What is this?"

"That," he pointed, "is my niece. Her name is Emma, and she's Robert's only daughter."

"Lovely, Noah, but what does she have to do with this?"

He couldn't keep the annoyance from his voice, despite her hand being inches from the pair of handcuffs. "I'm getting there. Just give me a damn second."

She glared but remained still. Noah composed himself, wiped his palms on the tops of his thighs and told her the entire story, starting with the night of Amber's death, the paramedic class that Jack had been in. He told her about Jack coming to visit him, stealing his medication. About the diner, the threat, and the photograph of Emma that she was now holding. He told her everything, with the exception of the gun that was tucked against his lower back.

Her lips twisted. She opened them to speak only to close them a second later. Noah tried to avert his eyes, gaze around the room while she sat in silence, the analytical part of her brain undoubtedly fried by what he had just told her.

Suddenly, she got up and grabbed the radio from the pocket of her coat.

"What are you doing?" Noah asked.

"We need to get a car on Emma." She pointed her radio at him. "And you were concerned about your own safety? You're disgusting."

He jumped up, hands in the air. "Wait, wait, stop."

She held the radio in front of her mouth, thumb above the button.

"You can't draw any attention to her yet. If Jack's watching—"

"Then we'll get him," she nearly yelled.

"I know, I know, I'm not saying that you won't, but just hold off. Please. Let me run a few things by you first. If you're not convinced, then you're in control, okay?"

Madsen lowered the radio, stepped close to him on her way back to her desk. "The fact that you would let your brother's daughter stay in danger is unbelievable. If something happens to her, you will have a special place in Hell all to yourself."

Noah couldn't control it. His hand shot out on its own accord, his fingers gripping her upper arm. The speed of it surprised her.

"I *live* in Hell, Detective. There is no other place for me."

He let her go. His cheeks burned as he looked to the floor and slowly pulled the seat away from her desk. They sat in silence until Noah reached into his other pocket and pulled out a clear sandwich bag. Inside, was the London Parliament postcard.

"He sent this to me. It was postmarked October 1. There's significance in that. It's the same date that the real Ripper sent a postcard to the central news agency. They called it the Saucy Jack postcard. I honestly don't remember why. Robert could probably tell you, but anyway. It mentioned the night with two murders. The double event. He is aligning himself perfectly with everything the real Ripper did."

"What does your brother say?"

Noah shook his head. "Robert doesn't know about it. About any of this."

Madsen said, "If he did, you'd have to explain about his daughter."

"Back me up, Detective. The third murder, the one that Rob and I almost caught him outside of."

"You mean the one your brother got shot at."

"Yeah," Noah said. "That one. Was it like the rest?"

Madsen whacked a pen against the edge of her desk. "Just like the real Ripper would have wanted it to be."

Noah rubbed the top of his head. Tried to think. Recall which article had described which murder. "It would have been the one where he got interrupted."

Madsen nodded. "Yes, we looked into that. The third victim of the real Ripper was found in a very similar state. As if something had startled him before he could do anything else."

Noah sat back in mild disbelief. This was actually happening. Hearing Madsen corroborate the events shifted everything from an idea to truth. It unnerved him.

"Well?" Madsen asked.

"If Jack senses a cop following Emma, then we will never catch him. He'll hide out until November 9, finish his whole deal, and then vanish. He's expecting us to do this. He wants to be chased; he wants to be sought after, like the real Ripper was."

Madsen nodded. Noah took her silence as a good sign.

"If we ignore him, pretend he doesn't exist, then he'll seek us out. Or me anyway."

"That's quite a gamble you're suggesting, Noah."

"I understand."

"And in all honesty," she continued. "I'm not sure that I buy it. Give me the name of the program you went through, and I'll have someone pull the roster from the company records."

Noah gave her the information. Madsen picked up her radio and called for someone. A few seconds later, an officer knocked on her door. She beckoned for him to come in and handed him the postcard. "Run the print. If you get a hit, tell no one but me, okay?"

He nodded, eyed Noah uneasily, and left.

"People don't seem to like me around here," he said.

"You're too deep in this, and they have police mentalities. I still think we need eyes on Robert's daughter," Madsen said.

"It's the only way," Noah said. "I don't like it either, but you know I'm right. If you thought I was wrong, you would have already sent someone up there, regardless. He wants to be chased, and if we don't play along, he will try and get us to."

She smiled. He could tell she was trying to fight it and losing.

"So, what now?" she asked.

Noah rocked back in the chair before pushing himself up.

"Now, I'm going to go buy a new truck and pick up a pay-as-you-go phone. When I do, I'll call you so you know what number to reach me at."

"If he's going to come after you, you're going to be the one reaching me," she countered.

"Right," he said and left.

Back in the lobby, waiting for an Uber, Noah looked up as Madsen came through the doors. She looked at one of the other officers who was standing with a mother and her small child before taking a seat next to Noah.

He sat straight, surprised and mildly uncomfortable at how close she was. Had they gotten a match already? That was absurdly fast. It took her a minute or so to say anything. In the preceding silence, Noah realized it couldn't have been anything good.

"I want you to know that we're releasing Amber's body to her mother and father."

They sat in silence, Noah staring at the patch of floor between his feet. After a long while, she offered him a reassuring touch to the shoulder and left, buttoning her blazer as she walked out of the foyer and back toward her office.

Noah cracked his knuckles and thought of his first date with Amber. The black clothes. The mourning. His mind flashed to his dreams of the church and the empty coffin on the altar. Next to death, caffeine and narcotics were candy and soda.

Maybe his real addiction was tragedy.

THIRTY-TWO

Robert didn't go to Amber's wake, at least as far as Noah could tell. Noah stood waiting for him in the parking lot, hands in the pockets of creased dress pants, leaning against the tailgate of a new truck. Perched there, just on the outside, he watched cars come and go for nearly half an hour. Everyone dressed almost identical with the same solemn expressions. Grim as they walked in, broken when they left. From where he was, it felt like the world existed around him, that he wasn't an actual part of it.

Amber's father stepped outside for a cigarette. Interrupted three times, the biker-looking man who didn't actually ride, shook hands and nodded thanks. He had aged since the last time Noah had seen him—when the appetizer plate was thrown to the floor, threats flying, and Amber screaming as they toppled onto the living room floor like high school boys, not grown men.

He dialed his brother's number again but, like before, the call went straight to voicemail. Disgruntled, Noah pushed himself off his truck and shut the tailgate with a *thunnnk.* Noah turned and nearly jumped backward, hand on his chest.

Detective Madsen raised an eyebrow. "Didn't mean to scare you."

Noah took a few exasperated breaths, though he wasn't sure why; the woman didn't scare him that badly. Truth be told, he was more surprised that she was actually there than that she had snuck up on him. He walked around to the passenger door and tossed his phone on the seat. When he turned back she was still standing there.

"Was hoping I imagined you," he said.

A brief flash of genuine hurt crossed her face but vanished as soon as she blinked. Noah was sure he had seen it. . . Hadn't he?

"Thanks," she said softly. "I can leave you alone."

She turned, but he caught her by the arm. "I'm sorry."

He dropped his grip and took a quick step back. It was so familiar: the grabbing, the apologizing. Why was it always the same? What did he have to do to change things? To finally cut that branch off the cherry tree and get it right?

"Are you okay, Noah?"

He nodded slowly. "Yeah. What are you doing here, Detective?"

She sucked in her lips and gave him a coy look. "If we really are on a first name basis, then it goes both ways."

"Sorry."

"You shouldn't apologize so much. You're not as bad as you think you are."

And there it was: Amber's words in another's mouth.

"Seriously, though," he looked over her shoulder, checking to see if anyone was watching them. "Do you think he would be here? I mean, I would be the only one who would recognize him."

"It's a possibility," she said. "A fairly good one. Though, my uniform in the car across the street and the one inside the actual funeral home is keeping an eye out. I'm not here to work."

"Then why are you?" Noah's voice trailed off. Their eyes met, and he took a presumptive breath while adjusting the waist of his dress pants.

"Come on," he said.

"You sure you're ready?"

"I'll never be ready for this."

Just inside the main doors was the coiled end of the procession. Noah recognized several people, a trio of nurses dressed in scrubs, either coming from or going into their shifts. He nodded to one of the physician assistants he recognized and stepped forward as the line crawled across the beige carpet, still a dozen yards from entering the actual wake.

Madsen was silent behind him. He wondered what people thought of her being there. But it was a stupid curiosity, because no one knew they were together. As far as anyone around them was concerned, they were strangers, drawn together by mourning.

Someone cleared their throat and in the silence that followed, *Stairway to Heaven* played through the speakers in the ceiling. He closed his eyes, half at the cliché of it, half in an effort to stop himself from crying.

A poster board of pictures was positioned between bouquets of flowers. Noah caught a quick glimpse of Amber's family, her mother with tears in her eyes, her sister stoic and vacant, and then her father, bald head reflecting fluorescent lights.

The photographs spanned the entirety of her short life: muddy jeans of childhood, awkward teenager, adulthood, the lake, smiling as she graduated nursing school.

"How long were you two together?" Madsen asked quietly.

Noah looked from a picture of Amber in a green prom dress to one of her in a flannel shirt straddling a quad. Slowly realizing that there were no pictures of them together. That the distance between him and her family and been solidified. "Almost six years."

He was suddenly exhausted. The weight of the world crushing his shoulders, pressing his arms close against his sides. Suffocation. Pain in his ribs. People all around him. Too many people for him to count. Where was the exit? Where could he—

"Noah." Madsen's voice was soft in his ear.

He tried to focus. Noticed the gap between him and the person before him. As he approached the casket, his palms dripped with sweat. His arms tingled and his stomach turned against him. He gagged, drawing the attention of those around him. Noah waved them away and cleared his throat.

It was his turn. He approached and reality instantly shattered, falling away like a broken mirror while each fragmented piece was slowly replaced by the haunted altar from his dreams. Adrian was suddenly next to him. The cloud of blackness, a fog of thick smoke, once again covered his face.

"I'm not singing," Noah said. His voice caught. Tears formed. "I can't, Adrian."

"You don't have to sing," Adrian replied. "It won't help. You have to say goodbye now."

Could the boy take him? Take him instead of Amber. Noah would. Without a second thought, he would. She didn't deserve what had happened to her, and he didn't deserve what *hadn't* happened to him. If Adrian took him, then it would all just be over. None of this would matter, and he wouldn't have to worry about solving problems or helping people. He could just close his eyes and rest.

"I'm just so tired," he said aloud.

"Um." Madsen stammered. She touched his shoulder gently, stirring him from hallucinations.

Noah looked, but he already knew Adrian was gone. There was no choice. This, where he was standing, was the choice that had been made, and now he had to live with it. He stepped up to the casket, lowered his head, and closed his eyes. When he opened them, he saw Amber's face. Calm. Peaceful. The post-mortem work unbelievable. Aside from slightly different pigments, odd shapes that were dressed with thicker makeup, there were no hints at her injuries. Her hair had been cut short, tied back to hide the singed edges. Noah's eyes honed on the slice in her ear. The odd way the lobe hung from her face. Had they tried to pin it back? Make it look as if nothing had happened?

Noah raised his hand, ready to stroke her hair, just slightly, one last time but voices around him were growing louder. Amber's family. Detective Madsen. They were questioning her. Wondering about leads. About suspects. They were crying. Screaming. Hushing one another. Noah leaned forward, kissed Amber on the forehead, and promised that he would see her soon.

***

"Noah, wait." Madsen called after him.

Noah ignored her. Unlocked his new truck—picked up the second his insurance check had cleared—and pulled open the driver's side door, backhanding tears from his cheeks. Her hand was on his shoulder. Noah spun. Sidestepped away from his truck and away from her.

"Noah." She frowned. "Breathe."

"I'm fine," he muttered.

"You're not, and that's okay. This is tough; I get it."

Noah shut the door. "No you don't. Just leave me alone. Go find Jack and arrest him. Do your thing or don't, whatever."

She stood there, dumbfounded. "What about Emma? Are you giving up on her?"

Noah scoffed. "For all we know, it's a fake. Some picture he got off Facebook or something."

Madsen narrowed her eyes. "Follow me."

"Detective," Noah said, exasperated. "I'm going—"

"One hour," she interrupted. "If after one hour you still want to call it a day, then fine. But at least give me that. You owe it to your niece. You owe it to Amber."

Noah clawed his fingers across the top of his head. "Where are we going?"

***

She led him to a light blue ranch in a quiet Sara's Point neighborhood. Noah pulled his truck to the side of the road just behind Madsen's unmarked car. Orange traffic cones blocked the driveway. Police tape was wrapped around the front porch. He left the gun in the center console and, with the reluctance of a child going to church, jumped out. He immediately noticed an unmarked cruiser parked in a driveway several houses down.

He recognized the neighborhood but not the house. Scattered piles of leaves dotted the front yard while a wooden fence with missing boards cordoned off the back. A woman jogged past, her dog on a leash by her side. Noah couldn't see her eyes through her sunglasses, and judging by the way her face tightened when she looked at the house, he wasn't sure he wanted to.

Madsen buttoned her blazer. Eyed Noah with slight surprise. "You don't know this place, do you?"

"Should I?"

Leaves blew across the road. His tie lifted off his chest and fluttered against his shoulder.

"It's been on the news quite a lot."

He shrugged. "No cable. Does that mean something?"

"Come on." She waved him forward, pulling two pairs of exam gloves from her pocket. "We have most of what we need, but just put these on, okay?"

Noah pulled the gloves on, suddenly unsure of exactly why she had brought him here and what exactly had happened inside. He tried to peer over the fence, but it seemed to be a normal backyard. Grass and a swingset.

Inside was a galley kitchen that led to a small dining and living room. Noah could see markings on certain things. Police tags. What had happened here? He followed Madsen into the living area, when he passed a framed picture on the wall and stopped dead.

"This is his house. You found his house."

Madsen ran a gloved finger over the top of a television. "We were able to pull the roster from your paramedic program and through a little work, we found him. His real name is Dennis Rowe. He's a freelance IT consultant. Does pretty well for himself."

Noah squeezed his fists tight. "So you have him? This is done?"

"No. But that bit about making up a personality? Being someone new? It was a bluff. There was a bag of cash in the washing machine downstairs. Forty-seven thousand. Or just about."

"He was gonna leave," Noah said.

"Most likely. Do his bit and go. But we got to him first."

"So then you have him," Noah repeated. He knew it wasn't true.

"We found the only car registered under his name at an airport parking lot."

"Then what? He's got a rental car under Lechmere?"

"Checked. Nothing. I hate to say it, Noah, but this guy is intelligent. He's right under us, and he still finds ways to stay one step ahead. After giving it some thought, I think your plan is golden. I think it's what we need to do."

Noah hesitated. As he did so, Madsen stepped past him and down the hall. "Come here."

She opened the door to one of the three bedrooms. It had been converted to an office with an L-shaped desk in the corner, and two bookcases on either side of the room. An LED fireplace was pushed against the wall opposite the desk, giving the room the facade of elegance and pretentiousness. Madsen slid the closet door open revealing an expensive scanner on a makeshift table.

"He was listening to everything," Noah said.

"He was," Madsen said. "It's how he knew the response times. We took a lot of evidence in already, one item in particular, a notebook. He logged response times for months. Where you responded from, how long it took you, how long the ambulance would take. He knew all of it."

Noah felt his chest twinge. Nerves fluttering upward from his stomach, trying to reach his throat. He tried to focus on the bookcases. The lines of novels and texts on each shelf. Spines with subjects covering history's most notorious killers. Manson, BTK, Son of Sam, Zodiac, an entire shelf dedicated to dear old Jack.

Madsen pulled open a drawer and dropped a handful of photographs on the desk. She wouldn't lift her gaze to meet his.

"The only reason these are still here," she said solemnly. "Is because there were dozens and dozens of copies."

He shifted through them, holding his breath as he tucked each picture behind the pile. When he couldn't thumb through them one at a time anymore, he flicked through them like a flipbook. His chest burned as his eyes took in shots of himself. His apartment. His car. The SUV parked at the Caligan firehouse. Amber. Amber in her apartment. In her shower. Talking on her phone. At work. Outside of Noah's apartment, replaced in the next shot by the physical therapist running away.

And then came Emma. His niece walking between classes at Northern University. Getting in her car. Her car without her in it, but the gas cap off and hose hanging out. Emma in her underwear crawling into bed.

Noah threw the stack of photos against the wall. Ripped the bookcase down, sending it crashing to the floor.

"Noah!" Madsen shouted. He stormed away until he was back in the living area of the house, framed photo of Dennis—the man he knew as Jack—and his dog in hand. Madsen rushed in just as he hurled it across the room, glass exploding from the frame as it smashed into the wall.

He reached for the detective's throat, stopping suddenly a few inches away, clenching and unclenching his fist. Their eyes remained locked on one another.

"We do this," Noah said. "We do it my way."

"Done."

With each huff the anger subsided, deflating Noah back to his normal self. His stomach gurgled, and he felt dizziness descend upon him.

"Whoa." Madsen grabbed his shoulders. "Are you okay?"

He pushed her away. "Yeah. Yeah, fine."

"Noah, when was the last time you ate anything?"

His vision swayed. Madsen linked her arm underneath his and led him from the room, shards of broken glass reflecting light from the bay window.

THIRTY-THREE

"I don't know what to order," Noah said.

"Well," Madsen raised two fingers in the air. A slim-looking man with long hair and a beanie walked over to their side of the U-shaped bar. "We'll start with this first. What's the oldest whiskey you have?"

The man looked over his shoulder at the rows of different colored bottles. "Depends what you're in the mood for. Got us Johnny Walker Green, which is fifteen years or Macallan twelve year; that's always a winner."

She sucked in her cheeks. A sound of disappointment.

"Not Macallan," Noah said.

Madsen nodded. "Scotch is good, but what about Irish whiskey? The real stuff?"

The guy walked to the array of bottles and reached into the middle shelf. He brandished a dark green bottle with an even darker green label.

"Jameson Limited Reserve," the man said as he held the bottle out. "Eighteen years old."

Madsen nodded, a smile on her face. "Two two-finger glasses."

The bartender hesitated before leaning forward, the bottle held at his side like some priceless artifact just dug from the depths of the Earth. "That's almost a hundred dollars for two drinks."

To Noah's—and the bartender's—surprise, Madsen laughed. Her credit card landed on the bar with a *thwack*. "Thanks for the warning."

Noah raised his hands as the guy grabbed two rocks glasses and filled them halfway.

"You really don't need to do this."

She raised her drink. "Don't worry, I'm banking on you hating yours."

He reached for the glass of amber liquid. The aroma pungent. It hit his nose as a twist of oak and vanilla with the sharpness of pure alcohol spiraled inside. Based on his numerous relapses, Noah was surprised the detective was doing this. Maybe she needed a release, and he was the closest person she had at the moment? What a sad thought that was.

"To…" Madsen's voice rang out.

Noah offered a meek smile. "Closure. And those we can't share it with."

Their glasses touched. He sipped. His lips curled back as the harshness descended past his tongue and into his throat. The whiskey face. Madsen laughed.

"I thought you were a drinker."

He lowered the glass to the bar, trying to salvage what remained of his tongue. "Why would you have ever thought that?"

"Because when I ran into you at your apartment, you were either drunk or high and carrying a liter of rum. Which means we probably shouldn't be doing this, now that I think about it."

Noah lowered his head quickly and nodded. "That—that wasn't really me."

"So who was it?" she asked as she took another sip, no liquor-bite visible on her face.

"The bad me," Noah said and choked down another swig. "Besides, you said you were buying me dinner."

"Right," she motioned for the bartender and ordered two burgers.

"What if I were vegetarian?"

"You're not."

"Yeah, but—"

Madsen rolled her eyes. "Just, take the free food okay?"

For several minutes they sat in silence while *In-A-Gadda-Davida* played over the jukebox. Noah watched people argue over the sports highlights that looped across the televisions. Their sense of pride tied with whatever team they supported. Finally, he asked, "What do you think they're saying?"

"I'm sorry?" Madsen replied.

"The song: *In-A-Gadda-Davida*, what do you think they're actually saying?"

She shrugged. "That. What you said."

"Nah," Noah said and swallowed another mouthful. "That's too easy."

"Alright," she countered. "What do you think it says?"

"I got nothing. Rumor has it the singer was really saying *in the Garden of Eden*, but the words got jumbled, and now we got what we got."

Madsen raised an eyebrow. "Interesting theory. You should be a detective."

Noah laughed. He laughed until it felt awkward to laugh. Noah reached for his phone but decided to leave it in his pocket. Instead, he adjusted his tie, finally loosening it.

"Six years is a long time," Madsen said.

"It was really more like four," Noah replied. "The last two, well, I don't really count anything after the accident."

She nodded.

"That was an incredibly difficult—"

"What happened to Adrian?" he interrupted.

She looked at him, puzzled. "The boy?"

Noah nodded.

"I don't know. He was under the care of her sister in Caligan. I'm assuming he was either given to her next of kin—"

"She didn't have any," he said bluntly.

"How do you know?"

He didn't answer, only stared at his glass.

"You looked into her? Have you been following him all along?"

With one harsh gulp, Noah swallowed what remained in his glass and put the back of his hand to his mouth expecting vomit. When nothing rose, he cleared the phlegm from the back of his mouth and choked it down.

"Believe it or not, I used to be a church going guy."

"Really?" It was evident on her face that there was not a single piece of her that believed him. "I thought the crucifix was just for show."

"Your memory's impressive. But no, not just for show. Every Sunday, hymns and all."

"Wow," she said.

He shrugged. "We all do what we have to do to survive right?"

"Speaking of," she waved to the bartender and pointed to both of their glasses. He hesitated, holding his hands out in a way of saying *are you sure?* Madsen pointed to both of their empty glasses with a slight glare in her eye. He shook his head and grabbed the bottle.

"You were saying?" She ushered him on.

"Church and all that good jazz," Noah said. "Used to go every week. Bow down and say my prayers. I was devoted."

The bartender slid two new glasses filled with whiskey in front of them. Noah bit back the bitter taste and swallowed three large gulps, ending with an exasperated gasp.

"You're supposed to sip that, ya know," Madsen said.

He forced a laugh. "Shows how much of a drinker I am."

"You're going to be wasted in fifteen minutes."

He raised one of his hands slightly off the bar. There was not a part of him that cared. He should have cared if Jack was watching them. Had he been at Amber's wake? Had the uniforms seen anything? Or did he skulk around the burial that had been open only to immediate family members? If he did indeed have his eyes on Noah, then that was fine. It would all play into the final wheelhouse.

"So what happened?"

"Hmm?"

"What happened that made you stop going to church? Was it the accident?"

"Amber had a miscarriage," he blurted.

"Oh." Madsen held her glass between both hands.

"Right after the accident. We were going to on vacation the next day. Camden. It had been her idea. A nice surprise. She was going to give me the news. We would celebrate. Except the trip never happened, and two weeks later helping me off the couch, she felt a pain in her stomach, and that was that. You know that saying when it rains it pours? Well, my life's a fucking hurricane."

Madsen paused, glass in the air. "How does Adrian fit into all of this?"

"He doesn't, really. I went to his mother's wake, followed him a little bit until I learned that her sister was adopting him. She seemed like she was a good parent, not the type of person who was taking him with reluctance, ya know?"

"Mhm."

"Explains why I recognized her. I knew I had seen her before, just must have lost it in the fog of two years. Time does that I guess."

"Among other things," Madsen added.

Noah winced.

"Can I ask you something?"

"On or off the record?" He smirked.

"Funny. What would you have done if Alexia hadn't seemed like a good mother?"

Noah frowned. "What?"

"You heard me: what would you have done?"

Noah took a long, slow sip of his drink. He couldn't help but feel like he was about to be interrogated. Her mind had flicked on. . . Or, he wondered, had it never switched off?

"Nothing. Probably just gotten more depressed, sunk a little lower." He looked right at her. "Hell, maybe killed myself."

The muscles in her face were like stone. "Jokes aside, you're lying."

"Whatever," he grumbled and took a drink. "You know, I don't know what you're trying to get at, but—"

He felt her hand on his wrist. Her fingers were surprisingly soft. Her grip gentle.

"It's okay. I wasn't trying to get at anything. It's admirable. You were trying to be his savior. I'm assuming the miscarriage happened before he was adopted?"

Noah nodded.

"It was transference."

Her voice trailed off and left Noah in a bubble of silence. He stared at the little alcohol remaining in his glass; the effects of what he had drank started to take hold. If he stood, he would teeter.

Madsen opened her mouth slightly, only to close it just as quickly.

"What?" he asked.

"Nothing." She shook her head.

"No, what?"

"I—My second year on the job, there was this guy who drove drunk and slammed his car into a pole. He was ejected, up and walking on the side of the road when we got there."

Noah smirked. "They always are."

"You're not kidding. So we—"

Madsen's phone rang vibrated across the top of the bar. She looked at the screen and rolled her eyes. "Detective Madsen."

She spoke for several minutes while Noah spun his glass between his fingers, catching words of the conversation as his buzz took hold. When she hung up, he asked, jokingly, if her husband was looking for her.

She gave him a disgusted look. "Don't start being an asshole now."

He apologized. "Did it have to do with Jack?"

"Yes. But nothing significant."

She began to resume her story. Noah spoke a fraction sooner, inadvertently cutting her off.

"A few more days—that's all we have to get through." He finished the last of his whiskey and stood, his legs rubbery.

Madsen smirked as the bartender put their burgers down.

THIRTY-FOUR

Noah caught himself on the railing of the stairs, drunk and in a fit of laughter. Madsen leaned into him, wrapped her arm under his shoulder and pulled him toward the top step, unable to stop her own laughter.

"But that's not how it went," Noah said. "You just—you just don't—ah, never mind; you weren't there."

"Of course I wasn't!" she exclaimed. "I've only known you for a month."

He leaned toward her, his weight shifting, forcing her to reposition herself in order to prevent them both from toppling.

"Doesn't it feel li-ssss so much long-er?" The last syllable came out as a belch; his face immediately felt hot, and he clasped his hand over his mouth. "So sorry. That's so gross."

Madsen laughed. "I'm a cop; I've been exposed to a lot worse."

"Like four dead women and the prom—mise of a fifth?"

They shared a grim look, before she answered with a simple yes.

"He was prob—probably doing the right thing, you know?"

Madsen's glare told him that no, she didn't know.

"No, no. I don't mean killing peoples is a good thing. I mean, the way they lived back then was bad. Like real bad. Over crowded. Poor health. Poor people. He killed hookers. Vigi—vigilante or something, right?"

"Something," Madsen said.

Rounding the corner to his apartment, she stopped. Noah looked up, ready to question why. Robert was sitting on the floor of the hall, a duffel bag next to him, mindlessly staring at the pages of a book. Something about the way he was sitting made Noah think he wasn't actually reading.

"Wha—What the hell, Robert?" Noah stumbled forward. Madsen reached after him but stopped and folded her arms against her chest.

"Where were you today? Or did you forget? Wasn't important enough, even though she took care of you when you were shot?" He stopped, going back in his head before correcting himself. "Or *was* going to take care of you, until she, you know, died."

Robert waited patiently for Noah to stop his drunken rambling. Madsen stood next to him, sober, and her protective wall back in place.

"Claudia left this morning," he said solemnly. "She took off when I was in the shower and took Mikey with her."

Noah's shoulders went slack. He wobbled to the side, catching himself before falling. "Oh."

Noah fumbled in his pocket for his keys and stepped past his brother, into his apartment.

"Well," he called back. "I only have one bed, so you can sleep on the couch."

"Do you know where they went, Mr. McKeen?" Madsen asked when they were inside with the door closed.

He shrugged. "I'm assuming her mother's. She's done this once before."

"Three times," Noah yelled from the bathroom.

"She's just never taken our son before."

"Is there any reason to believe she'd harm him?"

Robert shook his head. "No, absolutely not. She may be a little off-kilter, but she wouldn't hurt our kids."

Noah stumbled past. "Bitch is crazy."

"Come on, Noah," Robert said, his voice tense.

Madsen took a subtle step between them. "Why don't you give me her plate number, just in case, and I'll have my guys keep an eye out. If you don't hear from her, or for whatever reason you think something is wrong, call me."

Robert nodded and said thank you.

"Goodnight, gentlemen," she said.

"Wa—wait," Noah pushed himself away from the sink. "Where you going?"

"Home," she said. "Get some sleep."

"But I thought we were having fun."

"We'll talk tomorrow."

When she was gone, Noah spun around and shoved his brother against the counter.

"What the hell, Noah?"

"Why? Why are you here?"

Robert gave a snort of derision. "You forgot about Amber real quick."

"Fuck you," Noah said and shoved him again. "Least I know where the people I love are. Oh, where's Emma, by the way?"

"At school."

"Yeah," Noah nodded, biting his bottom lip. "You s-s-sure about that? Know who's s-h-e-e with, what she's doing?"

"Alright, Noah, what are you getting at?" His brother straightened, waiting for a response.

"Just saying," Noah shrugged, dropped his hands to his sides hard before storming to his bedroom and slamming the door.

***

When Noah woke, the pain in his head threatened to divide his skull in half. He opened his eyes; morning light outlined the rectangle curtains covering his windows. The room smelled of sweat and alcohol. He could feel the grease in his hair. Noah pushed himself up and nearly became sick as the room began to spin.

"Ugh," he managed to grumble.

His lips were dry, and all he wanted was a giant glass of ice water. And something greasy. And some Advil. And a shower.

It took close to an hour, but Noah finally managed to shuffle to the bathroom and into the shower. He couldn't find a comfortable temperature: the water needed to be hot to scald away the grime, but he wanted an ice cold shower to combat the sweating and the shakes.

In the living room, Robert was sitting on the couch, the same book in his lap, this time unopened.

"Hey," Noah offered with his head down. He moved slowly, afraid that turning his head quickly or looking from one place to the next would prompt him to heave.

"You must be feeling quite fantastic," Robert said.

"Oh, you know." Noah slugged down a glass of water, burped with his hand over his mouth in case anything attempted to come out with it. "Rob, I'm sorry about last night. I don't remember exactly what I said, but I know it was mean and wrong, and to be honest, I'm pretty damn embarrassed."

His brother waved him away. He came into the kitchen and slid his car keys off the counter. "Come on."

His voice was amplified by the pulsing divide in Noah's head. "Where?"

"To go get your truck."

"I don't really want to do that right now."

Robert shrugged. "Yeah, but if we go now, then you can buy me breakfast for being such a dick. And you can tell me exactly what it is that you have planned."

"I don't have anything planned," Noah said.

"Noah, I know you better than anyone. There is no way that you would let what happened to Amber go without retaliation."

"Maybe I've changed. Got nothing left to fight for, so why bother?"

His brother dropped the book onto the coffee table. "Don't be melodramatic. Tell me."

Noah exhaled. What did he say? Tell him everything? Except there was a good chance that Robert, if given the opportunity, would interfere. Do something that caused Jack to act prematurely. Either that or take him out—and that was something Noah had reserved for himself and no one else.

"Ah, see," Robert said. "You're hesitating. Tell me."

"Alright," he said. "I have an idea and Madsen's on board with it."

Robert's eyes lit up. "What is it?"

"If he follows the chain of actual events, what's next?"

Robert thought for a moment. "Well, if you believe in the validity of the—"

"Rob."

"The Ripper sent the 'From Hell' letter, along with half of a kidney. He claimed he ate the rest. But you know this. I saw it in the search history of your laptop. Sorry, I've been up for awhile."

Noah felt gas bubbles collide in his stomach. "Whatever. So, Jack delivers the package."

"On the sixteenth," Robert paused to remember what day it was. "That's in two days."

"Yeah," Noah nodded.

"And you're going to catch him when he does it?" Robert asked. "How?"

Noah smiled, sipped some water, and refilled the glass.

THIRTY-FIVE

Noah made it a point to only travel between his house and the package store until the morning of the sixteenth. Robert had camped out on his sofa and had yet to hear from Claudia or Mikey. Madsen had called the day after the drunken incident. Said she had an officer drive by Robert's mother-in-law's house, and his wife's car was indeed there.

"Thanks," Noah had said. "You didn't have to do that."

"Yeah, well, I still live in a world where we do favors for one another."

In an effort to keep Robert from focusing on his marital problems, Noah made him recount everything he knew about Jack the Ripper. Most of it was a re-hash of Noah's own research over the past few weeks, but seeing his brother talk with such enthusiasm was reassuring. Even if it was about something so macabre. But then again, Noah's own profession was built on injured people. If death were a chemical compound, it would out nudge oxygen.

"So," Noah said, leaning against his counter with Robert at the kitchen table, papers, photographs, web articles printed out and scattered in front of him. "Mary Ann Nichols."

"Number One," Robert said. "Of the canonical five, anyways. Was wandering around at around midnight, seen last at the pub before being locked out of where she was staying, due to lack of money."

"They could do that?" Noah asked.

"Whitechapel, London was bad. Real bad."

"Fair. So Nichols is found on Buck's Row."

"Hence our deer painting on the closet door," Robert said. "Found on August 31, by our man Charles Lechmere."

Noah opened a can of soda. Offered Robert one but his brother declined. "Okay, so number two is Annie Charlton?"

Robert looked up. "Chapman."

"Right." Noah thought of Alexia. Thought of Adrian and his traumatic childhood. Noah would have to follow up with Madsen about him when this was done.

"She was married, then separated. Husband—ex husband—died on Christmas day, and with him went her weekly allowance." Robert said.

"So she turned to drinks, which is why there were little rum bottles on the coffee table."

"Yup," Robert's voice became quiet. "He knows what he's doing, that's for sure."

"Don't," Noah said firmly. "Do not give him anything."

"Sorry," Robert said. "Number three was Elizabeth Stride. Now, she was actually seen with someone—a man with a hard felt hat, or so the records say. That's where the pictures come from. Some of them anyways."

"And he was interrupted," Noah added.

"Very good. Her body was clean, except for the cut across the throat, leading police to believe that the Ripper was scared or interrupted before he could cut her open. She would, however, be the first of two in one night making the double event."

Robert looked up. Noah met his gaze and after a second said, "What about number five?"

"Mary Kelly," Robert said. "Well, she went by a bunch of different names. That's the thing about back then: there were no IDs, no driver's licenses or social security numbers. Aliases were everywhere. If they wanted, someone could go to sleep one person and wake up a completely different one."

"How did he get Kelly?"

"She was a prostitute, just like the others. Poor, living in poverty. I don't remember the guy's name, but her landlord sent someone down to collect the rent. She was overdue by a couple weeks, I think. They found her dead inside. She had it the worst out of any of them. I mean he eviscerated her. Cut off both her breasts, emptied her abdominal cavity. Hacked her face almost completely off."

"Okay," Noah said quickly. But it was too late. The image of Emma, of his niece, sliced to a near unrecognizable state in her dorm room. It fit. She was on her own. A small cramped living space. Noah's nose twitched.

"What?" Robert asked.

Noah traded his soda for a glass of water. "Nothing. Sorry."

After a pause, Noah asked, "Why did she get it worse than the others? Did he know her? Was it someone supposedly close to him?"

"Probably not. I mean, there's no way to tell, seeing as we don't actually know who Jack the Ripper was. I mean, anything's possible, but the accepted theory is that because Jack was in the privacy of Mary's rented room, he didn't worry about anyone coming in and finding them, so he sort of took his time."

There was a knock on Noah's door. His heart skipped a beat. With his hand on his right hip, a quick grab away from Damien's gun, Noah pulled the door open. Madsen walked in quickly, and Noah shut the door behind her, but not before stealing a look down both ends of the empty hall.

"Well?" Robert was on his feet.

Madsen slid a tray with three coffees on the counter and took one for herself. She eyed the two full cases of beer and three unopened bottles of rum on the counter and nodded at Noah.

"Going to be a hell of a party when this is done," she joked.

They laughed uncomfortably.

"You been all right, though?" she asked.

He nodded. "Stumbling around for the past two days, making regular appearances on the balcony, looking slightly drunker each time. Your end?"

"We're good to go. I have two of Caligan's officers positioned about four miles away on standby."

"Okay, good."

Rob clapped his hands together. "Then we're set."

Madsen pulled two radios from her belt, tuned the knobs on top, and handed them over. "You are only to use these if you have an unquestionable visual on him. Let's assume he's watching us. That he thinks Robert and I are playing babysitter to your drunken bullshit."

"Hey," Noah furrowed his brow.

"You know what I mean. Let's just be cautious, okay?"

The three were quiet for a moment, each saying their own mental prayers. Robert broke the silence.

"So, what do we do if he doesn't show? If the package is delivered by mail?"

Noah looked at his brother. "Rob, it's Sunday. There is no mail."

"Right." He tried to hide his embarrassment. "And you really think he's going to take the risk and deliver this thing himself?"

Noah and Madsen shared a glance before both nodding.

"Alright then," Robert shrugged. "Let's do this."

"You have the rear stairwell leading to the fire door out back," Madsen instructed. "I'll be on the bottom floor watching the main door. Noah you will," her voice trailed off as Noah grabbed a beer from the pack, popped it, and dumped half of it in the sink. She nodded. "Yeah, that."

Before leaving, she reached over and ruffled Noah's hair until it looked unkempt. "Good luck."

"Gonna be a long day," he said.

***

Noah opened the slider door and stumbled out, half-falling against the railing, burying his head warily in his hand. It was a gorgeous October day. The air was crisp, refreshing with each breath, but he couldn't enjoy it. He had to appear drunk, on the brink and ready to jump.

After a few seconds, he tipped his head back and mock-drank the rest of the beer, placing the 'empty' bottle on the floor of the balcony before heading inside to fetch another.

It was nearing one-thirty when Noah returned to the balcony, a rum and coke—

sans rum—in his hand. He collapsed into one of the plastic chairs and sat there for ten minutes, swaying back and forth, belching into the air, sloppily gulping at the drink in his hand.

A door shut somewhere, and he wondered which of his neighbors were home and what they would think if they knew what was going on in their building. Background actors in the play that was their life.

Enough time had passed. Noah stalked back inside and placed the drink on the counter. He walked to his bedroom, stopping in front of the crucifix. Maybe this had all happened to him because he had abandoned his faith. If that were true, then what was the reasoning behind the accident? Behind his injury and the miscarriage?

He touched the bottom of the crucifix, closed his eyes to remember hymns and sermons spoken to him, passages that talked of truth and love and sacrifice, when a voice came from the doorway of his bedroom.

"It's all a lie."

Noah spun on his heels, eyes wide, and found himself face to face with Jack.

The man was rocking on his heels, hands behind his back. He had adorned the same gray suit. Looking calm and collected despite the raid on his house. *How?*

Noah's throat became dry. Goosebumps formed on the backs of his arms, and try as he might, he couldn't stop a chill from sending a spasm down his back.

"How did you—" Noah's voice caught. Anger coursed through him. This had been the plan and yet—he wasn't ready. This man shouldn't have made it past Madsen or Robert or the officers that were waiting. He cleared his throat. Spoke low. "How did you get in?"

Jack held his hand out, a silver key in his palm. "Amber was nice enough to leave me her key."

Fury filled him. All the rage and loss burning an endless fire. Noah yanked the gun from his belt and pointed it at Jack's chest.

Jack only smiled. "So, you're not as drunk as you seem."

"Stone sober," Noah said. "You're not the only one who can act."

"Clever. And while that's good, it depresses me that I was this predictable."

Noah reached for the radio clipped to his pocket, only for his hand to come up empty. Cursing himself, he visualized the device on his counter.

"Yeah, I don't think they're coming right this second," Jack said before backing into the bedroom. "We have a few minutes."

Noah stepped forward, opened his mouth to yell stop, but couldn't find the words. Jack reached behind the door and came back with a disposable white cooler held in both hands. "I brought you something. Just like I said that I would."

The man stepped forward and placed the cooler on the floor of the hall. Noah's hand gripped the gun. Shoot him! His muscles twitched, burning in a state of tense permanence.

"Open it," Jack said. "Please? It's rude if you don't."

Noah shook his head, stunned at the man's audacity. "No."

"But it won't mean as much if I open it for you."

Noah stared in disbelief.

Jack stepped forward, impatient, and knelt. "It's not a bomb, I promise. But it *was* difficult to obtain. Fortunately, though, with money comes ease. I suppose we can thank capitalism for that. They really should pay funeral home attendants more, though. Especially funeral home attendants whose significant others have lost their jobs. Could prevent all sorts of things getting stolen. Though, I didn't really steal it. Amber wanted you to have it."

Noah's chest and stomach pricked with nerves. As he watched Jack slit the tape and pull the top of the cooler off with a quick screech of foam on foam, he winched. His hand began to shake as his eyes saw nothing but red.

The cooler was filled with blood, a solid oblong shape in the middle, cut crudely in half.

"It's not all her blood," Jack said. "I had to swipe some of that from the hospital blood bank. She had been dead for so long, done up in that pretty makeup all ready for the funeral, there was nothing I could use for such a dramatic presentation. I had almost missed my opportunity all together. What a waste that would have been."

Jack laughed. That evil, smirking laugh that now made Noah's skin crawl. "She had a good heart, Noah. Believe me. I fried the other half and ate it."

Noah dropped the gun and lunged, his open hands landing on Jack's throat.

THIRTY-SIX

They toppled backward into the bedroom, Jack falling onto the foot of Noah's bed and sending them both to the floor. A knee in his side, pain exploded across Noah's chest as his broken ribs crunched together.

"Gah," he cried out, squirming and slapping the floor.

His palm hit the side of the cooler, his fingers inadvertently hooking the edge, teetering it until it fell. The blood, the soft tissue of Amber's heart, slid across his fingertips.

Jack drove his fist down, connecting with Noah's face. His vision flashed black. He saw Adrian. Amber. Both of them together. Noah wanted to melt into the oblivion. Be pushed down until he could join them as a family.

But suddenly, the weight was off him, the oppressing force of Jack's body gone.

"Everything," Jack spat with rage. He walked to the hall and picked the gun off the floor. "Everything I have done these past two months has been for you. And yet you still fight me."

Noah rolled, dragged himself to his feet while trying to avoid the blood that had pooled on the floor, his own streaky handprint running through it.

"Enough," Noah coughed. "This isn't for me. You killed someone I loved; how is that for me?"

"She was holding you back." The ferocity of Jack's voice took Noah by surprise. He suddenly felt a wave of fear. Jack stomped his foot on the ground.

"All you did was sulk and cry over her. You were pathetic. She had moved on. Why couldn't you? Instead you took the selfish, pitiful route that bordered suicide. That's what was next for you, ya know?"

Noah spat, not caring that he was inside. "You should have let it happen."

"Ahh." Jack gripped at the sides of his head. "How? How can you be so ungrateful? I saved your life, Noah. Just like you've done to others, so I did for you. Jack the Ripper gave investigators in Whitechapel the case of their lives. Now, I'm giving you yours."

Noah scoffed. Slowly looked up from the floor. "No, I'm alive and sober because of myself."

In the second that Jack looked away, rolling his eyes in disgust, Noah rushed forward. Jack turned back. Noah was almost there when his foot slid on the very edge of the blood, sending his leg out from under him. Jack parried, knocked him to the floor and pointed the gun at his chest.

"Please don't make me kill you, Noah. I like you. That's why I did all of this. It's why you're here with this little bit of fight still left in you."

Noah scurried back several feet and pushed himself off the ground, burying any fear he may have had. "Too bad."

He started walking forward. Jack took tentative steps back. "Noah, please. There is a plan here. I only kill like Jack killed. Just the women. Just the five. Especially not you. Noah, stop. Noah!"

The sound of the gunshot was deafening. Noah's ears rang with temporary deafness, but he felt no new pain.

Jack's face was frozen, horrified. "Did I? Oh God, Noah, I'm sorry."

But Noah remained unmoving, the bullet not in his body, but behind him in the kitchen wall. Jack's face turned stoic. Then angry.

"You shouldn't have made me do that," Jack hissed. "You selfish fuck."

Noah closed his eyes. Would Robert or the detective have heard it? If Madsen had been in the lobby. . . Noah silently counted to ten when behind him the door to his apartment flew open.

Almost too exhausted and too relieved to say it, Noah muttered. "We're done."

But as he turned to see Madsen rushing toward him, movement flashed in the corner of his eye and a sudden pressure was on his throat. Jack wrapped his arm around Noah's neck. Squeezed and pressed the muzzle of the gun against Noah's temple.

Jack edged forward, guiding Noah with each step. Madsen froze, her own firearm raised.

"Stop," she said. "Lay it down and put your hands up."

"Not likely, Alyssa," Jack said. "Now take a step back. One more, come on."

Noah swallowed, felt the pressure of Jack's arm. It was hard to breathe with his grip so tight.

"Dennis," Madsen said. "We know who you are. We know where you live. There's nowhere you can go at this point. Just put the gun down."

Jack snickered. Kept walking with Noah as his protective puppet. They were in the kitchen, Jack's back to the door when Noah saw something in Madsen's eyes. Something like relief.

"I have the world," Jack said.

There was a sudden thud. Jack's arm went slack from around Noah's neck, and Robert's voice behind him said, "No, you don't."

Noah sucked in air. His brother stood above a groaning Jack. Robert's hands were shaking as he bent to pick the gun off the floor. Madsen rushed forward, stowing her firearm and pulling out handcuffs, her hand on her radio when Jack grumbled. "Emma."

Robert's eyes narrowed. Noah panicked and kicked the withering man. It wasn't enough.

"You'll never find where I have her. She'll die because of you. Is that what you want?"

Noah put a hand on his brother's chest, pushing him. "Rob, back up."

"No," Jack said.

Madsen dropped to the floor, her knee on his chest.

Robert's face fell. "What about Emma?"

He looked from Jack to Madsen to Noah. Noah's heart began to pound. How far out were the other officers?

"Rob, she's fine. I didn't tell you, but he's been stalking us. It's how he knew the response times. It's how he knew I'd be here."

Madsen fixed her cuffs to Jack's hands and jumped up to grab her radio, calling for the two units on standby to run lights and sirens to Northern University. She gave a brief description, followed by Emma's dorm number and license plate.

"Noah," Rob asked, shockingly calm. "What is happening?"

"She's such a pretty girl," Jack said. He dragged his teeth over his bottom lip. "And she would have been fine. Just a few scratches. A cut here. A slice there. Now, well…"

"Where is she?" Robert demanded. Spit flew from his mouth. "Where did you put my daughter?"

"Rob," Noah yelled. "Stop. He doesn't have her."

"No," Jack said. "I couldn't possibly have taken her from her dorm on Dog Lane. Waited in her closet where she still keeps her purple prom dress because it reminds her of home."

"Shut up." Madsen stepped forward.

"The stuffed dolphin you bought her in eighth grade is on her bed. Did you know that?" Jack laughed. "It may have some red on it, though. I mean, think of Kelly, Robert. Think of what the Ripper did to her."

Robert raised the gun.

"Rob!" Noah exclaimed.

"Shut up," Rob yelled. Madsen inched forward, but Noah held his hand out.

"I waited for her to fall asleep on her little bed with her gray sheets and flower comforter that you and Claudia bought for her fifteenth birthday. Imagine Mary Kelly. They could barely recognize her, her face was so perfectly done. It was all because he had time. I had time, Robert. I had plenty of time."

Noah grinded his teeth together. He took a deep breath and tried to keep his voice from shaking. "Rob, what happened to Jack the Ripper?"

"What? Noah, I don't—"

"Rob, what happened to the real Ripper? Did he get arrested?"

"You know he didn't," he practically shouted. "He got away."

"Right, he got away. And all this man wants is to be Jack the Ripper. If he is caught and goes to jail, then he fails." As Noah said it, there was a burning in him to take the gun from his older brother, aim it at the floor, and pull the trigger. But in that moment it had become clear that there was only one way for the ordeal to end.

"If I shoot him, he fails," Robert argued.

Noah took a step forward. "No. Because eventually the real Ripper died. But he was never arrested and put in jail. Give me the gun, Rob."

Madsen echoed Noah's words. "Robert, give him the gun."

Jack laughed. "I watched her while she slept. She was beautiful, Robert. Would have made such a fantastic little whore."

"Rob," Noah pleaded. "Emma is fine. He wouldn't kill her before the real date. He's timed it all out. Please.

Think of Mikey. What's he going to do if you're in jail for the rest of your life?"

Robert's arm shook. Noah took another cautious step toward him, thought of a half-dozen times a gun had been drawn on scene, either by an officer or a junkie in one last stand.

Noah was almost there. He raised his hand to grab the gun, but Jack spoke first.

" I know you know the nicknames Kelly went by. Jack probably whispered them in her ear as he gutted her like an animal. What's to say I didn't whisper sweet little things to . . . Come on, you know at least one of Mary Kelly's nicknames. . . Fair little…"

Noah saw his brother's arm tense. He heard the faint sounds of sirens in the distance.

Robert closed his eyes and whispered, "Fair Emma."

Jack smiled as Robert pulled the trigger.

THIRTY-SEVEN

Noah sat in the back pew of Mary's Cathedral, tired with bloodshot eyes. He flicked the corner of the Bible in front of him. There were four others in the church, including Father Michaels. Sitting in front was the same elderly couple he had seen multiple times before. The man seemed well.

He heard the church doors shut. Detective Madsen slid in next to him. Elbows on her knees, she pressed her fingertips together. They sat in silence. Each observing, each accepting the world around them.

"They call this place a sanctuary," Noah said. His voice sounded heavy, even to himself. Exhausted. "Like four walls and a roof can provide security."

"To some it is," she said quietly.

He looked at her, his face stoic. "There are no sanctuaries, Alyssa. There's no safe haven for people to run to."

Noah flicked the back cover of the Bible a final time before allowing his hands to drop. Altar candles flickered in the early morning sun that refracted through stained glass windows. Upon hearing what Robert had done, Claudia came back from her mother's with their son in tow. Madsen had allowed the boy to see his father at the station while his arrest was being processed.

"He has a good lawyer, Noah."

"There such a thing?"

She nodded. "Everyone in the department hates her, so she must be good."

He forced a chuckle, then puffed his cheeks and let out an exasperated breath.

"I won't let it go unknown why he did what he did," she said.

Noah ran a hand through his hair. "How's Emma?"

"In shock. I don't think it's hit her yet, but she's with her mother and brother."

"Did you tell her everything?" he asked.

She shook her head. "Just that the man knew of her. No sense in scaring her into thinking she's unsafe."

Noah leaned back. "She is, though. We all are. Even home isn't safe anymore."

Alyssa forced a grim smile. Together, they watched Father Michaels as he spoke to the elderly couple. After a few minutes, Madsen stood. Noah looked up at her; a thousand things were on the tip of his tongue, the foremost being, *please don't go yet.*

She stopped outside the pew, took another look to the altar before saying, "You know, this place was built because of a person, not because the building itself is special in some way."

Noah looked at her, confused. She tilted her head toward the crucifix at the front of the cathedral.

"I don't understand?" he asked.

She looked at the ground before meeting his eyes. "Maybe sanctuary isn't a place. Maybe it's the people you surround yourself with."

When the cathedral door closed, her words still hanging in the air, Noah finally blinked. Father Michael looked toward him and nodded.

Noah thought of all the ghosts that haunted him, the people he hadn't saved, those he tried but lost along the way. He thought of how much time they'd had, and how much he may have left. The things they could do if given the opportunity.

Noah pushed himself to his feet and headed for the door, hoping to catch her before she was gone.

***

ACKNOWLEDGMENTS

In the calm that follows the chaos, I can take a breath and actually think about everything that was done to bring this project together from inception to completion. I am amazed at the collective work and support that went into forming a scattered idea—with maybe two scenes and no plot—to something you can hold in your hands.

Starting professionally, I want to thank Emma Nelson and Hannah Smith. From our first call, where I paced across my backyard with a notepad and my dog looking at me like I was off my rocker, the two of you have been an absolute dream come true to work with. I cannot thank you enough for your insight and for taking a chance on a manuscript that needed quite a lot of work. You guys rock more than you know. Also, thank you to Caroline Geslison and everyone else at Owl Hollow Press for taking me in and making me feel at home.

My parents, Christy and Al, thank you for pushing me while I was a kid and a teenager (God, that was an awful age; sorry about that guys). Thanks for showing me that things don't come free and you can do anything if you are willing to work for it. I'm really grateful for everything you've taught me, and I hope you know that. Thank you, also, to Aunt Mary Ann and Grandma Carole for your continued support and encouragement.

Liz, Mike, Ginny, and Judy, thank you for reading early drafts of the book and giving me feedback. It was invaluable in the editing process. Also, Mike and Liz, thanks for being incredibly supportive and, not to mention, a pretty rad pair of in-laws.

Mike, Michelle, John, Michelle, Roper, Caroline, Erick, and everyone else who's dealt with me missing drinks and nights out while I worked on this project, I'm coming back. Don't worry.

Matt, thanks for answering random questions, even when they came via one a.m. text messages. Caroline, thank you for reading bits and pieces and giving feedback; I owe you! Also, both of you, we need another round of *Letters from Whitechapel* to see who can play Jack and get away. Drew, thanks for helping with legal research. I still owe you a drink, buddy. Melinda, thank you for coming to Utah with us. I'm writing this prior to the trip, but it's going to be another awesome adventure (and hopefully not as hot as D.C. was)! And Brandi, I'm sorry this isn't three pages . . . but big thank you for answering my physical therapy questions and making me sound like I sort of know what I'm talking about. Thanks to everyone willing to help read an early copy—Monica, Caroline, Melinda, Caroline, Liz, Ginny, Rebecca, Carole, and Tony. Everyone else, I love you, guys; thank you for everything!

And that's about it. . . Just kidding (almost done though, I promise).

Max, I've actually sat staring at the screen now for about ten minutes, trying to figure out exactly what to say, and I'm not really getting anywhere, so…I'll say thank you. But that's not enough. You have been the most supportive brother I could ever ask for. But that's nothing new. We've always had each other's backs, even way before we were planning to take over the world—you, me, and Derek (aka Guns—HA! I did it.) From all-nighters playing *Quake III Arena*, *Mortal Kombat*, or *The Last of Us* (still the greatest game ever, next to *Doom*) or bingeing through *Star Wars* or *Alien* movies, getting into heated debates about world issues that we are totally unqualified to address, or just hanging out. Thank you. I'm proud of you and everything that you're doing, my friend.

And that leaves Eryka. My best friend. The person who makes me smile like no one else ever has. The girl who I can look at when we're out with friends, at some party, or just hanging out at home, and marvel at the fact that we're together. I couldn't be any luckier. Between the second date knock out that's still on YouTube somewhere, Max and I quoting endless movies (which over the years you have gotten better than us at!), the hiking, the concerts, the traveling—all of it is only as amazing as it is because I'm doing it with you. Thank you for listening to me go on and on about Jack the Ripper and murdered prostitutes for the past two years, for finding podcasts about Whitechapel to listen to, and for finding stuff to do while I worked on this project night after night. I love you, and wherever we have plane tickets to next, I can't wait.

Also, thank you to whomever you are who just read this book. I hope you enjoyed it.

ABOUT THE AUTHOR

Benjamin Thomas earned an MFA in creative writing from Albertus Magnus College while working as an Emergency Room Technician.

His short stories have appeared in publications such as Flash Fiction Online, Winter Tales: A Fox Spirit Anthology, and others. He can also be found reviewing books for Shoreline of Infinity, the Hugo-nominated speculative fiction e-zine.

Ben writes from New England where he unequally balances time between traveling, hiking, and quoting seemingly random movies. JACK BE QUICK is his first novel.

CONNECT WITH BENJAMIN

Website: www.bthomas7.weebly.com
Twitter: www.twitter.com/jigsawkid7
Instagram: www.instagram.com/benjaminthomas7
Facebook: www.facebook.com/jigsawkid7

If you enjoyed this book, please consider leaving a review. Thank you for reading!

ABOUT THE PUBLISHER

Owl Hollow Press, LLC publishes genre fiction, contemporary, and non-fiction books, with a yearly themed anthology.

For other OHP titles, visit us at www.owlhollowpress.com.

Twitter: www.twitter.com/owlhollowpress
Instagram: www.instagram.com/owlhollowpress
Facebook: www.facebook.com/owlhollowpress

WORLD-ALTERING STORIES, REAL AND IMAGINED

Made in the USA
Middletown, DE
05 May 2017